Destiny's Bridge

Carrie Carr

Yellow Rose Books

Nederland, Texas

ISBN 1-932300-11-2

First Printing 2003

9 8 7 6 5 4 3 2 1

*This story was initially published, along with the story *Faith's Crossing,* under the title *Destiny's Crossing.* Some parts have been changed from the original version.

Cover design by Mary D. Brooks

Published by:

Yellow Rose Books
PMB 210, 8691 9th Avenue
Port Arthur, Texas 77642-8025

Find us on the World Wide Web at
http://www.regalcrest.biz

Printed in the United States of America

Acknowledgments:

This book wouldn't have been here, if not for: my wonderful AJ, who tirelessly sat beside me as we read and edited (and edited, and edited); Lori L. Lake, a superb author and extremely talented editor/proofreader; and Cathy, the publisher who first tackled "the Monster," and graciously allowed me to re-edit it so that it could finally be printed in its proper form. Thank you all.

This book is for my mom and dad, who never stopped believing in me, even when I had; and, of course, to my beautiful AJ, the woman who makes everything right, and whose smile lights my way. Forever and always, my love.

Chapter
One

Raindrops pattered against the window and the midday sun hid behind dark clouds. Thunder rumbled ominously, punctuated by erratic flashes of lightning. In the cluttered office, nature's symphony was wasted on the heavyset man who sat behind the oak desk. Searching for a particular scrap, he rifled through the piles of papers that threatened to topple at any moment. His blue tie was stained, and the top two buttons on his shirt were loose. The matching jacket to his gray suit lay haphazardly across one of the visitors' chairs on the opposite side of the room. The ringing of his phone caused the man to pause in his search. Muttering curses, he picked up the receiver. "Yeah?"

As the voice on the other end of the line whined on, a smirk gradually formed on the pudgy man's face. He pulled a pen from his shirt pocket and scribbled furiously on a blank appointment sheet. "Do you think it'll work?" Nodding, he continued to write. "No kidding? I guess it couldn't hurt. Yeah. Sure. Whatever." He hung up the phone and tapped the top of the pen against his lips.

Rick Thompson was the manager of Sunflower Realty. He had been in charge of the real estate office since the owner, Anna Leigh Cauble, retired a few months earlier. Rick had been Somerville High School's star athlete more than ten years before, but his best years were obviously far behind him. The muscular build of his shoulders and chest had given way to a paunchy abdomen, and his dark brown hair was thinning. Resentful that his glory days had faded, he used his current position either to solicit favors or to settle old scores. The news he had just received was too good to ignore, and he wracked his brain for the perfect way to use it. Rick smiled malevolently when he decided what to do. He stabbed a button on his phone.

"Wanda, tell Amanda I've got something for her."

A few moments later, the door to Rick's office opened and a petite woman in her mid-twenties stepped into the room. In her black jeans, green silk top, and high-top sneakers, she looked more like a student than a real estate agent. The young agent brushed her hair away from her face and stood by one of the visitors' chairs. "Wanda said you wanted to see me?" Amanda Cauble had very little use for the office manager, having turned down his requests for dates more times than she cared to remember. Amanda was Anna Leigh Cauble's granddaughter and her grandmother's first choice for her replacement when she retired. She had turned down her grandmother's repeated offers and insisted that she start out as just another agent. Content to work her way up, Amanda felt she wasn't ready for the responsibility of managing the entire office.

"Yeah." Rick thrust a piece of paper at her. "I got a call a few minutes ago, and they want someone to come out today."

"In this weather?"

Mimicking her voice, he said, "Yeah, in this weather." Amanda glared at Rick, who rolled his eyes and continued, "Look, it's a huge ranch. Just go and meet with the owner." When Amanda's expression didn't alter, Rick exhaled loudly, as if irritated, and ran his finger across the information on the appointment sheet, pretending to verify the name. "The ranch is owned by L. Walters. Guess they're getting tired of the ranching business."

Amanda accepted the paper hesitantly. "Why me? If you got the call, why don't you want the client?" She didn't like the feel of this and didn't trust Rick any farther than she could throw him.

"Look, kid. I'm just trying to do you a favor. I know we haven't gotten along, and I'm trying to make it up to you." Rick could see skepticism reflected in her eyes. "Honest." Releasing a heavy sigh, the big man leaned back into his leather chair. Injecting just the right amount of grumbling into his voice, he added, "Besides, I don't want your grandmother pissed at me. I need this job."

Ah. Well, I guess that makes more sense. Amanda studied the paper in her hands. "From these directions, it looks like it's going to take me all afternoon. Are you sure this couldn't wait until the weather clears up?"

"No, it can't. They said if we don't come out, then they'll go somewhere else with their business." Rick propped his feet up on his desk and linked his hands behind his head. "Maybe you're not ready for such a big client. I could always give it to Stacy."

The comment stung Amanda's pride. She had passed her Realtor's exam recently and was quite proud of the license hanging on her cubicle wall. Although she hadn't gone out more than a few times to clients' homes, she knew she could do a much better job than her co-worker. The office gossip was that Stacy had a job only because she was sleeping with Rick. Amanda didn't know if it was true or not, but she knew she wanted a chance to prove herself. "Where else could they go? We're the only real estate company in town." Somerville was a small town of about ten thousand people, and Sunflower Realty was often hard-pressed for clients as it was.

"Hell if I know. Do you want the job or not?"

Amanda frowned. Her boss seemed a little too anxious for her to handle the appointment. Although gut instincts warned her otherwise, Amanda decided to give him the benefit of the doubt. "All right. But don't expect me to come back to the office today." She turned and left Rick's office and went to gather her things.

Smiling, Rick watched her leave. He was tired of looking over his shoulder, fearing that Anna Leigh would fire him and put Amanda in his place. *Once she meets with Walters, the fall-out will keep her off my back for a long time.* The owner of the Rocking W Ranch had humiliated him twelve years earlier, when they both attended the same high school. He'd tried several different times over the years to find a way to get even and hoped that this was his chance.

After gathering up her briefcase and purse, Amanda jogged around to the side of the building in a hurry to get out of the rain. The unyielding downpour was causing a section of the parking lot to resemble a miniature lake. A few steps before the young woman reached her 1967 Mustang, her left foot sank into an unseen pothole. Amanda staggered sideways and dropped her briefcase into another puddle before she was able to regain her balance.

Grimacing, she gingerly wriggled her foot, relieved that she didn't sprain her ankle. She picked up the mud-splattered briefcase and shook the excess water away before she opened the car door and escaped the storm. Amanda sat behind the steering wheel and laid the muddy briefcase on the front passenger's floorboard. She then proceeded to dig through her purse for her car keys. Finding them at the bottom of her bag, Amanda leaned back in her seat, grateful to be out of the rain. She patted the dashboard fondly. The classic blue car had been a graduation present from her beloved grandfather over five years ago.

She felt her heart constrict at the turn her thoughts suddenly took. *We almost lost him.* It had been six months since Jacob Cauble had been severely injured in an automobile accident. Amanda immediately moved from her parents' house in Los Angeles to her grandparents' home in Somerville to be at her grandmother's side while her grandfather was in the hospital. Now the only outward signs of the accident were a jagged scar on his forehead near his hairline and a pronounced limp that Jacob himself swore would not be permanent.

Amanda pulled the rear view mirror down to check her reflection and squinted at the hazel eyes looking back at her. "Drowned rat." She ran her fingers through damp hair that almost reached her shoulders and turned her attention to the task at hand. "Sitting here feeling sorry for yourself isn't gonna get the job done. Now get a move on and take care of business." Amanda started the car and backed out of the parking space.

In a large ranch house nestled in the foothills a few miles away, someone else cursed the unrelenting rain. Lexington Walters' long frame was sprawled comfortably on the porch swing, her muddy boots propped up on the rail that outlined the large wraparound porch. While they always needed rain, she knew that storms such as this one tended to cause problems with the fence surrounding the ranch.

Bored, Lex stood up, raised her arms over her head, and pulled on one of the supports above her. Stretching her body out, she was gratified to hear the gentle popping as her spine slid back into place. After releasing the support beam, Lex stomped into the house and grabbed her long brown duster and black cowboy hat from their hooks in the hallway.

"Martha," she yelled, "I'm gonna go check the fence down by the creek." She put the weather-beaten hat onto her head and almost had the door open when a plump woman in her mid-fifties came scurrying out of the kitchen, wiping her hands on a dishtowel.

"Lexington Marie Walters! Don't you be bellowing in this house. I raised you better than that."

Lex hastily removed her hat, looking properly chastised.

"I'm sorry, Martha. I didn't know where you were; that's why I yelled." She put on the engaging smile that usually got her out of trouble before shoving her hat back onto her head. "It won't happen again, I promise."

Not fooled for a moment, Martha just shook her head. The housekeeper had raised the young woman who was standing there doing her best to look contrite. Lex was four years old when Martha came to the Rocking W ranch, shortly before Victoria Walters died in childbirth, leaving Lex, an infant son, and Lex's older brother. *And for the last twenty-five years, Lexie has been using that smile on me. Maybe that's because it always works.*

Now twenty-eight, Lex had been running the Rocking W Ranch since her father had left home for a life on the rodeo circuit. Rawson Walters couldn't stand the fact that his daughter looked so much like his late wife, so on Lex's eighteenth birthday, he signed the ranch over to her and never returned. Martha was fiercely proud of Lex. Instead of focusing on the losses in her life, her "Lexie" had thrown all her energy into making the Rocking W a ranch to be proud of.

With motherly affection, Martha reached out and buttoned the duster closed. "Try not to get too wet, Lexie. You know how long it took you to get over that last bout of the flu." She stepped back and gave her charge a stern look. "And don't you dare be late for dinner. I'm cooking a big batch of chili, and I'm even making your favorite cornbread to go with it." With this, the housekeeper turned around and called over her shoulder as she bustled back to the kitchen, "And don't you be clompin' back in here with muddy boots. You're not too big for me to take my wooden spoon to!"

Lex looked after her fondly. "Yes, ma'am."

Straining to see through the rain that pounded against her windshield, Amanda's thoughts brought her back to the reason she was out in this horrible weather. "I don't know why I continue to let that jerk get to me." She used her hand to wipe the condensation from the inside of the window. "And I can't believe I'm actually out in this mess."

Without taking her eyes off the road, Amanda searched her purse for the directions that Rick had given her. Having not actually lived in Somerville before now, Amanda was not very familiar with the area. She had spent a lot of summers at her grandparents' house, but her time was spent with them, not running around the countryside with kids her own age. So, here she was, driving in the pouring rain on her way to an appointment that she didn't make and with directions she wasn't sure she could trust. It made her nervous. Rick looked too smug when he handed her the appointment sheet.

After a quick glance at the paper in her hand, she peered through the windshield. *Okay, that must be the small road on the left that the directions show.* Amanda turned onto the road and grimaced as mud spattered along the side of the car. *Sorry, baby. I'll give you a good wash and wax when we get out of this mess.* Up ahead, she could barely make out the shape of a large covered wooden bridge. "Oh, how pretty. I'd love to see this when the sun is shining." She slowed the Mustang down until it inched across the bridge.

Lex filled up the hole around the last post. As she had suspected earlier, a portion of the fence had been knocked down when the raging creek toppled a tree. After clearing away the tree with an ax, she spent an hour rebuilding the final section of fence. Now all she had to do was finish stringing the last strand of wire, and she could go back to the ranch house and get out of the foul weather.

Just then, a bright flash of lightning illuminated the creek, followed closely by a clap of thunder. "That was too close. I'm out of here." As she picked up the remaining tools, another flash of light caught her eye. "What the..." Her eyes narrowed under her hat. "Who in the hell would be fool enough to come out on a day like this?"

When the car was halfway across the bridge, a tree being forced downstream by the surging waters crashed into the center support beams. A large section from the middle of the old bridge crumbled, and Lex watched in horror as the small car fell into the creek. The tree and all its knotty branches shoved it downstream.

Cursing, Lex dropped her tools and ran to the nearby Jeep. She stripped off her coat and hat and traded them for a long rope. The cold rain quickly soaked through her thin tee shirt, and she shivered. She looked up and saw that the car was hung up on debris about twenty yards away on the far side of the creek.

Lex tied one end of the rope around an oak tree and the

other end around her waist. With a running start, she jumped feet first into the creek and allowed the violent current to take her to the half-submerged vehicle. The same tree that had caused the car to plunge into the raging water now pinned it between the branches and the bank. Lex wasn't certain how long it would stay in one place. The nose of the automobile was already under water, but she was able to climb onto the trunk to get out of the swirling current. Squinting through the rain, Lex used her gloved hands to brush debris away from the rear window and saw the driver slumped over the steering wheel. Glad she hadn't removed her boots, Lex desperately kicked the rear window, which cracked, but popped inward in one piece.

While she crawled through the open window, a smaller tree slammed into the car and tossed her headfirst onto the soggy backseat floorboards. She pulled herself up, hoping that the car would stay put for just a few more minutes, and reached over the front seat to gently shake the driver's shoulder. "Hey."

There was no response. The driver remained hunched over the steering wheel, oblivious to her plight. The car lurched sideways again, and Lex saw that she was quickly running out of time. She jostled the woman a bit harder. "Hey!"

Still not receiving a response and knowing time was running out, Lex weighed her options. She knew it was never a good idea to move an accident victim, but a quick glance through the window showed that the creek was continuing to rise. Her decision made, she carefully put her hands on the driver's shoulders and pulled her away from the steering wheel. Other than a small lump and a slow bleeding cut on her left temple, the woman seemed free from external injuries. The water level was rising inside the car and was already up to the unconscious woman's knees. Lex quickly unbuckled the seat belt, gripped under limp arms, and pulled the driver between the seats. She leaned the woman upright in the rear seat, and then edged out feet first through the busted out window.

Lex struggled to keep her balance on the slippery trunk as she reached back into the car. She pulled the still form through the window and set her onto the trunk just as the front of the vehicle slipped more deeply into the water. She quickly pulled off one of her leather gloves and checked the woman's pulse, which was strong and steady. Lex wiped the wet hair out of her own eyes then replaced her glove. Untying the rope from around her waist, she wrestled the unconscious woman up onto her own back and draped the loose arms around her neck. After tying the rope around them both, Lex positioned the woman's head beside her own and slowly dropped into the racing water. Thankful that the other end of the rope remained securely tied around the oak tree, she used her gloved hands to pull them across the churning creek.

They'd made it over halfway across before Lex instinctively looked upstream and saw a large object rumbling right for them. Without conscious thought, Lex turned her body so that she could protect her passenger from what appeared to be part of a barn. Taking a direct hit to the chest, Lex nearly passed out from the pain. She managed somehow to hang onto the rope, only to feel frantic arms wrapped tightly around her neck. Loosening one hand from the rope that had become their lifeline, Lex tried to pry the convulsive limbs from her throat before she was choked to death, while keeping a tenuous hold with her other hand. "Stop," she shouted. "Don't choke me!" Coming to her senses, the frightened woman quickly released her death grip on her savior.

Ten minutes later, Lex pulled them both up onto the muddy creek bank. Exhausted and trembling, she untied the rope from around them and turned slightly, allowing her passenger to slip from her back. Her strength depleted, Lex collapsed on elbows and knees to the soggy ground and rested her head on her forearms. When she heard another sound mixed in with the thunder and rain, she lifted her head and saw that the other woman was on her knees with her arms wrapped around herself, rocking back and forth and crying.

"Oh, God!" Amanda's eyes searched desperately from side to side as she attempted to get her bearings. "What happened?"

Lex attempted to push herself up but the sudden pain in her chest caused her to drop back to her knees. "Damn." She twisted her head to look at the woman beside her. "Hey, are you okay?" Lex struggled into a sitting position, grunting from the pain. She laid a muddy hand upon the distraught woman's shoulder. "Shhh. Everything's okay now." Bracing her right arm across her chest, Lex slowly rose to her feet and offered her other hand to the woman. "Let's get out of this damned rain."

Amanda glanced up and made eye contact with her rescuer. "Okay." Lex pulled her to her feet but this obviously made Amanda dizzy, and she fell forward.

"Take it easy there." Lex caught her, but the movement brought another sharp pain to her chest. She silently cursed the debris that had injured her. She wrapped her left arm around the

other woman, while she tried to keep her own balance. The two
of them trudged slowly through the mud back to the Jeep.

Once they had settled in the Jeep, Lex handed her brown
duster to the trembling woman. "Here. This should help ward
off the cold 'til we get back to the house."

Amanda shyly accepted the offer. "Thanks. But what about
you?" She snuggled under the oversized coat, relieved to be less
frozen. "Ah. Much better."

"Don't worry about me." Lex wiped the wet hair out of her
eyes again. "It's not that far." She leaned over and dug into one
of the pockets of the coat and pulled out a dark blue bandanna.
"Here, try this." She applied a steady pressure to the bleeding
wound on the woman's temple. "I promise it's clean."

Amanda took hold of the bandanna. "Thanks." She tried to
think of something to say. "Thank you for saving my life." Tears
welled up in her eyes. "I don't...I just..." She took a deep
breath. "I'm sorry. Reaction, I guess. I want to thank you, but I
don't even know your name."

"Lex. And you're welcome." Lex turned the key in the igni-
tion, and the Jeep sputtered to life. The incessant rain pounded
a loud beat upon its hard top.

"My name's Amanda." She dabbed at her injury, wincing
when she pressed a little too hard. "I can't believe this happened. If you hadn't come along when you did—" Amanda
choked tearfully on her words as she realized how narrowly she
had missed being killed.

Lex reached for the gearshift, which caused a sharp pain in
her chest. She tried to, but couldn't, suppress a groan as she put
the vehicle in gear.

Concerned, Amanda placed her free hand on Lex's wrist.
"What is it? What's the matter?"

"Nothing. Just a little sore." The Jeep lurched as it went
down what was left of the road.

Amanda turned slightly in her seat so she could observe the
woman beside her. "Uh-huh. If you say so."

Lex gave her a raised eyebrow in response. Diverting the
subject away from herself, she posed the question that had been
bothering her since she'd first spotted Amanda's car. "What in
the hell were you doing driving around country roads on a nasty
day like this?" Lex braced herself as the Jeep hit a deep rut in
the road. "And why were you driving across my bridge?"

"Your bridge?" Amanda was silent for a long moment.
Then she giggled.

"What?"

Amanda laughed harder. "Sorry, but I just got the funniest picture in my head."

Lex just glowered at her. "C'mon, let's hear it."

"No, really, it's not important." Amanda shifted her position and tried to look as if she had completely dismissed the thought that she had found so funny, until another giggle pried its way out of her mouth.

That earned her another glare from the driver of the Jeep.

"Okay." Amanda wiped the tears from her eyes. "I just had this mental picture of you as a troll, waiting for the Three Billy Goats Gruff." She wheezed, trying unsuccessfully to contain her laughter.

"Cute, real cute." But Lex was relieved. The head injury couldn't be too bad if the woman beside her was able to make jokes.

They drove along the muddy road in silence. Amanda had apparently worn herself down with the giggling fit, and was now quietly curled up in the passenger's seat. The thunderstorm still raged, making the darkened sky appear like late evening instead of late afternoon.

While Lex maneuvered the Jeep along the slippery road, Amanda took the opportunity to study the woman beside her. The glow of the dash lights flickered across Lex's face, high-lighting her features. Amanda could clearly see the pain and exhaustion on her rescuer's face. Her own head was still aching, and she felt a little bit sick to her stomach. Before she could open her mouth to speak, Lex turned the steering wheel sharply to the right.

"Hang on!" The Jeep slid sideways in the mud as Lex desperately tried to avoid a tree lying across the road. The left front tire hit a large branch, causing the Jeep to tilt dangerously to the right as it skidded to a stop.

"Dammit!" Lex shoved the Jeep into a lower gear. A high-pitched whine answered her as the tires spun helplessly in the mixture of mud and water and leaves. She laid her head against the steering wheel and closed her eyes. "Some days it just doesn't pay to get out of bed." Lex raised her head and looked over at Amanda who had one hand braced on the dash and the other with a death grip on the door. "Sorry. I guess I'm not real good at this rescue business." She looked out through the rain-spattered windshield. "Look, the house isn't that much farther, maybe a mile or so at the most. Hard to tell how long it will take in this weather, though. Feel up to a little walk?"

"Sure." Amanda looked down at the muddy black sneakers on her feet. "Don't think my shoes could get any wetter, anyway." She silently thanked her grandmother for insisting that she dress casually for work, instead of wearing the dress and heels she had originally picked out.

Lex ran her hand through her hair as she thought about what to do next. "We'll cut through the woods. It'll shave some distance off the trip. Not to mention that this road is obviously too much of a mess to get very far." She fished into the back seat to grab a large flashlight and her battered cowboy hat. After Lex crammed the hat on her head, she reached for her door. "Let me go around and make sure your side is clear before you try to get out." She pocketed the keys and opened the door, easing herself out.

Thunder and lightning blasted their way across the sky. Lex slipped in the mud three times on her way around the rear of the Jeep. Every slip brought renewed agony to her chest. Once she arrived at the passenger side of the Jeep, she was thankful to see it relatively clear of debris. She opened the door and offered her hand to Amanda. "Careful, it's kinda slippery out here."

Amanda accepted the proffered hand and joined Lex on the side of the road. "Thanks." She slipped out of the coat and tried to hand it to Lex. "Here. You're only wearing a tee shirt, at least I've got a long-sleeved shirt on."

Lex studied how the other woman was dressed. Her black jeans were pasted to her body by the rain and mud, and her long-sleeved silk shirt didn't look very warm. She shook her head and pushed the coat back into Amanda's hands. "No, you wear it. I'm pretty warm-natured, anyway." Lex waited until Amanda had the coat back on and then led her away from the dark road. As they walked into a copse of trees, she asked about Amanda's head wound.

Amanda pulled the coat tighter around her body and considered the question seriously. "Not too bad. Aches a little." She peered through the rain and gloom, and without realizing what she was doing, gripped Lex's hand. "Is this safe? Walking through all these trees during a thunderstorm?"

"Safer than the road. There's probably a lot of washed out places, and it would be nearly impossible to walk on all the mud there." Another flash of lightning and rumble of thunder interrupted her. She felt the grip on her hand tighten. "Hey, it's okay. We'll be back to the house before long. It's just a little rain."

Amanda sheepishly loosened her grip on the other woman's hand, but made no move to let go. "Sorry. I've never really liked storms." The hand holding hers tightened.

"No problem. I think the worst is over for now. That last blast sounded pretty far away."

They reached the top of a slight rise, and Amanda saw that the trees gave way to open fields. "Is your home much farther?"

"Not too much. In no time at all, we'll be in front of a nice, warm fire." She met the slightly foggy eyes peering at her. "Unless you'd rather take a break for a few minutes. You're not looking too good."

Amanda thought about waving off her rescuer's concern, but then noticed Lex had become increasingly pale and drawn herself. "The thought of getting out of this rain is tempting, but I'm afraid if I don't rest for a few minutes I'll fall flat on my face." She didn't miss the fleeting look of relief that passed over the other woman's features.

"Yeah, you're probably right. We might as well take advantage of these trees for a short break. The rest of our walk will be out in the open, and the rain doesn't seem like it'll be slowing down any time soon." Lex released Amanda's hand and dropped to the ground, then sagged against an old oak tree.

Amanda sank down beside her and mimicked her posture. "I never knew how wonderful sitting in the mud could be." She flicked a blob of mud off her knee. "I know this stuff is supposed to be good for your complexion, but I think I'll just take my chances without it." She wrapped the oversized coat tightly around herself. "Are you sure you're warm enough? I feel really bad that I'm hogging your coat."

Lex waved off her concern. "No, really. I'm fine. I only had it with me because Martha threatens to whack me with a wooden spoon when I leave it at home." She also didn't want to try to slip her arms into the coat, dreading the pain it would bring to her chest.

Amanda was about to continue this line of questioning when she heard what Lex had said. "A spoon? Who's Martha?" She hazarded a guess. "Your mother?"

"Nah, more like my nanny." Lex looked pensive for a moment. "She's actually our housekeeper, but she's just about the only mother I've ever known. And believe me, she can sure swing a mean spoon." She playfully added, "I learned not to get on her wrong side when I was just a kid, something that I still can appreciate all these years later."

"Remind me to be on my best behavior then." Amanda patted Lex's knee. "Maybe I *should* give you this coat back. I'd hate to get you into trouble."

"I'd probably get into more trouble if I brought you home without it. 'Sides, I think she'll be okay. Just be prepared to be clucked over big time."

Amanda nodded and quietly studied her companion's condition. The longer they sat there, the worse Lex looked, her pain evident in her voice. "Hey, maybe we should get started again." The temperature felt as if it was beginning to drop even lower, and she noticed Lex unsuccessfully trying to repress a shudder.

Lex was grateful when Amanda rose and offered her a hand. *I can't stay out here too much longer. I'm going to pass out from the pain if I start shivering again.* With Amanda's assistance, she slowly and carefully climbed back to her feet.

As the minutes passed, the duo slogged through the mud in silence, each lost in her thoughts. Lex was moving slower in deference to the sharp stabbing pain in her chest, and it was getting harder for her to breathe normally. She spared a glance at her companion. Amanda was moving fairly well, although she kept tripping over the long coat she had wrapped around her body.

Amanda kept a close eye on Lex also. She could see that the other woman's breathing was more ragged with every step she took, and that her pace continued to slow by the minute. Afraid Lex would soon be too weak to continue, Amanda purposely stumbled and then halted.

Lex paused and studied Amanda with concern, she asked, "What's the matter? Is your headache getting worse?"

Amanda gazed up innocently. "I hate to bother you, but do you think I could hold onto you? It seems like I'm having a bit of a balance problem."

Not fooled at all, Lex was too tired and hurting too badly to call her on it. "Sure." She carefully raised one arm and draped it around Amanda's shoulders.

Amanda eased her body under Lex's arm, wrapping one arm around her waist. She couldn't restrain her amusement at the difference in their heights.

"What?" Lex couldn't see anything particularly funny about their situation.

Amanda peeked up from her position under Lex's arm. "You're quite a bit taller than me. I feel like a little kid next to you."

"Well," Lex drawled, "in that coat, you kinda look like

one, too." She leaned even more on Amanda.

Feeling the pressure, Amanda congratulated herself. *There's more than one way to skin a cat.* Amanda could tell that Lex's voice was weakening, and it had an exhausted, raspy quality to it. *That doesn't sound good at all. I hope we have some way to get her to a doctor once we're back to her house.*

The open field they came upon was carpeted with a thick winter rye. It was too dark for Amanda to see much, but it was still more pleasant to struggle through the rye than the mud they had waded in earlier. She estimated that close to two hours had passed since she had crashed into the creek, and if the sun had been shining, it would be close to dusk by now. Her head still ached, although it was more like a dull throb at the moment. She continued to support Lex's weight, amazed that neither one of them had collapsed. Through the infrequent flashes of lightning, Amanda was able to see just how exhausted her companion was. Something nagged at the back of her mind, though. *What was she doing out in this weather? And just how did she get hurt? Guess I could just ask.* Amanda cleared her throat. "Lex?"

Lex flinched slightly. *Damn. Almost dozed off there.* "Yeah?"

Amanda tightened her grip. "You haven't told me why you were out in this nasty weather. Or do you usually hang around raging creeks waiting to rescue women who happen to float by?" She felt Lex attempt to stifle a laugh.

"No, not usually." Lex was thankful for the distraction. "I was repairing a break in the fence when I saw that tree smash into the bridge." She gave a slight shrug. "Then, when I saw your car fall in, I really didn't even think." She looked down at the woman snuggled close to her side and smiled. "Right place, right time, I guess."

Amanda looked up in surprise. "You jumped into a creek feeling the way you do?"

"No. I was okay then. A little tired from chopping up a tree and digging a few post holes, but okay."

"All right. Then what happened? And don't try to tell me you're fine." Amanda tightened her grip. "You're about to fall over, I can tell." The look she gave the rancher dared Lex to argue with her. Amanda wasn't real sure where this sudden protective streak for a virtual stranger came from, but at this point, she really didn't give a damn. Lex has risked her life for her, and she was determined to get her back home safely.

Lex looked down at the grass they were walking through. "Ah, well. When I was pulling us across the creek, right before you came to, I sort of got hit by some debris." She suddenly stopped, due to the arm wrapped around her.

"Debris? What kind of debris? Where did it hit you?"

Lightning flashed, giving Lex a clear view of the deep concern etched on the face below her. Although it deeply touched her, she didn't want to go into any more detail at the moment. So, Lex turned to start walking again. She twisted wrong and collapsed to her knees in pain, black spots swimming in her vision. "Damn."

Amanda followed her to the ground, landing beside Lex on her knees. "What's wrong?" She put her arms around the woman and tried to offer some comfort.

Lex leaned forward with her left arm wrapped tightly around her chest and face hidden by the cowboy hat. Amanda pulled the battered hat away and allowed Lex to rest her forehead on her shoulder. "Just give me a minute," Lex gasped, trying to remain conscious.

"Rest for a few minutes, okay?" Amanda eased herself down and pulled Lex onto her back so that she lay against her. She repositioned her arms around Lex and offered the exhausted woman her strength.

"No, I'm all right. We're almost to the house." Lex tried in vain to get back up, but she couldn't seem to gather the energy needed. It felt so good to be held. The thought raced through her head that she wouldn't mind being hit with the broad side of a barn everyday, if Amanda would be there to hold her afterwards.

Amanda tightened her hold on the rancher and tried another tactic. "Well, if we're that close, then a short break can't hurt now, can it?" She looked up and tried to see the house in the distance. Unfortunately, between the oncoming darkness and the driving rain, she could barely see a few feet ahead. "Look, if you'll just point me in the right direction, I'll go and get some help." She glanced back down at Lex, whose eyes were closed. "Lex?" Amanda used her hand to brush the rain from Lex's face and was relieved to see the woman's eyes finally open.

"Sorry. Guess I must've moved the wrong way." Lex inhaled cautiously. The shallow breath wasn't too painful, so she breathed more deeply.

Worried about the pale woman in her arms, Amanda

implored, "Please, let me go and get some help." She brushed the damp hair off Lex's face and smoothed it back.

"It won't do any good. Only person at the house is Martha. My brother doesn't live there anymore, and the ranch hands are gone to the big livestock show this weekend. Thought I could handle things until they got back on Sunday."

"I'm sure you could have, if I hadn't needed you to rescue me."

"I'm sure it was worth it." Lex reached up with her right hand. "Wanna give me a hand up? I'm really getting tired of this damned rain."

Chapter
Two

Finally, the lights from the big ranch house came into view.

"Wow." Amanda's eyes widened. "It's enormous." Even in the rain and darkness, she could tell the home was impressive. Two-story, with a wraparound porch and a balcony on the second floor, the stucco structure would be equally at home in the high rent district of Somerville.

Lex led her around to a side entrance. "We'll go in through the mud room." She opened a plain-looking door and led Amanda inside. "No sense tracking in half the ranch through the house." She closed the door behind them and flipped on a light switch.

The soft light was almost blinding after being in the rain and darkness, and it took Amanda a moment to adjust. The ten-by-ten-foot-square room was plain, yet clean, with a bench along one wall and hooks by the door for hanging items.

Unable to stand any longer, Lex wearily lowered herself to the bench.

"Well, it sure feels great to finally be out of the rain." Amanda brushed dripping hair out of her eyes as she dropped beside Lex. She noticed her companion was leaning back against the wall with her eyes closed.

"Oh, yeah. Gimme a second, and I'll get you something dry to change into." Lex's eyes never opened.

In the decent light, Amanda took the opportunity to study the quiet woman sitting next to her. Even covered in mud, Amanda could tell Lex was a strikingly beautiful woman. Her long dark hair was still gathered in a loose ponytail. She already knew that her rescuer was tall, but now she could see Lex's broad shoulders and muscular build. *That tee shirt can't disguise a body like that.* Then Amanda noticed something else. The drenched tee shirt had a dark stain starting just below her breasts and spreading down her right side.

"Lex?"

Tired blue eyes, so dark they were almost violet, slowly opened, and Lex turned her head to focus on the other woman. "What's the matter? The weariness and pain made her voice sound low and raspy.

"I...I...think you're bleeding." Amanda reached for the shirt, but pulled back at the last moment. She wanted to do something, but wasn't certain what. "Why didn't you say something earlier?" Amanda's casual observance now turned to near panic.

Lex groggily looked down at her chest. "Didn't know. Must not be too bad." She blinked a couple of times, trying to clear her head. "C'mon. Let's get the mud off our feet and go find Martha. She'll get you something dry to wear." Lex was about to reach down and remove her boots when Amanda slid off the bench to kneel on the floor below her.

"Here, let me." Amanda tugged the muddy boots and socks from Lex's feet, then pulled off her own mud-encrusted shoes and drenched socks as well. "Yuck." Finally warm, she stood and removed the heavy coat and hung it by the door. "That thing must weigh fifty pounds now." She helped Lex to her feet. "Did you say something about dry clothes?"

Lex allowed Amanda to help her to the door on the other side of the room. "Oh, I think that can be arranged. And we'll get you some hot food, too. Let me warn you, though. Martha will probably stuff you like a prize heifer, so I hope you're hungry." Her housekeeper's answer for anything was food, no matter what the circumstances. Lex considered herself lucky that she was so busy around the ranch; otherwise, she would weigh as much as one of her horses.

They walked through the door and into the kitchen. Across the room, a short, heavyset woman was talking on the phone, obviously very upset.

"No, Mr. Hubert, she's not back yet, and I'm really beginning to get worried. It's been several hours since she left." Martha turned around and stifled a gasp. "Oh, my Lord! Lexie, what have you done to yourself?" She hung up the phone abruptly and rushed over to the two women who were dripping enough muddy water to make puddles in her kitchen.

Lex still leaned heavily against Amanda. "Hey, Martha. This is Amanda. Do you think you could find her some dry clothes?"

Amanda gave Martha a friendly smile and held out her hand. "Hi, Lex rescued me out of the creek today when my car got tossed in." Amanda looked at Lex with the kind of pride that showed Martha that the tall rancher had achieved hero status on this rainy afternoon.

"Yeah. Then she followed me home. Can I keep her?" Lex joked.

Martha laughed in relief. "My goodness Lexie, you always did have a habit of bringing in strays." She quickly closed the distance between them and shook Amanda's hand, releasing it after a long moment. "You both look like you could use a warm bath and a cup of hot coffee." She gently cradled Lex's cheek. "Do you think you could take your friend upstairs, while I fix you something warm to drink?"

"Sure, Martha." Lex clasped Amanda's hand and led her through the kitchen and into the hallway. "C'mon, let's go. After you've had a hot shower, I'll find you something to change into." Amanda placed her arm around Lexington to help steady her as they ascended the oak staircase. Halfway up, Lex stumbled. She would have fallen except for the tight grip Amanda had on her waist.

"Okay, that's it." Amanda forced Lex to sit down on one of the steps. "Now you sit right here and don't move. I'm going to go get Martha so she can help me with you." When she saw Lex open her mouth to protest, she gave her a look that caused the injured woman to snap her mouth shut. "Please don't try to argue with me." She patted the seated woman on the head and turned to go back down the stairs. Nearly whispering, she said, "Good girl. I'll be right back." Amanda hurried back down the stairs and disappeared into the kitchen.

Lex slumped to the side against the wall, her eyes following the lithe body. *Is it my imagination, or are there now two women in my life who can tell me what to do? This one's quite a little spitfire, eh?* She closed her eyes and struggled to fight off the pain.

Amanda burst back into the kitchen and grabbed the housekeeper's arm. Martha spun around from where she was stirring something on the stove. "What's the matter, dear? Did you get lost?"

"No, nothing like that." She pulled her out of the kitchen. "Lex is hurt, and I need some help with her. She practically collapsed on me."

At the foot of the stairs, Martha looked up. When she saw Lex, she ran up the steps until she could kneel beside her. "Lexie? Can you hear me?" She gently turned the quiet woman's face toward her.

"Hmm?" Lex and rubbed her eyes with one hand. "Guess I'm a little tired." She tried to sit up, but the pain in her chest pushed her back down. "I suppose a little help would be good." She looked at Amanda, who was standing in front of her looking worried, and thought to divert some of the attention away from herself. "And I bet you could use some aspirin, right?"

Amanda blinked in surprise. Lex was on the verge of completely collapsing, but here she was, concerned about her. "Yeah, for some reason I seem to have the darndest headache." She reached to help as Lex allowed Martha to pull her to her feet. The housekeeper wrapped an arm around her, and Amanda moved to support her other side. The three of them climbed the remaining stairs slowly.

Martha led them down the hallway and into the master bedroom. Amanda couldn't help but glance around in awe. The room was impressive—a large fireplace framed in rocks took up one entire corner, and there were two comfortable stuffed chairs in front of it. A fire was already blazing, which made the whole area look cozy and inviting. The wall opposite the door held a bay window, complete with a padded window seat. The front of the room had French doors that opened up to the balcony she had seen from outside. But the thing that most caught Amanda's attention was the enormous king-sized bed that almost took up a quarter of the room. It was a four-poster oak bed with a massive carved headboard, and it seemed to her that an entire family could sleep on it.

Lex noticed where her companion's attention was. "It was my mother's. Dad had it made for her as a wedding present." She stifled a groan when her two 'nurses' placed her on the object in question. It didn't take but a few seconds for Lex to lie back and close her eyes.

Amanda sat down on the foot of the bed. She turned so that she could keep an eye on Lex. Martha noticed the bloodstained shirt for the first time. "What happened here?"

"I'm not real sure." Amanda's eyes took in the exhausted woman. "I was driving across this beautiful wooden bridge when all of a sudden something hit it and sent my car crashing into the creek. I must have hit my head, because the next thing I

remember is being tied to her back and pulled across the water."
Her hand caressed the damp denim leg next to her. "She told me
she had gotten hit by some debris, but I never did find out
exactly what that was."

The housekeeper rolled her eyes. "Some things never
change. I swear I've spent half my life patching this girl up."
She looked down at the woman who was obviously asleep.
Then, to Amanda she said, "Let's get you some dry clothes, and
you can help me with her." She walked over to a large oak
dresser, which, by the design, appeared to have been by the
same person who made the bed. Opening the bottom drawer,
Martha dug around until she pulled out a pair of maroon sweat
pants with matching sweatshirt, each sporting a Texas A & M
University logo. "Here. Go hop in the shower and then put
these on. Lexie hasn't worn them in years, but she never could
manage to get rid of them. Just leave your wet clothes on the
floor, and I'll get 'em washed up for you." Amanda was about
to protest when Martha shook her finger at her. "Now, don't you
be giving me any lip. I do the cooking and the washing around
here." She gently pushed Amanda in the direction of the bathroom. "Hurry up. I'll probably need all the help I can get with
little Lexie. She hates when I fuss over her."

Little Lexie? That's sweet. "I'll be right back." Amanda
walked into the bathroom and closed the door behind her. *Good
grief! It's almost as big as my bedroom at home.* She walked
past the large dressing area complete with a long gray marble
counter with two separate sinks, one at each end. One corner of
the bathing area had a jetted garden tub and a very large free-
standing clear glass shower with a built-in bench. Another door
showed her a hidden lavatory. She opened the shower door and
her eyes widened. *Wow! Two people could shower in here.*
Amanda shook her head, trying to snap out of it, when she realized she was mentally picturing that second person. *Good grief,
Amanda! You're covered in mud, cold to the bone, with a headache that would fell a moose, and all you can think about is
showering with tall, dark, and unconscious in the other room?
Get a grip!* She turned on the water, quickly removed her soggy
clothing, and piled it by the door as neatly as possible.

Stepping into the steaming water, Amanda couldn't help
but moan. *Never thought that standing under more water would
feel so good.* Although she was tempted to spend the rest of her
life standing there, feeling the hot water sooth the muscles in
her back, she finished her shower and dried off. When she

pulled on the sweats, the sleeves fell several inches below her fingertips, and the pants promptly fell to her knees. Amanda chuckled, then tugged the pants back up to her waist. She tightened the drawstring and tied it into a bow, and then rolled the shirtsleeves up a few turns until she could see her hands. After she ran a comb through her hair, Amanda walked back into the bedroom, where she saw Martha trying to peel Lex's jeans from her legs.

"Am I ever glad to see you." Martha stood up and wiped her brow with the back of her hand. "I'm having the hardest time with these blasted jeans. They normally fit her like a second skin, and now that they're wet, well..." She shook her graying head. "Lexie was trying to help, but it got to hurting her so bad that she passed out again."

Amanda stepped up beside her. "I think that between the two of us, we should be able to handle it." She grabbed the bottom of the jeans. "I'll pull from here, and you try to work them from her hips."

It took them several minutes to rid the unconscious woman of her jeans. Martha brushed the drying hair off Lex's forehead once they were finished. "Poor thing. We might as well go for what's left of this shirt." She began to peel the damp shirt off, but stopped when she saw that it was stuck to Lex's skin. *There's no telling what we're going to find.* Martha glanced at the woman standing beside her. Fearful that Amanda's pale complexion meant she might faint at any moment, especially if Lex's wound was as bad as it looked, she decided it was time for a distraction. "Amanda, honey, could you bring me a few warm washcloths from the bathroom?"

Amanda had been staring intently at the prone woman, worrying more and more about her condition. But when Martha asked for her assistance, she looked up eagerly. "Sure." She rushed into the bathroom, wanting to do whatever she could to bring aid to the woman who had saved her life.

A few moments later, Amanda returned with a pair of damp washcloths. Martha stood over Lex with a clinical air. She had removed Lex's shirt and covered her legs with a colorful quilt, leaving her torso exposed. A white cotton bra clung to the unconscious woman's breasts, which rose and fell in a slow rhythm. Blood, both drying and fresh, coated the area over Lex's ribs. And the mud that coated her everywhere made the rancher look like she'd been beaten within an inch of her life.

Martha accepted one of the clean cloths from Amanda.

"Thanks. It looks a lot worse than it actually is, I believe." She cleaned the area around the wound, relieved to see the limited extent of the damage. The long, paper-thin slice started just below Lex's breasts and edged down her ribcage. The beginnings of a very large bruise surrounded it. "Just scraped up a little, but I don't think her ribs are broken." Martha gestured to the other washcloth Amanda was still holding. "Why don't you wash her face and arms while I go get something to put on this?" Not waiting for an answer, Martha stood up and left the room.

Amanda stood for a moment looking down at her rescuer. As she wiped off the evidence of their harrowing afternoon from Lexington's face, her heart moved her to whisper, "You jumped into the creek for someone that you didn't even know. You nearly got your beautiful self killed, too." Amanda paused for a moment as she fought back tears. "Thank you." She smoothed a lock of Lex's hair and lay it gently against her pillow. Then she resumed washing the dirt from Lex's face, unaware that she was still speaking words of comfort and gratitude out loud.

The housekeeper slipped back into the room. She was touched to see the tender care Amanda was giving Lex. *Ah, she's a sweet one, that girl. I wonder what business she had that brought her to us.* "I told you I wouldn't be long." Martha stepped over to the bed carrying a jar and several strips of cloth.

"What's that?"

"Just some homemade salve that I've used on her since she was knee-high to a grasshopper. And since I didn't have enough gauze on hand, I cut up an old sheet instead." Martha sat next to Lex and gently dabbed the ointment onto the bleeding wound. "Could you climb up on the bed on her other side, and help me sit her up?" She waited until Amanda was in position. "Let's lift her forward, slowly now." Lex moaned, but didn't waken. Amanda sat behind her and held her upright while the housekeeper wrapped the strips of sheet around her torso. "This should keep the wound clean and give her a little relief from those ribs." After they laid Lex back against the pillows, Martha used the quilt on her legs to cover her up completely.

Amanda eased herself off the bed. "You do act like you've done this before." *I don't think I could stay that calm, especially if I were as close as they seem to be.*

Martha sighed. "Oh, goodness, yes. That little mite was always coming home with some sort of scrape or bruise." She eyed Amanda carefully and then tugged on her arm. "Now, you come on in the bathroom and I'll check out that bump on your head."

"Oh." Amanda reached up to touch the spot. "I'd forgotten all about it." She followed Martha into the adjoining room. "It hardly hurts at all now."

"Hop up there," Martha ordered, assisting her guest onto the wide bathroom counter. She looked Amanda in the eye. "Don't worry, dear. This won't hurt a bit."

Put at ease by Martha's soothing manner, Amanda braced her hands on either side of her legs and leaned forward. "I know."

The housekeeper gently cleansed the area around the small cut, put some of her homemade salve on it, and then covered it with a large adhesive bandage. "That should keep it from getting infected." Martha reached behind her and grabbed a bottle and glass. She poured out two white tablets from the bottle, then filled up the glass with water. "Here, these should help with your headache."

After taking the medication, Amanda jumped down from the counter and turned in a circle. "I feel like a little kid playing dress up in her clothes." She pulled the material away from herself, showing how baggy they were.

Martha chuckled. "Don't you be worrying about it, dear. You look just fine." She went into the bathing area and returned with the wet clothes. "Now I'll just go take care of these and Lexie's wet things."

Amanda held out her hands. "No, really. I can take care of those. Just point me in the direction of the laundry room."

Martha moved around her. "Nope, I'll take care of this. You just go lie down and rest." When Amanda began to argue again, Martha placed a hand on her shoulder. "You could help me by keeping an eye on Lexie. Watch to see if she develops a fever. I'll just get these started and then bring you both something to eat."

"Okay, I'll do that. But shouldn't we get her to a doctor?"

Martha shook her head. "That bridge that you came over on is the only way on or off this ranch. And until this weather lets up, they can't even bring a helicopter in."

Amanda froze. "You mean, we're trapped here? What if she's hurt worse than you think? What can we do? What—"

Her babbling was stopped by a light squeeze of her shoulder. Martha looked deeply into her eyes to reassure her. With a steady voice, she said, "It's going to be okay. Yes, it's true it's

just the three of us here for now, but we've got more than
enough supplies, and we do have a telephone. So don't you
worry." Martha gathered up the rest of the wet clothes and
headed for the door. Remembering how gentle Amanda had
been with Lex a few moments before, she said, "It would be easier to keep an eye on her if you laid down beside her. It's a big
bed." She walked out of the room, with a perplexed Amanda
staring after her.

Amanda watched Martha leave, and then switched her
attention to the bed. "She's right. That thing's huge. And I am
worn out. Maybe I'll just lie down for a few minutes." She
walked around to the other side of the bed and lay down. *Oh, I
could be in serious trouble here—this is way too comfortable.*
Amanda rolled over onto her side and noticed the color return-
ing to the sleeping woman's face and reached out to brush her
fingers against Lex's cheek. Within moments, Amanda joined
Lex in sleep.

Lex woke up, disoriented at first. She looked around and
recognized that she was at home and in her own bed. *Yeah, now
I remember trying to come up the stairs.* Her mind was still a little fuzzy after that. Hearing soft snoring, she turned her head to
find Amanda asleep on the pillow next to her, with her right
hand tucked under her cheek, and her left hand...*holding my
arm?* Despite the ache in her chest, Lex reached to Amanda and
ran her fingertips across her forehead and down her cheek as
she studied the woman sleeping next to her. "You got us home,"
she whispered. "Thank you."

Hearing Martha's footsteps on the stairs, she stopped stroking Amanda's face and tried to disengage her arm from
Amanda's grip. Before she could do so, Martha walked in carrying a large wooden tray laden with food.

"How are you feeling, Lexie?" Martha placed the tray on
the bedside table, and sat carefully next to her "patient." She
brushed the hair off Lex's forehead, also using the motion to
check for fever.

"I'm fine, Martha. Don't worry so much." Unable to lie
still, Lex disentangled herself from Amanda's grip and rose to a
sitting position.

"Oh, sure. You were so 'fine' that *we* had to undress you.
You probably don't even remember it."

Lex stretched cautiously, satisfied that the pain was manageable. "I think I was more tired than actually hurt." She noticed that the worried look was still on Martha's face. "Honestly, I feel much better now." Leaning slightly forward, Lex tried to peek around her. "Is that food I smell?"

Martha patted her on the leg. "Oh, Lexie, you're gonna be the death of me yet."

Awakened by the sound of voices, Amanda opened her eyes. "Hey." She sat up and rubbed her eyes. "How long was I asleep?" She looked outside, but it was still dark and raining.

"Only a couple of hours." Martha reached for the tray and placed it in the middle of the bed.

"*A couple of hours?* Oh, no!" Amanda made a move to get off the bed but Lex grabbed her arm.

"What's the matter?"

"My grandparents—I really need to let them know I'm okay." Amanda was nearly frantic. "They'll be worried sick. Especially with this weather."

Martha halted her babbling with a wave of her hand. "Now hold on there." She picked up the cordless phone that was on Lex's bedside table. "Here. The last time I checked, the phone lines were just fine."

Amanda took the phone gratefully. "Thanks. I'm sorry, I don't usually fall apart this easily." She dialed her grandparents' number, and after three rings it was picked up.

An older woman's voice answered. "Hello?"

Relief flowed through Amanda. Just hearing her grandmother's voice was soothing. "Gramma? It's me, Amanda."

"Mandy, are you okay? We were getting a little worried. You're usually home before now." Anna Leigh's voice was muffled for a moment while she addressed her husband. "Yes, Jacob. It's Mandy. I will." She returned her attention to Amanda. "Where are you?"

Amanda wondered what she could tell her grandmother without lying or making her worry. "Actually, I went out for an appointment today."

Anna Leigh interrupted her. "You went out in this awful weather?"

"Yes, Gramma. Rick gave me the appointment sheet—"

"That pompous ass! I'd fire his worthless hide, if only you'd agree to run the office." Anna Leigh's voice shook with emotion. "So, where are you now? You're not still out somewhere in the rain, are you?"

"Gramma, I've told you I'm not qualified to be an office

manager just yet. And no, I'm not out in the rain. I'm, uh, kind of stuck at a friend's house." She looked over at Lex and Martha and shrugged her shoulders.

"Where? Are you okay? You didn't get the car stuck, did you?"

Amanda blanched. She had been so worried about Lex, and so disoriented after bumping her head, she had completely forgotten about the car. "Oh. Well, yes, Gramma, the car is stuck," *in a creek.* Her mind finished the sentence, and then she chastised herself for misleading her grandmother.

"Well, don't you worry. Jacob will be the first to say that you're much more important than some old car. Besides, we'll just wait until it dries up some and have Randy down at the garage take care of it."

It'll probably take a lot of drying out. "I know, Gramma. I guess I'm just a little tired."

"That's perfectly okay, Mandy. When will you be home? Do we need to send a cab for you?" Even though his leg cast recently had been removed, Jacob still had not been cleared to drive, which frustrated him to no end. Anna Leigh refused to leave him at home alone, afraid that he would need something and try to drive anyway. And she certainly didn't want to get him out in this weather. She could tell their granddaughter wasn't telling the whole story, because she sounded far too upset for the car just to be stuck in the mud.

Amanda's voice trembled. "Well, that's kind of hard to say. I guess you could say I'm stranded."

"Stranded? What exactly do you mean by that? Are you sure you're okay?" Anna Leigh was becoming upset as well.

"Uh, well." Amanda looked desperate. She covered the mouthpiece with her hand and whispered to the women looking on. "I don't know what to say, and I don't want them to worry."

Lex covered Amanda's hand and gave it a squeeze before pulling the phone out of her fingers. "Hello? This is Lexington Walters." She paused and listened to the woman on the other end of the line. "Yes ma'am, that's right, Mrs. Cauble. I've been on the Historical Committee with you."

Hearing those words, Amanda's jaw dropped. *Lexington Walters? Historical Committee? My grandmother? She knows my grandmother?*

"Yes ma'am. Amanda is here at the ranch with me, but I'm afraid she'll be stuck here for a while. Excuse me? No, nothing like that. Seems our old bridge was washed out, and your lovely

granddaughter got stuck on this side of the creek." Lex mischievously raised an eyebrow at Amanda.

Lovely? She thinks I'm lovely? Wow! Amanda closed her
eyes as a sudden wave of shyness washed over her, and when she
opened them, Lex smiled at her and winked.

"No, ma'am, it'll be fine. It's only Martha and me out here
right now, so she'll be good company. The boys are at the stock
show. Do you need our number? Oh, that's right. I forgot that
you already have it." Lex saw an incredulous look cross
Amanda's face. "Yes ma'am, I will. I think Amanda has calmed
down now. Yes ma'am. Nice to talk to you again, too. Good-
bye." She handed the phone over to a very curious Amanda.

"Hi, again, Gramma. I'm sorry I fell apart like that. Guess
being stuck out in the rain today wore me out." Amanda leaned
back against the headboard, finally able relax.

"Don't apologize. I'd probably be the same way. At least we
won't worry about you. Lexington is one of the sweetest people
I have ever met. She's a good person, no matter what others
might say." Fearing that she'd said too much, Anna Leigh
stopped. Rumors abounded about the Walters girl. Some said
she was unnatural, running the ranch when she had an older
brother perfectly capable of it. And the fact that she didn't date
much in high school and still wasn't married spoke volumes as
far as the town's gossips were concerned. *Not to mention that
unfortunate wild streak she had a few years ago.*

Amanda paused. *What others might say? Well, if Gramma
thinks she's a good person, that's all that matters to me.* "I know
what you mean. She practically took me in today. I'll give you a
call in the morning to see how you're both doing, okay?"

"Why don't you make it tomorrow evening? Your grandfather and I have a few errands to run tomorrow. He has his physical therapy; then we thought we'd take in an early movie."
Anna Leigh didn't want her granddaughter to think she had to
be with them every minute of every day. *She's sweet, but she
really needs to get out more and meet people her own age.
Maybe this is the perfect opportunity.* "And you try and get
some rest. You sound tired, Mandy."

"I will. Don't go out if it's still raining too hard, please?"
She paused, forcing the lump out of her throat. "I love you,
Gramma. Please give Grandpa Jake a big hug and kiss from
me."

"We love you, too, dearest. I promise we'll stay home if the
weather's too bad." Anna Leigh hung up the phone, touched by

her granddaughter's protective nature.

Amanda turned off the phone and handed it back to Lex. "Thanks. I feel much better now." She suddenly slapped Lex's arm.

"Ow! What was that for?"

"You didn't tell me you knew my grandmother."

Lex shrugged her shoulders. "Well, since we didn't exchange last names, I didn't know either, until I recognized her voice on the telephone." She shook a finger at Amanda. "*You* didn't tell me you were Jacob and Anna Leigh Cauble's granddaughter."

Amanda shrugged. "Okay, you got me there." Thinking out loud, she continued, "It's so weird that you know my grandparents, but we've never met." Deciding a change of subject was in order, Amanda reached for the tray and grabbed a bowl of chili. "Mmm," she mumbled with a mouthful. "Dis is fantastic!" She took another bite.

Lex leaned over slightly to pick up her own bowl. "Oh, yeah. Martha makes the best chili I've ever eaten." She looked up as the woman they were talking about approached, carrying a cotton nightshirt.

Embarrassed by the high praise, Martha tried to appear gruff. "Put that down and put this on. I don't want you to catch cold."

"Why? Isn't quilt-wearing fashionable this year?" Never one for modesty, Lex set down her bowl and allowed Martha to help her remove her bra. Amanda tried not to watch Lex raise her arms while Martha slipped the nightshirt over her head. "This is a lot easier to eat in, that's for sure." Lex picked up her bowl and began to eat again, ignoring the burst of laughter from the woman on the bed beside her.

Martha swatted Lex on the leg. "Smarty-pants. I'll just drag out your quilt the next time you say you have nothing to wear." She turned and headed for the door. "After you girls finish that tray, give me a buzz and I'll come back to clean it up. I've got some laundry to finish in the meantime."

"Do you think she would be too mad if I took the tray downstairs? I don't want her to be waiting on me hand and foot," Amanda asked between mouthfuls of chili and warm cornbread. "Although if I stay here too long, I'll weigh too much to get down the stairs."

Lex laughed, then stopped and held her arm up to her chest. "Ow! Don't make me laugh. She'll fuss about it, but she rarely gets mad." She finished her bowl and set it down. "I've been trying for years to stop her from fussing over me, and nothing has worked yet. I even offered her the chance to retire and travel. Bad idea."

"Why?" Amanda took one last bite of the cornbread and licked the butter off her fingers, unaware of the affect it was having on Lex, who was watching her intently.

Transfixed, Lex asked, "Why what?"

"Why was it a bad idea to ask her to retire?"

Lex blinked and forced herself to remember that they'd been talking about Martha. *Way to go, Lexington.* "She was not about to leave me alone on this ranch, and she let me know that. Loudly. I've never heard so much yelling in my life. So now, I let her fuss. It seems to make her happy."

Amanda finished up her bowl and placed it on the tray as well. "Let me take this downstairs before she makes another trip." She got up off the bed and started to pick up the tray, but a loud gust of laughter stopped her. "What?"

"Sorry." Lex was trying, without much success, to control herself. "It's just you...you..." She wrapped both arms protectively around her aching chest. "Ouch!"

"Me, me, what?" Amanda was beginning to get a little angry.

"You look funny in my old sweats." Lex lay back on the bed, rocking silently with laughter, except for the very frequent "Ow!"

Amanda rolled her eyes. "Serves you right, making fun of me." Then wondering what kind of picture she presented to the beautiful rancher, she asked, "I don't look that bad, do I?" She set the tray down and walked into the bathroom to look in the full-length mirror. "Oh, good grief!" The clothes had to be at least three sizes too big.

Lex finally calmed down, but when Amanda walked in giggling, she started up all over again. Lex groaned and wrapped her arms around her chest, in pain. "Ugh."

Amanda continued to laugh as well while she staggered over to the bed and sat down next to Lex. "Shh! You're just gonna hurt yourself worse." She placed her hand on the injured woman's shoulder in an effort to help calm her.

Finally winding down, Lex struggled to catch her breath and closed her eyes. "Damn. That hurt, but felt really good." She took a semi-deep breath and opened her eyes to look at Amanda's face. "Thanks."

All of Amanda's senses were captured the moment Lex opened her eyes. "For what?" It was her turn to lose all thought.

"For being such a good sport and not smacking me when I started laughing. I wasn't really making fun of you, you know."

"I know. You were making fun of the clothes. I just happened to be wearing them at the time. Besides, I do look like a little kid in these things. But they're really comfortable." Doing an exaggerated imitation of a model, Amanda walked around to the other side of the bed and picked up the tray. "I'm going to try again to take this tray downstairs." She started to walk away, then turned back to face Lex. "You didn't hurt yourself laughing, did you? Should I ask Martha to come up and check your bandage?"

Lex dismissed her concern with a wave of her hand. "Nah, just a little sore. I'm fine."

Amanda had her doubts, but decided to keep quiet. "Okay, then I'll run this downstairs. Why don't you try and get some more rest? I'll be back in a little bit."

Now that she wasn't in such a rush, Amanda had time to look around while she descended the stairs. The walls of the house were covered in a light maple paneling and had old oil paintings scattered among framed pictures of children. The floor of the ranch house was a dark oak that appeared to have seen better days, although she could see that it had been well maintained. She had just made it to the bottom of the stairs when she heard Martha's voice echo around her.

"All right young lady, just what do you think you're doing?" The housekeeper stood at the end of the hall with a stack of clothes in one hand. "Well?"

Amanda continued until she was standing a few feet away. She felt like a four-year-old who'd been caught doing something naughty, and gave the other woman a bashful look. "I thought I'd save you a trip upstairs."

Martha took pity on Amanda and decided to lighten up on the teasing, just a little. She led her into the kitchen where she placed the stack of clothes on a nearby stool and took over removing the dishes from the tray. "I'll let it slide this time. How are you feeling?" Martha efficiently stacked the dirty dishes in the sink then wiped down the tray with a dishcloth.

Realizing that she wasn't needed, Amanda sat down on the other stool. She picked up her clean socks and slipped them on her feet. "I'm feeling much better. I don't know how you did it, but thank you for finding my socks and washing my things. You didn't have to, but I do appreciate it."

Martha wiped her soapy hands on a dry dishtowel and turned to face her. "You're more than welcome. I found your socks when I was cleaning up the mud room. I was washing Lexie's things anyway and thought you might need something clean to wear." Her amused gaze traveled over her guest's outfit. "Although you look like you're mighty comfortable right now."

"Actually, I am. These," she plucked at the shirt, "may be big, but I think I'm addicted to them already."

The housekeeper patted her on the leg. "Well, I don't think Lexie will mind. She hasn't worn them in years."

Amanda couldn't help but be curious. "Even though I don't know her very well, she doesn't seem like the type to keep things that aren't useful. Why would she keep these?" She looked down at the Texas A&M logo on the shirt. "Did she go to school there or something?"

Well, better she ask me than Lexie. Martha picked up the clothes on the spare stool and sat facing Amanda. "No dear, she didn't go to college. She wanted to, but her father left her in charge of the ranch and then took off to ride in the rodeos."

"She said she has a brother. Why didn't she let him run the ranch while she went to school?"

Martha lowered her voice, anger in her tone. "Now this is my opinion, mind you, but that man would have run this ranch right into the ground within a year. He's a smart enough pencil pusher, but Hubert doesn't know enough about ranching to fill a thimble." She cleared her throat. "Besides, Lexie is a natural. I don't think there's anything that girl can't do. Just don't let on that I told you. She's a pretty private person, and I didn't want you to upset her by asking her about it."

"Thanks for letting me know, Martha. I would never intentionally hurt her. If I'm not being too nosy, what was she planning on studying?"

"She wanted to be a veterinarian. That girl has always had a way with animals. I think if she didn't feel so responsible for everyone who works here, she would have sold this ranch years ago and gone to school anyway. But no, Lexie will stick with this place until the end of time." She looked over at Amanda, who had a strange look on her face. "What's the matter?"

"That sorry..." Amanda trailed off, anger beginning to flair in her eyes. "He probably knew she'd never sell and just wanted me to make a fool out of myself."

"What are you talking about?"

Amanda shook her head apologetically. "I'm sorry, Martha. It just dawned on me that someone was trying to make me look like an idiot, and probably trying to get Lex riled up as well." *I'll bet that Rick knew all of this, and anticipated how it would make Lex feel to talk about selling the ranch.* "You see, I work for my grandmother's real estate agency."

Martha placed a hand over her mouth in dismay as understanding dawned on her weathered features. "Oh, no."

"Oh, yes. The manager, Rick, gave me an appointment sheet and directions to find my way out here earlier today—"

The shocked housekeeper interrupted her. "Rick? That wouldn't be Ricky Thompson, would it?" Small towns had their bad points, too. Everybody knew everyone else, and there were few secrets.

"Yeah. He's had it in for me ever since I refused to go out with him." She shivered. "I can't help it. The man makes my skin crawl. Why? Do you know him, too?"

"I guess you could say that you and Lexie have something in common with him. When Ricky was a senior and Lexie was a sophomore, she turned him down for dates quite a few times. He wouldn't take no for an answer and started to get a little physical about it, so she basically flattened him in the main hall in front of most of the school. I probably would have never known anything about it, but she got suspended from school for three days." Martha paused, trying to gather her thoughts. "I was pretty upset at first, until the school counselor called me and explained. They had to suspend her for fighting as a matter of school policy, but they made sure she didn't miss anything important in class. I think they were impressed that someone finally stood up to Ricky. He was such a bully in those days. Poor Lexie. Since then, he's always been looking for a way to get back at her."

"He sure hasn't changed much." Things came together in Amanda's mind. "That would explain why he sent me out here today. I was supposed to meet with 'L. Walters' to discuss putting the ranch up for sale. Rick told me that the owner was tired of ranching." She clenched her fists. "That rat! I ought to—"

Martha stood up next to the angry woman. "Now, now dear." She rubbed her hand lightly on Amanda's back. "Everything turned out okay, didn't it?" *Other than this poor child nearly dying in a flooded creek.*

Amanda made a conscious effort to calm down. "You're

right. I would have probably never met you or Lex otherwise, so maybe I should call him up and thank him." She smiled evilly. "Wouldn't that just twist his shorts?"

The housekeeper hugged her. "Oh, it certainly would. I'd love to see his face. Unfortunately, we're all three stuck here until the weather clears up enough to start rebuilding that bridge, or the creek goes down enough to walk across."

"Well, at least we're dry and safe." Amanda stood up and took the folded clothes. "I'll just go put these away for now, since I'm pretty comfortable in my present outfit." She headed for the doorway. "But please, let me know if there is anything I can do to help around here. I feel bad that you're doing all the work."

Martha walked back over to the sink. "If you can keep Lexie occupied without her driving me crazy, I'll consider it a fair trade." She put her hands back in the water, then turned and looked over her shoulder. "Try to keep her still for as long as possible. Even though they're not broken, I'd really like to give those ribs a little time to heal."

"I'll try. But she seems like the type who doesn't like to stay still."

The housekeeper agreed. "Mercy! Have you got her number. Now go on and get some rest yourself."

"I will. See you later." Amanda left the kitchen with her mind set on keeping a certain someone occupied.

She tiptoed quietly to the bedroom, in case Lex was sleeping. Amanda peeked around the door and looked inside, seeing only an empty bed. *Now where could she be?*

The bathroom door opened and a slightly damp Lex made her way slowly into the bedroom. She had a towel around her neck and was wearing boxer shorts with a faded blue nightshirt.

"What do you think you're doing?" Amanda stood in the doorway and crossed her arms over her chest. She hated the way she sounded, but her worry overrode all good sense. As she watched the ease with which Lex moved across the room, Amanda gave up being upset, and followed her to the sitting area of the bedroom.

Lex slowly maneuvered herself into one of the chairs in front of the fire. "I felt pretty grimy after that swim in the creek and the mud bath, so I thought I'd take a real bath." Realizing that wasn't much of an answer, she hurried to explain. "Don't worry. I was real careful and didn't even get my bandage wet."

Amanda sat in the opposite chair. "I'm sorry, but Martha

asked me to keep an eye on you, and I didn't want anything to happen on 'my watch.'" She took a moment to study the woman across from her. "You do look a lot better than you did."

Lex leaned back in the chair gingerly. "Yeah, amazing what warm water and soap can do for a person." She was a little surprised at the concern Amanda showed, considering they hadn't known each other for very long. It felt good to know that someone besides Martha cared about how she felt. But, deciding not to delve too deeply into those thoughts, at least not tonight, Lex made a point of looking at the clock sitting on the mantle. "It's getting late, and you're looking a little tired yourself." She stood up slowly in deference to the complaints from her aching body. "C'mon. Let's go get you tucked in." Lex offered her hand to Amanda, who blushed at her choice of words.

Stop that Amanda—she doesn't mean anything by it. Still, she was affected by the attraction she had felt ever since she'd first laid eyes on Lex. Struggling with her feelings, Amanda didn't take Lex's hand, but got to her feet on her own. "Okay, point me to the couch."

Lex felt a little hurt by the rebuff, but mentally shrugged and led her guest across the hall. She reached inside the doorway and flipped the light switch. "Here's the guest room. We just finished remodeling it, so you're our first guest."

Amanda walked behind her into the room and was pleasantly surprised by what she saw. Almost matching Lex's room in size, about the only things missing were the fireplace and the French doors. A large brass bed sat against one wall. Its yellow comforter was decorated with a bright flowery design. There were two large picture windows with window seats that matched the bed, and several nice oil paintings adorned the elegantly papered walls. The corner sitting area held a comfortable chair and lamp within reaching distance of a well-stocked bookshelf.

Disturbed by how quietly Amanda was taking in her surroundings, Lex asked, "What? It's not that bad, is it?"

"Not that bad? It's beautiful, Lex. Did you do the decorating?"

This earned her a snicker from her host. "Oh yeah, right. Not." Lex led Amanda to a door on the other side of the bed. "You've seen my room. This was all Martha's doing." She opened the door to a more modest bathroom, but well equipped, all the same. "There should be everything you might need here. Martha's always real thorough."

Amanda turned around and looked up into Lex's eyes. "Thank you. I don't think I'll ever be able to say it enough. You saved my life, took me into your home, and have taken care of me. I don't know how I'll ever repay you." Wanting to do more, she merely took Lex's hands in hers and squeezed them gently.

"You don't owe me anything. I'm just glad I was there." A sudden surge of tenderness brought Lex to place a gentle kiss on Amanda's forehead. "Now try to get some sleep. I'll see you in the morning." She turned and walked out of the room, then closed the door quietly behind her.

The soft touch brought out strong emotions in Amanda as well. *Oh, my God!* She drew a shaky hand through her hair. *And I'm supposed to be able to sleep after that?* The feel of Lex's lips on her forehead and the scent of Lex's skin awakened long dormant feelings. The attraction she had been feeling for Lex up until that moment seemed insignificant by comparison. It had been years since a woman caused her heart to speed up like that, but she told herself that it was probably due to the day's circumstances. Dismissing her feelings as foolishness, Amanda went into the bathroom to get ready for bed. After going through her nightly routine, she came into the bedroom and crossed over to the door. She opened it and looked across the hall. *Light's already out. Guess one of us will get some sleep tonight.* Closing the door behind her, Amanda made her way over to the bed and crawled under the clean sheets. Moments later, in spite of her racing thoughts, she fell deeply asleep.

Chapter Three

It was dark and very cold, and whatever was holding her down was too strong for her to break free. Unable to see, she could hear a roaring sound coming nearer, but for some reason her legs would not move. The thundering drew closer and closer, and no matter how hard she struggled, she was held tighter and tighter.

Noooo!

Water lapped at her feet, as the tumultuous noise got louder and louder. *Help me!* The strap holding her in place seemed to get tighter, and the water was now over her thighs and still rising. *Please help me!* The cold, dirty water was up to her chin. The band constricted around her chest. *I can't breathe. Nooooo!*

Amanda screamed as she jerked upright, and found herself wrapped in strong arms. "Shhh. You're okay," a low voice murmured in her ear. Warm hands rubbed her back soothingly.

"Oh, God. What happened?" Amanda's eyes blinked open, and she was startled to find Lex sitting on her bed, holding her tightly.

"You were crying out. Must have been one doozy of a nightmare." Lex's dark hair was in disarray, and she appeared to be half-asleep herself. She sat back a little, but still kept up the soothing motion on Amanda's back.

Amanda took a shaky breath. "S..s...sorry." She began to cry. "It was dark. I couldn't get loose. And then the water—" Needing the comfort, she fell forward into Lex's arms.

"Hey, it's all right." Unsure of what to do, Lex held her hands out behind Amanda for a moment, then placed them on her back and patted her awkwardly. It was one thing to comfort someone in the throws of a nightmare, but she wasn't sure how her touch would be taken now that Amanda was awake. "Shhh.

You're safe now." Amanda clung to Lex as if her life depended
on it. Strangled sobs racked her body. Although the position
they were in caused her ribs to ache, Lex never even considered
letting go of the distraught woman. She pulled her closer and
rubbed her cheek on the top of Amanda's head, relishing the
feel of the woman clinging to her.

Shortly, Amanda quieted. She was half asleep, enjoying the
gentle touch. Suddenly she realized how tightly she was
attached and released her stranglehold. "Thanks," she sniffed.
"I...I don't know what came over me. I haven't had a nightmare
since I was a little kid." Amanda pulled away, regretting the loss
of physical contact. To compensate, she loosely held both of
Lex's hands. They were different from other women's, with
thick calluses formed across the palms from years of hard work.

"You've had a pretty rough experience today. Any normal
person would have nightmares. Add the knot on your head, and
the fact that you're sleeping in a strange bed, it's only natural."
Lex squeezed the hands in hers, offering comfort and understanding.

"Hearing it put that way, I don't feel so bad now. I'm just
sorry that I woke you." She saw a flicker of pain cross Lex's
face. "Are you okay?"

Lex felt uncomfortable at the scrutiny. "I'm fine. Are you
doing better now?" She couldn't seem to look away from those
trusting eyes.

Amanda noticed Lex's glassy look. "Let me help you back
to bed." She stood up and pulled the other woman up with her.
"Besides," she touched the bandage on her temple, "I could use
a few more aspirin." On impulse, she wrapped her arms around
Lex and squeezed, which garnered an almost inaudible grunt in
return. "Thank you, again. You seem to always be pulling me
out of scary places."

Although her ribs ached from the contact, Lex returned the
hug. Finally she drew out of the embrace, missing Amanda's
warmth as soon as their bodies were separated. "Glad I could be
of service, ma'am." She tipped an imaginary hat and winked.

"You nut." Amanda kept one arm wrapped Lex's waist and
led them to the door. "Let's get you tucked in."

They made their way through the doorway and across the
hall easily. Amanda led her companion to the bed then placed
her hands on Lex's shoulders. "Down you go." She gently
pushed until Lex sat back on the bed.

"This isn't really necessary, you know." But even as she

said this, Lex allowed Amanda to lift her legs, swing them around, and then cover her body with the sheet and comforter. "You gonna tell me a story, too?" She smiled to take the edge off the teasing words.

"Only if you want me to." Amanda sat down on the edge of the bed next to her. "Any requests?" The two women locked eyes.

Several requests ran through Lex's mind, none of which could be voiced without embarrassing them both. Feeling the heat rise from her neck to her cheeks, she cleared her throat. "Yeah, go get your aspirin."

Amanda stood up. "Good idea." She patted a nearby leg. "Be right back." She stepped into the bathroom and Lex heard the sound of water running. There was a short pause, and then the tap was running again. Amanda stepped out of the bathroom with a glass in one hand. Her hair was slightly dampened around the back of her neck. "I've had mine." She opened the other hand and gave Lex two white tablets. "And here's yours."

Lex raised a questioning eyebrow at Amanda's dampened neck, but took the offering without complaint. She tossed the pills into her mouth and tilted her head back, then swallowed the contents of the glass. Placing the empty vessel on the nightstand, Lex patted the bed on the other side of her. "If you're gonna tell me a story, might as well get comfortable." Lex had a feeling Amanda was still shaky from her nightmare, and she was determined to help her.

Amanda blushed, but walked around and climbed up on the other side of the bed. She rolled over onto her side, and propped her head up on an upraised hand. "Okay, what story do you want me to tell?"

"Oh, I don't know." Lex turned her head and looked at the amused face across from her. "How about a happy childhood memory? You know, something to take your mind off what happened today?"

Amanda was touched that Lex was trying to help her get over her bad dreams. She turned over onto her back. "I can do that. Close your eyes, now. What good's a bedtime story if your eyes aren't closed?"

Lex chuckled, then reached up and turned off the bedside light. "Okay, I'm ready." She closed her eyes and laced her fingers together, resting them on her stomach.

Amanda laid back on the bed and folded her arms beneath her head while she thought of a story. "A happy memory, huh?

Let me think." *How about, no, that's not that much of a happy story. Oh, I know.* "The summer before I turned sixteen was one of the best I can ever remember. My parents took their normal trip to Europe, and my older sister Jeannie went on a church camp retreat. I was given a choice of going either place, but I chose to spend the summer with my grandparents instead.

"Anyway, the day after I arrived at their house, my grandfather suggested that we pack up a lunch and take a drive. No matter how hard we begged, he wouldn't tell us where we were going." She turned her head to look into Lex's amused eyes. "Our curiosity nearly did us in, but Gramma and I managed."

"You look like the curious type," Lex mused. "I'm sorry, go ahead."

"Thanks. As I was saying, he took us on a mysterious drive, and we ended up a couple of hours away from home at some old property. We drove down an overgrown road that led to an abandoned farmhouse. There were weeds and wild bushes everywhere, and it looked like it had been deserted for ages.

"Come to find out, my grandfather actually owned the place. Some time before, he had done extensive cabinetry work for a man who hadn't been able to finish paying him. Mr. Tucker vowed to my grandfather that somehow or other he'd honor his debt, so, when he passed away, he willed his property to Grandpa."

Lex yawned and rubbed her eyes. "That's pretty cool. So he brought you out to see the place?"

"Yes. We explored the property for most of the afternoon, and then had a picnic lunch out under the trees behind the house. We saw what looked to be a barn, and, after we finished eating, we decided to go check it out.

"Inside it was a cornucopia of junk. There were all sorts of rusted tools hanging from the walls, and in one corner was this great big thing covered with a grimy tarp. I finally got up the courage to peek under the cover, and what we found was something none of us expected."

"Piles of bodies?" Lex hazarded a guess, her voice heavy. She was fighting sleep, but still wanted to know the end of the story.

Amanda reached out in the dark and lightly slapped her companion's arm. "No, silly. It was a 1967 Mustang hard top, up on blocks and partially restored. There were no front seats, and the car was a patchwork of primer and old paint, but something about it called to me. My grandfather suggested that we take it home and work on it together over the summer. I was so excited I thought I was going to burst."

She paused for a moment, reliving the memory. When Anna Leigh agreed to let them use their garage for their summer project, Jacob had picked up his wife and spun her around the room. *I was so lucky growing up. Grandpa and Gramma were the best examples of two people in love I could ever know. Much more so than my own parents.* Her mother and father never showed affection to each other, at least none that she knew of. Most of their conversations had to do with business, the running of the massive house in Los Angeles, or where they were going on their next trip. *What my grandparents share is the true definition of love. Maybe someday I'll find someone who'll make me feel like that.*

Amanda looked over at Lex, who had just drifted off to sleep at the end of her story, and she sighed. *Yeah, maybe I will find that person.* Then she closed her own eyes and dreamed of her grandparents, dusty old cars, and cool summer days.

Early the next morning, Lex awoke at her usual time. She turned her head to check the digital clock beside the bed. *Just once I wish my internal alarm had a snooze button.* It was dark outside, and the previous night's thunderstorm had settled down to a more peaceful rain. She cautiously took a deep breath to see how her ribs were doing and was pleased when she only felt an ache and not the sharp pains of the night before.

In no hurry to get up, Lex glanced across at her companion and noticed that Amanda had gotten over her nightmares and was sleeping peacefully. Her youthful features were unlined, and Amanda's face wore the open look of someone with no worries in life. Now dry, her hair was slightly lighter than the almost brown of the day before. One strand was lying across Amanda's face and Lex had the urge to brush it out of the way before realizing that Amanda was holding her hand. *It seems so natural to have her here beside me. Was it just yesterday that we met? Maybe it's the ordeal that we went through together, but—* Her thoughts drifted off when Amanda pulled their joined hands to her chest and snuggled deeper into her pillow.

Lex stayed right where she was for a little longer, not wanting to take the chance of ruining the moment and ending the contact Amanda sought in her sleep. As Lex continued to gaze at Amanda, she felt the beginnings of something stirring deep within her. It was akin to the feeling she had when Amanda had held her and comforted her out in the mud and the rain. Telling herself that it was just the extreme situation they had been in, and that strong emotions were a natural result, she fought to push her feelings aside.

Besides, lying here isn't going to make the day go by any faster, Lexington. Disgusted with her woolgathering, Lex gently pulled her hand from Amanda's grasp, rolled out of bed, and padded quietly into the bathroom. After making herself more presentable, Lex came out of the bathroom, took a final peek at the sleeping woman, and slipped silently from the room. Still sore from the previous day's adventure, Lex took the stairs slowly and followed her nose to the kitchen, where she could smell fresh coffee brewing.

Martha was already up and into her daily routine. She hummed a nameless tune while she pulled several items from the refrigerator and carried them over to the counter.

Grinning mischievously, Lex waited until she was directly behind the older woman before speaking. "Morning, Martha."

The housekeeper whirled around, one hand covering her heart. "Blast it Lexie. You're gonna be the death of me one of these days." But she was smiling, and she raised her hand to cup the cheek of the other woman in an affectionate gesture. "How are you feeling this morning?"

Lex covered the hand on her face with one of her own. Martha Rollins was so dear to her. She was the only maternal figure Lex could really remember. Lex did have a brief memory of a beautiful dark-haired woman sitting at the piano in the drawing room and singing to her as she sat next to her on the bench. But the woman standing in front of her now was the one who raised her. It was Martha who cleaned her scraped knees, spanked her with a wooden spoon when she misbehaved, and listened to her hopes and dreams as she was growing up.

She remembered when she was about eight or nine, and the housekeeper held her as she cried over the cruel teasing she received in school. Not having someone to make a Mother's Day card for, Lex's young mind decided that she must be too bad to have a mother and came home completely upset. Martha wiped her tears and assured her that wasn't the case, and that she loved Lex as her own. From that moment on, Lex showed Martha all the love and respect a daughter would show her parent.

Lex snaked her arms around Martha and pulled her close.

"You know, I don't think I've told you lately that I love you."
She felt her hug fiercely returned. "Thanks for being here for
me. I do love you, you know." Lex leaned down and placed a
tender kiss on the graying head. Pulling back slightly, she could
see tears springing up in Martha's eyes. "So, is that fresh coffee
I smell?"

Relieved for the change of subject, Martha patted her gently on the stomach then bustled over to the stove to start breakfast. "Of course it is. Help yourself."

Upstairs, Amanda awakened feeling completely rested. She
was embarrassed at falling asleep in Lex's bed and was a little
concerned what her host thought of her. She looked around the
empty room. *Now where has she wandered off to?* Then the
aroma of coffee and sausage reached her senses. *Mmm. I think I
know where she might be.* She climbed out of bed and walked
across the hall to the guest bath.

Feeling more human, Amanda jogged down the staircase
and followed the enticing smells of breakfast. She noticed Lex
at the kitchen table while Martha was busy at the stove. "Good
morning." Amanda walked over to the counter where the coffeepot sat.

Martha glanced up from her cooking. "Good morning to
you, too. Cups are in the cabinet above the coffeepot. I hope
you like scrambled eggs, sausage, biscuits, and gravy."

Amanda filled her cup and leaned back against the counter
top. "That smells great. Is there anything I can do to help?"

Lex raised an eyebrow. She knew how territorial Martha
was about the kitchen and waited for the fireworks to begin.

But to Lex's amazement, Martha gestured to the counter
beside her. "Well, you can take the plates and silverware to the
table for me, if you want." She turned back to the stove, purposely ignoring the sputtering noises coming from the table.

"What? You never let me help you." Lex's tone was indig-
nant.

Amanda carried the requested items to the table and casually set three places. "Maybe you just never asked the right
way." She stuck her tongue out at Lex and winked.

Martha placed platters and bowls of food on the table.
"Now calm down, Lexie. You've got enough to do around here
without helping me in the kitchen. Besides, don't you remember
what happened the last time you tried to cook?"

Lex blushed, and stared silently at the plate in front of her.

Amanda looked on, charmed by this new facet to the woman she found herself fascinated by. "Oh?"

Lex mumbled something, but didn't look up.

Martha patted her shoulder, then sat down in the chair next to her. "Oh, my. That had to be what? Twelve or thirteen years ago?" She looked at Lex for confirmation.

Wanting to be anywhere except in the kitchen, Lex could only nod.

"Oh, please. Share." Amanda couldn't help but tease Lex, who rolled her eyes in disbelief.

"I was just a kid, Martha! I can't believe you're still holding that whole thing over my head." Lex gave Martha her most desperate pout, which didn't work.

They all started filling their plates as Martha began her story. "I guess little Lexie was about fifteen or sixteen. She wanted to do something special for me. I believe it was Mother's Day, wasn't it?"

"Yeah, but see what you get this year."

Martha chuckled, and continued on, unimpeded by Lex's display of discomfit. "Why she decided on cooking when she *hated* working in the kitchen was beyond me—"

The object of the story quietly interrupted. "I just thought since you had to cook for everyone else all the time, someone should cook for you for a change."

The housekeeper nodded. "Ah, so that's it. Anyway, she must have spent half the night in here, trying to make pancakes. The little imp couldn't find a recipe, so she used a cake recipe instead."

Lex defended herself. "Well, they're called pan-*cakes*, aren't they?"

Amanda covered her mouth to keep from laughing. "Oh, no."

"Oh yes. She must have used ten different pans, and flour was everywhere."

Here Lex tried to help. "They never said how hard it was to mix all those different things together. I thought you had to use one egg *per* pancake. And I think the stupid mixer I used was stuck on high speed. Do you know how hard it is to sift cake mix with the mixer out of control?"

Martha laughed out loud. "By the time I got up to fix breakfast, Hurricane Lexie had completely demolished the kitchen. I opened the door, and kneeling on the countertop trying to wipe dough off the cabinets was this powdered apparition. She looked so sad."

"I was trying to get the mess cleaned before you got up. But it took me most of the morning. I just knew Dad was gonna whip me for sure over it." She looked to Martha for confirmation. "You talked him out of it, didn't you?"

Martha patted Lex's hand fondly, her eyes growing misty. "Yes, I did. Your daddy never did understand why you did it. It was just about the nicest thing anyone ever did for me."

A pained look crossed Lex's face. *Oh yeah, he did.* She remembered the conversation with her father the week before Mother's Day. She had wanted to do something special for Martha, and made the mistake of telling her father as they cleaned stalls one afternoon. Rawson got very upset and grabbed Lex by the shoulders, shaking her and telling her that Martha wasn't her mother, and not to treat her like one.

Lex took exception to that, and told him Martha was the only mother she knew. When he yelled that she was just the housekeeper, Lex yelled back. In a moment of outrage, Rawson slapped one of his children for the first time in his life. Lex, already taller than her father, told him in no uncertain terms to never touch her again. After that, the rancher avoided her. She never knew if it was out of shame for what he had done, or out of fear of what she might do. All she knew was a little over a year later, her father left the Rocking W and never looked back.

Amanda saw a flash of pain in Lex's eyes. She reached over and touched the other woman's wrist. "Hey. What's wrong?" So quickly she thought she might have imagined it, the look was gone.

"Huh?" *Snap out of it, Lexington. That's old history.* "Sorry. Guess I'm just not completely awake yet."

Not believing her for an instant, Amanda decided to let the subject drop. "Maybe you should go back to bed then."

Lex stood up. "Can't. Gotta go down to the barn and feed the horses, take some hay to the cattle in the far field, then do a quick fence check." She carried her plate to the sink, challenging Martha to say something.

Martha let her get away with it this time, knowing that Lex was trying to get a rise out of her. *Brat.* Then she noticed the look on Amanda's face. *Or, maybe I'll just let this one take care of her. I have a feeling that Lexie has met her match.*

"What?" Amanda practically leapt out of her chair. "You should be resting, not out gallivanting around in the rain." She picked up her plate and deposited it in the sink.

"I'm fine. Besides, I'm the only person here that can do all that. You don't want the stock to go hungry, do you?"

Amanda chewed on her lower lip. She hated the thought that innocent animals could be neglected. "I suppose not. But at least let me go with you to help. No arguments, okay?"

"Okay, but I think we'd both better get dressed first. It's pretty cool out this morning." Lex looked Amanda over critically. "I think I can find some clothes to fit you, if you don't mind wearing boys' clothes."

"Hey, if they're warm, I don't care." Amanda put her hands on her hips. "Just as long as you don't make fun of me anymore. I don't think your ribs could handle it."

Lex headed for the doorway. "Nah, I won't laugh. I think I was just overtired last night." She stopped and turned around. "You coming?"

Amanda looked over at Martha, who was still seated at the table. "Thanks for breakfast. Are you sure I can't help with the dishes?"

Martha made a shooing motion with her hands. "No, get out of here. Try to make Lexie behave herself this morning. I've got this all under control."

Once upstairs, Lex steered Amanda to a door down at the far end of the hall. She paused to calm the anxious feeling that was creeping up inside her, and then opened the door.

Amanda could see it was a young boy's room. There was a twin bed against one wall, a bookcase with model cars and airplanes decorating it, and a small desk with a reading lamp sitting on top. The walls were adorned with posters of airplanes and horses, and a faded baseball cap sat on a hook by the bed. Amanda looked at Lex. She was staring at the cap with a faraway look in her eyes. Then she shook her head slightly and went to the closet door, pulled out a pair of jeans and a flannel shirt, and turned to Amanda.

"These should fit you just fine. You're about the same size." She hunted around for another moment. "Don't think I can find you any shoes, though. You'll probably have to make due with yours."

Amanda ached at the pain in Lex's eyes. "These will be fine. Are you sure it's okay? My wearing these?" She had to stop herself from reaching out and giving the other woman a hug. *She looks so sad. I wonder why?* "Whose clothes are these?"

Lex grabbed two more pairs of jeans out of the closet, along with several shirts. She walked over to a small dresser and opened the top drawer. After pulling out several pairs of socks and closing the drawer, she moved to the bed and sat down heavily. "This was my younger brother Louis' room." She reacted to the pain that seemed fresh again. "He...he died nine years ago."

Amanda sat down next to Lex and gently held her hand. "I'm sorry—"

"Martha still cleans his room. I know I should just pack this stuff up." Lex closed her eyes. "I've completely remodeled the entire second floor of this house, but I can't bring myself to destroy," her voice faded to a whisper, "the only thing I have left of Lou." Silent tears tracked down her face.

They both sat quietly for a few minutes. Amanda entwined her fingers with Lex's, lending her support as Lex wiped at her face with her other hand. "Sorry. I must still be tired from yesterday. I don't normally do this."

Amanda released Lex's hand and put her arm around her, hugging her gently. "Don't apologize. Are you sure you want me to wear these clothes? Martha already washed my shirt and jeans."

"No. You'll be more comfortable in these. Besides, I think he would have loved to have shared with you." Lex stood up and then pulled Amanda up next to her. "Come with me. I'm going to show you how to run a ranch."

Chapter
Four

Amanda struggled to keep up with Lex's long legs. "So, just how big is this ranch of yours?" She adjusted the hood on the raincoat she wore, another hand-me down, this time from Lex.

"It's a little over a thousand acres. I've been slowly adding to it over the past few years." Lex turned to talk to Amanda, then stopped when she noticed that the shorter woman was wearing herself out trying to catch up to her. "Why didn't you ask me to slow down?"

"I didn't want to bother you. I just kind of forced myself on you this morning." Amanda tried to look down at her shoes, but a firm hand gently tilted her chin up.

"You are not a bother, and with my ribs as sore as they are, you'll most definitely be a big help to me." Lex wrapped an arm around Amanda. "C'mon. I'll introduce you to my friends." She led her into a massive barn and along a clean concrete walkway that ran between a row of stalls. There were ten stalls on each side, but only half of them were occupied.

Lex noticed the unspoken question in Amanda's eyes. "I've been trying to gradually phase out the cattle. I'm working on making this a horse-only ranch." She opened an interior door where the feed was kept.

Amanda looked around, fascinated by all the sights, smells, and sounds. "Are these all the horses you have?" she asked, as Lex opened a 55-gallon drum. She watched the rancher take the top metal bucket from a stack beside the drum and dip it inside, then pull out a full bucket of oats.

"Well, these are the working horses." Lex handed the bucket to Amanda and grabbed an empty one to dip into the barrel. "The rest of the horses are in the far pasture. We bring in a few at a time, break them, then take them to auction." She led the way back into the main part of the barn and dumped the contents of her bucket into a trough in front of one of the stalls. Amanda pointed to the next occupied one, received a nod, and followed suit. They repeated this procedure until all ten horses were fed.

"Okay, boss." Amanda brushed her hands off. "What's next on the agenda?"

Lex pulled her gloves out of the pocket of her duster. She walked to the back of the barn and opened a door that led outside. "Next," she held the door open for her companion and pointed to another building about twenty yards away, "we go to the hay barn and take breakfast to the cattle and the other horses."

The rain had faded to a slight drizzle by the time they reached the structure, which was twice the size of the previous barn. Lex opened the double doors and waited for Amanda to go ahead of her.

"This place is huge." Amanda pushed the hood off her head and looked back at Lex. Bales of hay were in stacks that almost reached the ceiling in some places, and an old blue pickup truck sat in the middle of the room. "Now what?" She followed Lex to one side of the truck.

Lex eased in on the driver's side. "Just let me back this up to the hay, and we'll get started loading." The truck rumbled to life, and the gears ground in complaint when she shifted it into reverse. Once it was rolled back into position, Lex grabbed another pair of gloves and slid out from behind the wheel. She moved to the rear of the truck and dropped the tailgate before climbing into the back, then tossed the extra gloves to Amanda. "Well? You want to stand there all morning, or are you going to help?"

Amanda put on the gloves and jumped up into the rear of the truck beside her. "What do you want me to do?"

Lex pulled off her coat and laid it over the side of the truck, leaving her upper body clad in only a dark blue tee shirt. Amanda couldn't help but notice the play of muscles along her back before she straightened up and turned around.

Lex said, "We need to load up the truck with bales of hay then take it over to the next pasture." She was about to grab one of the bales when a hand touched her arm.

"Do you think it's wise for you to be hefting these things around?"

"I'm just a bit sore, and it's not like I have much of a choice, Amanda. With all this rain, we need to make sure the cattle have enough to eat. Otherwise, they have a tendency to knock down the fence looking for something to munch on, and I've already had my fill of fence building this week."

Amanda removed her hand. "At least let me help you." She grabbed the other side of the bale that Lex had her hands on, and together they pulled it into the truck. "See? That wasn't so hard, was it?"

Lex hated to admit it, but Amanda really was a big help, and she didn't think her ribs would appreciate her tossing the bales around like she usually did. "No, but you may be singing a different tune by the time we get finished today."

Amanda glowered at Lex and crossed her arms, taking a defiant stance. "I'm a lot stronger than I look, you know." Then she reached for another bundle of hay.

Lex stopped her with a hand on her shoulder. "I'm sorry, I didn't mean anything by it. I just don't want you to hurt yourself." She looked a little lost. "I really do appreciate all the help. I don't think I could do it by myself today."

Amanda patted the hand resting on her shoulder, instantly feeling regret for her sudden flare of temper. "I'm sorry, too. I guess I've spent so long trying to prove myself, that being defensive about my size is second nature to me. In my whole life, only my grandparents have ever believed in me." She turned and gestured in the direction of the remaining bales of hay. "So, are we going to stand here chatting all day, or get those animals fed?"

"Feed the animals. Yes ma'am." Lex gratefully gave up the argument and helped Amanda drag the bale down to the bed of the truck.

A couple of hours later, after they unloaded the last of the hay, the rain started up again in earnest. Both hurried back into the truck, each heaving a great sigh of relief to finally be out of the weather. Lex leaned back in the seat and closed her eyes. "How much longer can this damned rain last?" She wasn't going to tell Amanda, but her ribs were really beginning to bother her.

Amanda pushed the hood off her head. "I know what you mean. I keep expecting to see the animals begin pairing up."

"Yeah, and at this rate, we may want to book passage for ourselves." Lex turned her head and opened her eyes. "Thanks again for all the help. I'd probably still be piling hay in the truck if you weren't here."

"Well, I thought I'd better begin to earn my keep somehow. What's next on the program?" *Hopefully lunch figures in pretty soon. I'm starving.* Amanda absentmindedly plucked a piece of straw from her coat and started to chew on the end of it.

Lex raised an eyebrow at her. "Well," she drawled, "I was going to suggest lunch, but I didn't know if you were hungry or not." Nodding her head at the hay that Amanda was munching on, she added, "I guess I'd better get you something to eat before the rest of the livestock have to do without." She smirked when Amanda blushed. "Guess that's a yes." Lex leaned forward and started the truck.

After they rinsed off their boots outside, Lex and Amanda came in through the mudroom to hang up their soggy coats. As they stepped into the kitchen, the housekeeper turned around with an agitated expression on her face.

Puzzled by the anger she could feel emanating from the housekeeper and hoping it wasn't directed at them, Amanda offered, "We cleaned our feet. We didn't track in mud, Martha. Honest."

Martha softened her expression for a moment and then said, "I'm so glad you're back, Lexie. Your brother called, and he's in some sort of tizzy. He wants you to give him a call as soon as possible. Didn't even ask how you were, just demanded that you call."

Lex clenched her jaw in order to keep her opinion of Hubert to herself. The last time he'd visited the ranch, he barged into her office, sat at her desk, and demanded that Martha "fetch" him a cup of coffee. When it wasn't to his liking, he yelled at the housekeeper until Lex happened into the house and jerked him to his feet. She threatened to snap his head off, and Martha had to pull her away from him to keep Lex from making good on her threat. They hadn't seen Hubert since. "Was he rude to you again, Martha?"

Martha shook her head. "No, he wasn't. I think you scared him out of all good sense the last time." She noticed that Amanda seemed a little bewildered. "Come on, dear. Help me set the table for lunch."

"Sure. Just let me go upstairs and clean up a little." Amanda hurried out of the kitchen, still not sure what had just transpired.

Lex waited until Amanda left before continuing the conversation. "Did Hubert give you any clue as to why he called?"

Martha sat down on a nearby stool. "Yes. I just didn't want to get into it while Amanda was here." She paused to gather her

thoughts. "He said his old friend Rick called him and told him
Amanda would be staying out here for a while. Apparently, Mrs.
Cauble had called Rick to let him know Amanda wouldn't be at
work for a week or so." She could see Lex visibly tremble in an
attempt to control her anger.

"Amanda works for Rick?" Lex's voice was barely above a
whisper. She fought the feeling of betrayal that started to take
over her emotions, wondering if Amanda was trying to take
advantage of her somehow. She thought about how easily she
had already begun to care about the young woman, and the idea
that it was all to serve a purpose made her feel raw and exposed.

"Yes. Didn't she...oh. That's right. You were asleep when
we talked about that last night. Seems like Ricky thought it
would be fun to send Amanda out here on a wild goose chase
saying that 'L. Walters' was tired of ranching and wanted to sell
the place. When she found out what he'd done, she was pretty
upset."

That explains a lot of things. "Okay, that makes sense. I'll
deal with him later." *She could have been killed because of him.
What a rotten bastard!* Lex took deep cleansing breaths to calm
down. Relieved that her fears about Amanda were groundless,
she was furious with Rick for attempting to use the young realtor for his own sick amusement, especially since the two women
had hit it off so well. Remembering Martha's irritation, she
shifted her attention to the source of her housekeeper's aggrava-
tion. "So, what's Hubert's problem?"

Martha was almost afraid to say what Hubert told her. But
she had never lied to Lex and wasn't about to begin now. "He
said he didn't want a repeat of the Linda fiasco." She waited for
the eruption. But it didn't happen. When Martha looked into
Lex's eyes, she saw quiet defeat there. *Oh, no. Please don't give
up, Lexie. That's what he wants.*

"Okay. Thanks Martha. I'll just go give him a call and get it
over with." Lex left the room and walked to her office.

Amanda met her in the hallway. "Hey, 'bout ready for some
lunch?"

Lex looked pale and drawn, and her words came out
soberly and low. "I'm really not all that hungry right now. You
and Martha go ahead. I've got to call my brother back." She
resumed her trek down the long hallway, leaving Amanda to
stare after her.

Amanda continued to the kitchen, where Martha was busy
at the stove. "Martha? Is Lex all right?" Amanda picked up

three plates and some silverware. "I just met her in the hall and she wasn't looking too well."

"I don't think she is. That older brother of hers has always been a thorn in Lexie's side. He resents the fact that Mr. Walters put her in charge of the ranch instead of him, since he's seven years older than she is. And he is always trying to guilt her into doing whatever he wants."

In another part of the house, Lex closed the office door behind her and paced near her desk for a few moments. *Might as well get this over with.* She sat down behind the heavy oak desk and dialed the number for the house in town. She had signed over her half of it to Hubert, with the stipulation that he'd move completely out of the ranch house.

It took several years, but Lex remodeled the ranch by using money from the trust fund her mother had left for her. Her favorite addition was the cottage she had built for Martha just off the main house. The housekeeper had refused to take the newly remodeled guest room, so Lex trumped her by deeding her the cottage and the land surrounding it.

Lex tapped a beat on the desk as she waited for Hubert to pick up the phone. On the fourth ring, he finally answered.

"Hubert Walters." His voice had an annoying nasal tone to it, which became worse whenever he complained, which was most of the time.

"Yeah, Hubert. This is Lex. You wanted to talk to me?" Restless, she picked up the letter opener from the desk and cleaned her fingernails while she listened.

"'Bout damn time you called. Or did your 'maid' forget to give you my message?" He knew her weakness where Martha was concerned and wasn't above exploiting it to irritate Lex.

"Yeah, Martha gave me the message some time ago," she lied, "but I was busy." *Two can play this game, Hube ol' boy.*

"Busy? Doing what? Playing with your new little 'friend'? That's what I was calling about. I don't want you dragging our family name through the mud, like you did before."

"Shut up, you bastard."

Hubert sniggered humorlessly. "What was the little trollop's name? Lulu? No. Loretta? Nah. Oh, yeah, Linda. That was her name, wasn't it?"

"You know what her name was, Hubert. She dumped you, didn't she?" Lex couldn't help but bait him in return.

"Oh, yeah. But that's okay, 'cause she played for the other team. Was she good in the sack, Lex?"

Creak. Lex looked at the stainless steel letter opener she had just bent in half with one hand. "I couldn't complain, but you wouldn't know anything about that, would you Hube?"

Hubert knew he had pushed his sister just about as far as he dared. "Okay, okay. Look. I just don't want your hormones to get you into trouble again."

"What the hell are you talking about?" Lex slammed the bent letter opener onto the desk and stood up, looking around the room for something to throw.

"Rick told me she's a cutie, but she must be like you, 'cause she wouldn't even go out with him."

"Why do men think that if a woman isn't interested in them, she has to be gay? In Rick's case, all it proves is that she has good taste."

Her brother wasn't so easily dissuaded. "Rick knows what he's talkin' about, Lex. The little queer won't even socialize with anyone from the office. Just spends all her time with those two old farts."

Lex saw red. "Now you listen to me, you son of a bitch. You will *not* speak of her *or* the Cauble's that way. They're good folks. A lot better than that scum you run around with." She paused to let her words sink in. "*And,* if I hear of you even *thinking* badly of any of them, I *will* make you regret the day you were born. You got that?" She slammed down the phone before he could reply. Lex suddenly felt the walls closing in on her. *Gotta get out of here for a while.* She stomped down the hallway and out through the rear door.

Martha and Amanda sat together in silence at the table and ate their lunch. Lex was conspicuously absent, although they could hear her raised voice through the house from time to time. Hearing footsteps down the hallway, they looked up and saw a glimpse of a fleeting figure right before the back door slammed. Both women jumped up from the table and hurried over to the window just in time to see Lex practically run through the yard. She went into the barn and came out a few moments later astride a black stallion. Horse and rider quickly disappeared into a countryside obscured by the steadily falling rain.

"He must have really upset her. She never rides Thunder unless she's going to ride really hard." Martha stepped away from the window. "Let's get these dishes cleaned up, and then we'll sit and visit for a spell. She'll probably go check the fence by the creek again."

Amanda allowed Martha to lead her away from the window, but her thoughts went out to the woman out in the elements. She could almost feel Lex's raw emotions.

Lex and Thunder rode hard for thirty minutes, until she could feel him begin to tire. "Old boy, I'm gonna have to get you out more often if you're already winded." She also felt the need to slow down due to her own body's complaints as well. They rode through the winter rye fields, and then through the stand of trees she and Amanda had walked through last night. She pulled the horse to a stop before they got to the road, not wanting to risk injuring either one of them in the mud.

Looking at the felled tree and partially flipped Jeep, Lex was surprised they weren't both seriously injured. The Jeep leaned precariously on three wheels, the tree sitting almost on top of it. Lex used her knees to guide Thunder back to the creek, deciding she might as well see what kind of damage was done to the bridge.

The old bridge was not in as bad shape as Lex had feared. Only the middle section was gone, and it wouldn't take long to repair. She looked downstream and saw the tail of the little Mustang sticking up out of the water. With Amanda's story the evening before still fresh in her mind, an idea formed that lit up Lex's face. She turned Thunder around and headed back for the house. "Come on, fella. I've got some planning to do."

"And then she hands me this piece of paper and says, 'Happy Birthday, Martha.' I tell you, I was never so surprised in my life. She even had me pick out everything to decorate it with. It sure was a big change from that little room off the kitchen." Martha wiped her eyes. She had just explained how Lex surprised her with the deed to her little cottage, where they now sat drinking coffee. Martha thought it was the best place to wait for Lex since they could sit in her living room and see the main house and barn through the picture window.

Amanda and Martha had spent the afternoon getting to know each other better. Amanda told her about her grandparents and some of her more favorite stories from her childhood, including the summer they found her car. That sparked a small burst of tears when she thought that it was probably miles downstream by now. Martha related several humorous stories about Lex, and how hard it was to raise a girl on a ranch full of men. She also told of the sad young girl who never fit in at home or at school, how she slowly closed herself off from the pain of being different, and the loneliness of running a ranch.

"My grandmother said Lex is about the sweetest person she's ever met. That reminds me. How did she get involved in the historical society?" Amanda had been wondering about this since her talk with Anna Leigh last night.

"Actually, Lexie did it out of spite, at least at first. Hubert had been really nasty to all of us here at the ranch, and he decided he was going to become a big real estate developer. So, he picked out the old Taylor house to buy and level to the ground. I think he wanted to turn it into a shopping center or some such nonsense. Anyway, Lexie had gone into town to get the cast taken off her arm—"

"What?"

"Oh, she broke it instead of one of the horses," Martha said matter-of-factly, as she brushed some stray hair out of her eyes. "Where was I? Oh, yes. She was coming out of the doctor's office and nearly tripped over your grandmother, who was hanging up a sign in the window. She was chairing a meeting of the historical society that evening to discuss the historical significance of Loren Taylor's old house. Lex read the sign, asked Mrs. Cauble about the gathering, and ended up going. Afterwards, she decided that preserving the house was important from an historical standpoint, not just an excuse to get back at her brother. Now she tries to help out whenever they need her. You should see her in her boots and jeans at one of their little tea parties. I don't know who has more fun, Lexie or the ladies. It's really a sight to behold. She's even hosted a couple out here, trying to get me interested."

Amanda giggled at the mental picture. She could just see the ladies in their matronly dresses and pearls, and Lex with her denim jeans and flannel shirt. "Oh, I bet that's a riot. My grandmother invited me to their meetings before, but I was afraid I'd be the only one there under sixty. I wish I had taken her up on the invitation. Maybe I would have met you and Lex sooner."

"I don't know. Sometimes things are just meant to happen a certain way." Martha peered through the window. "And I think we should get back to the main house. Lexie just took Thunder back into the barn, and I'd hate to not be at the house when she comes in." She stood and took her coffee cup into the kitchen with Amanda hot on her heels.

A short time later, Lex walked out of the barn and looked at the house. It had been over two hours since she stormed out of the house, and now she was nervous. As she walked, she berated herself for her childish actions. "Running out of the house like my tail was on fire. Real adult, Lexington. What will Amanda think?" She slowly opened the back door and stepped inside. Hearing voices coming from the kitchen, Lex saw her chance to pass by unnoticed.

Martha and Amanda sat at the table drinking coffee and looked up when they heard footsteps in the hall. "Did you have a good ride, dear?" Martha asked. She stood up and walked over to the stove. "I kept your plate warm, just in case." She turned and looked at Lex, who had the most confused look on her face. *I do so love keeping her off balance.* "Now you go upstairs and get some dry clothes on, and I'll have your lunch ready." When Lex opened her mouth to argue, Martha put her foot down. "Don't argue with me, Lexington Marie. You've spent way too much time out in the elements the past couple of days, and I don't want you adding pneumonia to your other ills." She shook a finger in her direction. "Now git!"

Lex looked over at Amanda, who had her hand over her mouth to stifle a giggle. She shook her head and turned and left the kitchen.

"Oh, Martha. You are absolutely vicious." Amanda was unable to hold back her mirth. "The look on her face—"

Martha resumed her seat at the table. "She really is like an overgrown child sometimes. I know she was expecting to get yelled at, so—" Martha shook her head. "She's already whipped herself about storming off, and I know her brother can be such an ass." She picked the carafe from the center of the table and refilled their mugs. "Lexie is always tougher on herself than I ever have to be."

Minutes later they heard Lex's footsteps on the stairs. Martha got up, moved over to the stove, and pulled a plate piled high with food from the oven. She sat it at the empty space at the table just as Lex walked in. "Sit down and eat. Don't let your lunch get cold." As Lex silently took her place, Martha stopped and kissed the top of her head. "Now I expect you to eat every bite of that." Martha patted Lex on the shoulder and headed for the door. "I've got some chores to do, so I'll see the two of you later." She gave Lex a backwards glance that dared the young rancher to disobey her and left through the doorway, humming to herself.

Lex pushed the food around on her plate. "I'm sorry for running out like that earlier." She glanced up at the woman sitting beside her. "I just needed to get out for a while, and I wanted to check the fence down by the creek to see if my patch job held up."

Amanda did her best not to show her enjoyment of Lex's expression, which did remind her of a child who knew she was in trouble. "That's okay. Martha and I had a good chat. She is such a wonderful person." Amanda made it a point to look at Lex's plate. "But she might come back and throw a fit if you don't eat your lunch. How's the fence?"

Lex took a bite of food. "The fence is fine. And the bridge looks like only the middle is gone, so it shouldn't be too hard to fix. 'Course I'll have to check the supports and make sure they weren't knocked too loose to be used again."

"How are your ribs? All that riding couldn't have made them feel any better." Amanda knew that Lex more than likely had pushed herself to the limit today.

"Hmm?" The touch of Amanda's hand on her arm broke Lex out of her musing. "Ribs?" She swallowed another bite. "Oh. Ribs. Right. A little sore, but not too bad."

"So, what do you have planned for the rest of the afternoon?" Amanda lightly squeezed Lex's arm, then took a sip of coffee. "Is there something I can help with?"

Lex finished her lunch, not even realizing she had been hungry until she had begun to eat. "Well," she leaned back in her chair, "I thought we'd take it easy for the rest of the day." She interlocked her hands and laid them on her stomach. "It's too muddy to do anything outside, and there's not much else to do. Besides, I've got a large collection of movies in the den, and I just recently finished wiring the surround sound system. Been wanting to try it out." She stood up and carried her dishes to the sink.

"Sounds like a plan to me." Amanda followed suit and placed her cup in the sink.

Lex looked around and, seeing that the coast was clear, ran hot water. "Shhh." She placed a finger to her lips before sticking her hands in the soapy water. "I just gotta tweak Martha somehow."

Amanda bumped her with a hip. "Scoot over. I'll rinse and dry. No fair you having all the fun."

They made quick work of the dishes and had just put them away when Martha came into the room. "What are you two up to?"

Amanda hid the dishtowel on the counter behind her back. "Who, us?"

"Nothing, Martha. We were just going to go into the den and watch movies. You interested?" Lex stepped in front of the housekeeper, trying to keep her away from the sink.

Knowing that Lex rarely took time off, a concerned Martha reached up and touched Lex's forehead with the back of one hand. "What's the matter? Are you not feeling well?"

Lex took Martha's hand. "I'm fine. It's just too nasty to do any work outside, and I thought Amanda would enjoy the break." She pulled her into a surprise hug. "You care to join us?"

Martha returned the hug, confused by the sudden change in Lex. *It's been a long time since Lexie has been this affectionate. Usually, she doesn't allow anyone within ten feet of her. She sure is touchy-feely lately. Not that I'm complaining.* "No, that's quite all right. But if you're going to relax today, is it okay for me to go over to my place and get some things done?"

"Martha, you don't have to ask me if you want to do something. You know that."

"I know you say that, but you run this ranch and I respect that."

Lex thought about Martha's words. Although the ranch was in her name, she always felt like the woman standing before her was in charge, and couldn't be happier about it. "Not exactly."

"What do you mean by that?"

"You're the one who runs this house, Martha. I just work the ranch." Lex motioned for Amanda to follow her out of the kitchen, leaving Martha sputtering behind them.

Amused by the fact that she had finally left Martha speechless, Lex led Amanda into the den and pointed to the wall where a bookcase full of videotapes and CDs awaited their selection. "Go on and pick us out something to watch. I'll go beg Martha's forgiveness and nab some sodas and popcorn."

Amanda was so intent on studying the room that she didn't even notice her host had left her alone. In the far corner, there was a massive rock fireplace that was larger than the one in Lexington's bedroom. One wall held a large entertainment unit with a big screen TV and other electronic components. Next to that was a closed door. A wide, dark red leather sofa sat facing

the television equipment. There were matching plush chairs sit-
uated on either side of the sofa, and a heavy oak coffee table
was centered in front of them. She wandered to the bookcase,
amazed by the large selection of videos. "Comedy or drama?"
Amanda shook her head in disbelief when she saw that the movies were grouped alphabetically, except some that were grouped
by series. "Mel Brooks? She has the entire collection of Mel
Brooks? *Indiana Jones*, *Die Hard*, *Star Trek*—someone's an
action junkie." She continued to browse through the titles, looking for something lighthearted. *Sleepless in Seattle*? *While You
Were Sleeping*? *A Fish Called Wanda*— "I love that movie!"
Amanda pulled the tape from its designated spot and placed it
on the coffee table.

Lex returned from the kitchen with a tray loaded with
goodies, which she set on the coffee table. "Hope you like butter
on your popcorn. Did you find something to your liking?" She
noticed the tape on the table and picked it up. "Great. That's
one of my favorites." She took the tape and crossed the room to
the entertainment center and inserted it into the VCR. After taking the remote control from atop the TV, Lex sat down on the
sofa next to Amanda. "I figure we could just set the bowl
between us and share, but I brought some extra bowls if you'd
rather not."

Amanda scooted closer to her. "No. Why dirty up more
dishes? Unless you think we can get away with washing these,
too?"

"No way. I'm lucky to have escaped the kitchen with my
rear intact as it is."

"Was she really angry?" Amanda hated to think that she
helped get Lex into any trouble.

Lex tried to keep the smirk off her face while she pointed
the remote at the TV and turned it on, along with the surround
speakers. Martha had threatened her with cooking utensils for
as long as she could remember, but had never actually spanked
Lex once she got to be a teenager. It was more of an inside joke
that they shared in reaffirmation of the child-parent bond they
enjoyed. "Not really. But she did make threats." She leaned
back and propped her sock-covered feet on the coffee table.
"Might as well take your shoes off and get comfortable."

Amanda knew she had been tweaked. She made a silent
promise to get back at her new friend, then put her feet up on
the table next to Lex's and settled back to enjoy the movie.

A few hours later, Martha came back from her cottage and

thought the house was entirely too quiet. She was about to start the evening meal, but decided to go see what Lex and Amanda were up to first. She peeked inside the doorway to the den and saw Lex asleep on the sofa with her feet propped on the coffee table. *Well, at least she wasn't wearing boots this time.* The television screen had gone blank sometime earlier, and only a hissing sound emanated from the stereo speakers. Lex's arm was draped over Amanda's shoulders. Amanda was curled up against Lex, asleep, using one shoulder as her pillow with her arm wrapped tightly around Lex's waist. They were turned so that they were almost facing each other with Lex's other hand on her back, hugging Amanda close to her while they slept. Smiling at the tender scene, Martha decided to let them rest and tiptoed back to the kitchen.

Amanda woke a little time later, feeling groggy. She was warm and quite comfortable, at least until she recognized where she was. She was still studying her companion when the arms around her tightened, and she felt her body being pulled closer to Lex's. Not wanting to startle her, Amanda allowed Lex to continue to hold her while she soaked up the feeling of being in the other woman's arms.

In the shadowy state between being asleep and awake, Lex had started to nuzzle Amanda's hair when her eyes blinked open. For a moment, she looked as confused as Amanda had been upon wakening. Becoming fully alert, she thought about how it must seem to Amanda and hurriedly removed her arms from around her. "Um. I'm sorry about that." She struggled to sit up. "I didn't mean..."

Amanda gently patted her stomach. "Don't worry about it. I pretty much climbed all over you like you were my own personal mattress." She sat up and stretched. "That was a good nap, though." While outwardly pretending to be unaffected, Amanda ached for Lex to hold her again.

Relieved that she hadn't frightened Amanda off, Lex stretched as well. "Yeah, it was. Guess I was still pretty tired from last night."

Amanda looked at the clock on the wall. "Me, too. It's early evening, don't you think?"

"Yeah, I guess so. Why?"

"Well, if it's okay with you, I'd like to call my grandparents and see how they're doing."

"You don't have to ask permission to use the phone." Lex stood up and held out a hand. "Here. I'll let you use the phone in the office so you'll have some privacy."

Amanda allowed herself to be pulled up. "Thanks."

Lex led her through the door by the entertainment center and into the office. She guided Amanda around a heavy oak desk and pulled out the leather chair. "Have a seat. Just push a button for an outgoing line. We have three lines coming in, but the computer is hooked up to the third." She turned to leave. "Take all the time you need. I'll be in the kitchen harassing Martha."

Amanda enjoyed the gentle sway of Lex's hips as she left. Pulling herself back from where her thoughts were taking her, she dialed her grandparents' number and tried to concentrate on the call.

The phone rang twice, and her grandfather answered. "Hello?"

"Grandpa Jake? How are you feeling?"

"Just great, Peanut. We got back from the movies about twenty minutes ago. How are you doing, sweetheart?"

"I'm doing much better today, Grandpa. I helped Lex feed the horses, and then we took hay to the cattle." She paused, her mind's eye going back to waking up in Lex's arms. "After lunch we sat down and watched a movie."

"Sounds like you've had a busy day."

"Well, not really. I'm trying to keep Lex from overdoing it because of her injured ribs."

Jacob's muttered curse wasn't intelligible, and then suddenly Anna Leigh's concerned voice came over the line as she picked up an extension. "Mandy? Is everything okay?"

Amanda hid her face in her hand. Her attempts to cushion them from the worst of yesterday's events kept going horribly wrong. "I'm fine, but Lex bruised her ribs yesterday."

"Is she all right?"

"She's sore, but I think she'll be okay."

Jacob found his voice again. "Peanut, how did she get injured? Was she in an accident?"

Amanda rubbed her eyes. "Not exactly. Well, sort of. I'll tell you, but you've got to promise to stay calm, okay?"

"Of course, dearest. Go ahead." Anna Leigh's calm tone soothed her granddaughter.

"You remember when I told you I was on my way to Lex's yesterday because of an appointment sheet Rick gave me?"

"Yes. I still have half a mind to chat with Mr. Thompson about that," Anna Leigh grumbled.

Amanda continued her story. "I followed his directions, and finally found the road I was supposed to take. I was crossing an old wooden bridge when a tree came out of nowhere and crashed right into it." Amanda waited to see if her grandfather was going to comment while she steeled herself to tell the next part of the story.

"Go ahead, Peanut. I know it's hard," Jacob encouraged.

"Well, the middle of the bridge kind of collapsed, and my car fell into the creek. I must have hit my head, because the next thing I remember is being tied on someone's back and being pulled across the creek." She only heard breathing from the other end of the phone, so she tried to rush the rest of her story. "Once we were about halfway across the creek, Lex was hit in the chest by some debris."

Jacob finally spoke up. "Are you okay? Why didn't you tell us this last night, Peanut?"

"I'm fine. I just didn't want you to worry."

Anna Leigh sighed. "Mandy, please don't feel that you have to protect us from things. I'm just glad you're all right." Her voice took on a quieter timber. "Lexington is a very special young woman. I'm quite thankful that she wasn't more seriously injured."

"I know." Amanda's voice grew thicker with emotion. "She's becoming very special to me, too." She had to tell someone how she was feeling. Her grandparents knew she was gay and had always been very supportive of her. "There's something about her that makes me feel like I've known her forever, or that I want to know her forever. It feels so natural to be here with her. Do you think it's just misplaced hero worship? She did save me. Maybe it's the head wound. Maybe I'm just crazy."

Although amused by his granddaughter's assessment, Jacob's voice was sympathetic. "Honey, I felt the same way the first time I saw your grandmother. She became my whole world the first time our eyes met. She still is."

Anna Leigh joined in. "That's true, sweetheart. I felt as if we were destined to meet. Is this what you felt when you met Lexington?"

"Exactly. I feel so—" Amanda couldn't continue. She didn't know how to put her new feelings into words. They were too overwhelming.

"I understand completely, dear. Does she know how you feel?"

Amanda gasped. "Oh, good Lord, no! I'd probably scare

her out of ten years!"

"I don't think so, sweetheart," Anna Leigh answered.

Amanda was at a loss. "What do you mean by that?"

"Oh, Peanut, I keep forgetting you don't know local history," Jacob said. "Lexington certainly shook up the town gossips a couple of years ago. But I think you should ask her about it." He gave her a minute to think about that. "Let me put it this way: I don't think anything you could say would shock her."

Anna Leigh took over. "True. The poor girl has been through a lot in the past couple of years. She deserves so much happiness. So do you, dear."

Amanda choked back a sob. "Yes, she does, Gramma. When I look at her, I find myself wanting to be the one to make her happy. We're just becoming friends, but I already know that I want us to be so much more. I can't seem to stop myself from touching her, and when I'm near her, I feel a happiness that I never felt before."

Her grandmother clucked. "It does sound serious. Now you listen to me. I think she's a wonderful person, but she has a tendency not to think that way."

Jacob spoke up. "Is there anything we can bring to you, Peanut? I'm sure we could find a way to get it across that damned creek."

Amanda laughed out loud. "No, Grandpa Jake. Lex and Martha have made sure I have everything I need. But thanks for asking. And, thanks for listening. I guess I'll let you go now."

Both grandparents laughed. "Okay, sweetheart," Anna Leigh said, "but let us know if you need anything, okay? Give us a call again tomorrow. We'll just be puttering around the house."

"Okay. I love you both. I'll talk to you tomorrow. Goodnight." She hung up the phone, somewhat relieved that she had told them the truth about her accident and about her developing feelings for Lex. *They took that well. Guess it didn't sound so bad, since I'm still alive and kicking.*

Chapter
Five

Martha heard footsteps enter the kitchen and turned from the pantry to greet Lex, smiling sweetly at her. "Did you enjoy your movie dear?" She picked up an armful of items to carry across the room, only to have them taken out of her hands.

"What do you mean by that?" Lex followed the housekeeper like a lost puppy. "Where do you want all of this?" She was continually amazed at how Martha could take such an array of foodstuffs and turn them into a wonderful meal.

"Just set it on the counter there." Martha patted Lex on the back. "And I didn't mean anything by what I said. Just asked a simple question. Why are you getting so defensive?"

"I'm not defensive!" Lex snapped, and then sighed. "Yeah, I guess I am. Sorry, Martha. You didn't deserve that." She leaned on the sink and stared out the window, vaguely noticing the rain had finally stopped. "This can't be happening."

Martha wrapped an arm around her. "What's that, sweetheart?"

Lex turned and looked down at the slightly wrinkled features. Trusting the woman who'd raised her to know what she meant, all she could say was, "Amanda."

The housekeeper nodded knowingly. "And you're scared?"

"Terrified," Lex whispered. "I don't think I could go through that again. I don't know if I *want* to go though that again." She shook her head. "Moot point, anyway." She ran her fingers over the back of a chair while she shoved her feelings back down to where she could manage them. "Anyway, I came to ask a favor of you. I need you to keep Amanda occupied for a couple of hours tomorrow. I'm working on a little surprise for her."

Martha accepted the abrupt change in topics. "Okay, I'm sure I can come up with something, but you have to tell me what you're up to first." She stood back and placed her hands on her ample hips, trying to assume a threatening manner.

Lex was amused by Martha's attempt to intimidate her. She cleared her throat. "Did she tell you about the car she was driving yesterday?"

"My heart nearly broke in two when she said that it was probably gone forever," Martha admitted. The look on Lex's face puzzled her. "What?"

"As unbelievable as it may sound, her car is still in the same place it was when I pulled her out of it yesterday. And by tomorrow, the creek should be down enough for me to tie it to the Jeep and tow it back to the house."

"You're not—"

"Yep. Figure I can hide it in the maintenance shed until I get it running. Then we can take it into town and have the inside cleaned."

Martha loved a good surprise. "You *are* devious, aren't you? She'll be thrilled. But how long do you think you can keep this a secret? That little girl is pretty darn sharp."

"I know. That's why I'm going to need your help. She really wants to help you out around the house. So, maybe—"

"Okay, I'll try to keep her busy. But do you think you'll be able to pull that car out alone? That's quite a nasty wound you have." Martha crossed her arms over her chest. "And that reminds me. You *are* going to go upstairs right now and let me put some more salve on that, aren't you?"

Lex knew when she'd been beaten. "Yes, ma'am. Right behind you, ma'am. Whatever you say, ma'am."

Martha lightly backhanded her in the stomach. "Enough of your lip, young lady. You're not too big for me to use my spoon on, you know." They both snickered as they went upstairs.

Amanda stared at the receiver after she hung up the phone. Both her grandparents seemed quite fond of the young rancher, and it appeared that they had known her for some time. She turned her attention to the desk. It was clear except for a U-shaped piece of metal. Amanda picked up the letter opener and tried to straighten it out, but even with both hands, the steel would not budge. She had a pretty good idea when it had been bent. The thought of that kind of strength mixed with anger should have frightened her, but for some reason it didn't.

She heard footsteps above her and looked up at the ceiling.

I wonder what those two are up to now? Then she heard a shriek. Amanda was out of the office and up the stairs in a flash. She skidded to a halt at the master bathroom door, where the scream seemed to have originated.

Lex stood in the bathroom, her shirt off and wearing just her bra and jeans, with her back against the wall. "Dammit, Martha! Have you been storing that mess in the freezer or something? It's ice cold!" She ineffectively tried to slap Martha's hands away from her in an attempt to keep the cold salve from her skin.

Undaunted, Martha continued her efforts to apply the salve. "Stop your complaining Lexie. I'm almost finished."

They both turned to see a breathless Amanda standing in the doorway. "I heard a holler," she puffed. "Is everything all right?" She supported herself against the doorframe while her heartbeat returned to normal.

"Lexie was just being a big baby."

Now that Martha was finished, Lex crossed her arms over her chest in an attempt to salvage her dignity. "Hey, you'd scream too if she smeared that frozen gook all over you."

Amanda continued to rest against the door and shook her head. "I thought something horrible had happened." She couldn't help but notice the strong body that leaned against the wall and the firm breasts that pressed against Lex's folded arms. *Down, Mandy. You'd just give her another reason to scream.* But then something her grandparents had hinted about drifted into her mind. She realized belatedly that someone was speaking to her. "Sorry, what?"

Martha fought to keep the smile off her face. She saw where Amanda's attention had been focused, but didn't want to embarrass their guest. "I was just wondering if you were still interested in helping me around the house. I was going to enlist Lexie's aid in cleaning out the cabinets and pantry, but she's usually more of a hindrance than help."

The person in question started to object, only to gasp as Martha began to wrap the bandage tightly against her chest. "Ouch! You trying to kill me?"

The housekeeper gently slapped Lex on her good side. "Hush! I'd be finished a lot faster if you didn't squirm so darn much." She pulled the material tight again, getting a groan. "There. Amanda, could you hand me the safety pins on the counter, please?" She held out a hand.

Amanda stepped further into the room to pick up the pins.

She handed them to Martha, then picked up the flannel shirt that had been lying next to them. The blue fabric was soft, and held a hint of the scent of its owner. It was all she could do to keep from raising the shirt to her face and inhaling deeply.

"Stay still, or I'll end up poking you, Lexie." Martha admonished her patient. "I swear, you're worse now than when you were a child." She finally completed pinning the bandage and stepped back.

Amanda moved forward and held out the shirt to Lex. "Here, put this back on, it'll help warm you up." Her own body temperature felt as if it had risen several degrees just by being in close proximity to Lex, and she was afraid her feelings showed on her face.

"Thanks." Lex felt the same tension as she took the shirt with trembling hands. She slowly pulled the clothing on, but her hands were shaking so much she couldn't seem to get it buttoned. *What's going on with me? This is ridiculous!*

Amanda noticed the difficulty Lex was having, but assumed it was due to pain or the aftereffects of the cold salve. "Here." She stepped closer. "Let me give you a hand." Amanda took over the buttoning duties and was able to finish the job quickly; that is, as long as she kept her mind on the buttons and not on the person who was wearing the shirt.

Deciding that three was a crowd, Martha slipped unnoticed out the door. *Moot point, eh Lexie? I don't think so.*

Lex looked down into Amanda's face. Being this close, she could see the golden flecks that floated in the brownish-green eyes. When Amanda edged closer, she almost lowered her head to kiss her. The loud ring of the telephone broke the spell they were under.

Both women jumped. Amanda stepped back, startled by what she had almost done. *Stupid, stupid, stupid! Where's your head, Mandy?*

Disgusted by her own feelings, Lex moved out of the bathroom and over to the bedside table. "Excuse me. I'd better see who that is." The phone had only rung once, and she was reasonably certain that Martha had picked it up. *Saved by the bell—if I'd stayed in there much longer, I might have scooped her up and tossed her on the bed.* She ran a shaky hand through her hair as she picked up the cordless phone.

Martha was speaking calmly to Hubert. Lex wasn't surprised. Her brother's timing was never very good, and he only called the ranch whenever he wanted something. "It's okay,

Martha, I've got it. Hello, Hubert. What do you want now?" She waited until she heard the other phone click. "Well? Did you call for a reason, or are you just trying to piss me off for the second time today?"

"Nice talking to you, too, sis. Do I have to have a reason to call?" Hubert's nasal tone oozed insincerity.

"You always have. Now what have you called to complain about?"

"You are such a hard ass, dear little sister. Okay, as a matter of fact, I do have a reason for calling." Hubert seemed to be enjoying the banter, which was never a good sign.

Lex ground her teeth in an attempt to keep control. "Are you going to tell me sometime tonight?"

"Loosen up, sis. I just came across some property on the county books, and I think we could pick it up for a song. I need a little extra capital to get the ball rolling."

Lex was about to let him have it, when she felt a light touch on her arm. "Why would I give you money for another one of your real estate schemes? I told you months ago that I wasn't going to lend you any more. What makes you think I'd change my mind now?"

Amanda watched Lex get angrier by the moment. After finding the letter opener bent earlier, she was about half afraid of what Lex would do. Acting braver than she felt, Amanda sat on the bed and pulled Lex next to her. She slid her hand along the tense arm, opened Lex's fist, and placed her small hand in the larger one.

Hubert started to sound more desperate. "I just thought you would help me out, since I'm willing to help you out."

Lex's voice trembled with suppressed rage. "And just *how* are you supposedly helping me out?"

"Well, since you've got a house guest out there, I'm offering to try to keep it quiet for you. No sense in her reputation being damaged, right?"

Lex shot off the bed. "You sonofabitch! If you cause any trouble for Amanda or her family, I will personally take care of any aspirations you may have about fatherhood, brother or not!" She paced back and forth across the room, her face flushed with anger. "So don't you dare try to blackmail me for your idiotic little schemes, you little shit!" She turned off the phone and slammed it onto its base, then turned and, still seething, looked over at Amanda. "I'm sorry about that."

Amanda's eyes were wide with shock. "What was that all

about?"

Suddenly exhausted, Lex walked over and sat in one of the chairs by the fireplace, which had been lit and was burning brightly. "Why don't you come over here and sit. It's kind of a long story."

Amanda noticed the warmth emanating from the fireplace and couldn't figure out when Martha had time to do the things she did, yet stay mysteriously out of the way. She shook off her musings and sat in the chair opposite Lex.

Weary and resigned, Lex wiped a hand over her face. "I'm not sure where to start," she muttered, gazing into the flames of the fire to avoid the trusting face across from her. *Well, it was fun while it lasted.*

Amanda cleared her throat. "You really don't have to tell me anything, if you don't want to. I mean, it's really none of my business."

Lex hesitantly met the intense gaze directed at her. "Yes, I do. It does pertain to you in a roundabout way."

"But I just met you yesterday. And I don't even know your brother. What could he do that would have an effect on me or my family?"

Lex looked down at her own hands, clenched together in her lap. "He threatened to spread the word around town that you were staying out here with me."

"So, what's the big deal? For God's sake, Lex, you saved my life!" Amanda was beginning to understand where this conversation was heading, and she could almost feel the fear and pain radiating from the other woman.

"He would probably forget to mention the fact that you are actually stranded out here." Lex paused for a moment, thinking. "I've got the supplies. I can start first thing in the morning and get at least a walkway built across the bridge by the late afternoon. You can call your grandmother to come and pick you up."

Amanda slipped out of her chair and knelt at Lex's feet. She looked shyly at Lex's face. "Tired of me already?"

Lex looked down and became momentarily lost in Amanda's eyes. "No, of course not!" The denial came out sharply. "I just don't want your name dragged through the mud. My brother is quite good at that." Without her conscious permission, Lex's hand found its way to the kneeling woman's cheek.

Touched by Lex's gentleness, Amanda laid her hands on a denim-clad thigh. "I really don't think you should start to work on the bridge until you've had more time to heal. I'm perfectly happy here."

Lex removed her hand from the soft cheek. "Your reputation might be tarnished. Hell, if my brother has anything to do with it, it would be ruined." She looked away, unwilling to show how much the thought hurt her.

"Why?"

"This might take awhile to tell."

"So? I don't see us in any hurry to go anywhere. Unless you don't want to talk about it."

Lex resigned herself to the thought that her houseguest would jump across the creek after what she was about to say. "A couple of years ago, when Hubert was still living here at the ranch, he had gone to Las Vegas on what he called a 'business trip.' A week later, he came home with a young woman he had met at the blackjack tables, who had given him some hard luck story about being dumped by her fiancé." Lex's eyes took on a faraway look. "They hit it off immediately, and Hubert invited her to come home with him to *his* ranch." Here she sighed. "He must have really played it up. The ranch was only about half the size it is now, and we hadn't begun remodeling yet. Needless to say, it was a little...rustic." Lex slipped out of the chair and onto the floor next to Amanda. "I guess Linda felt a little betrayed by Hubert's exaggerations, because she started coming on to me." She looked over at Amanda, expecting shock or disgust, not the accepting smile she was receiving.

"Um hmm. Go on."

"Well, she told me she and Hubert had decided to break off their relationship and were going to be just friends. I was young; I believed her. It's a shame she forgot to tell Hubert." Lex's expression saddened. "So, she stayed here at the ranch with me for about six months." Mentally bracing herself, Lex quietly added, "As my lover."

In the total silence that followed, Lex thought she could hear her heart pounding throughout the room.

"So, what happened? Why isn't she still here?" Amanda gave the strong leg under her hand a slight squeeze.

Feeling somewhat relieved at Amanda's question, Lex continued. "Hubert had moved to the house in town, and Linda started asking me to take her on trips. I tried explaining to her that this was a working ranch, but she always cried about being bored and tired of living out in the middle of nowhere. Later on, I figured out that she was just a little gold-digger, and the luster wore off when she found out I really didn't have the kind of money Hubert had hinted at." She ran her hand through her hair. "I came in from tagging the cattle one evening and found all of her stuff gone. The note that she left said, 'Been a great ride, going to Atlantic City for a change of pace.'" *It still hurts, all these years later. I thought it was love. What a joke I must have been to her.*

Lex said, "Hubert was pretty vocal in town about what went on here at the ranch. And now he's telling me that if you stay here, people may think the same of you." She felt her hand grasped and looked into Amanda's eyes. "I don't want your grandparents to hear nasty rumors about you. I'm sure they've already heard all the stories about me."

Amanda's eyes sparkled with unshed tears. "I am so sorry you had to go through something like that." She squeezed Lex's hand. "I really don't care what anyone says about me. And my grandparents have never cared much for gossip." She longed to take Lex in her arms and hug the hurt away. "So, if you don't mind, I think I'd like to hang around here for a while. You need help with the chores, don't you?" She paused to let her words sink in before looking Lex directly in the eyes. "And I don't walk out on my friends just because someone *may* say something derogatory about me."

Lex returned the squeeze. "Are you sure? My brother can get pretty nasty."

"Puleez! He's the very least of my worries." Her stomach growled. "See?"

Lex laughed and stood, pulling Amanda up with her. "So I hear. Let's go invade the kitchen. Martha probably has dinner cooked by now."

Once she was on her feet, Amanda wrapped her arms around Lex and squeezed gently. She felt warm arms surround her as the hug was returned.

"Thanks, friend." The whisper was so quiet that Amanda thought she might have imagined it. Then she was released and led to the door. "C'mon. Let's go get underfoot. Martha just *loves* when I do that."

Chapter Six

Dinner was quite an animated affair. Amanda and Martha traded humorous stories back and forth, while Lex sat back and absorbed it all quietly. Lex had been half-afraid that their guest was going to run off screaming into the night after hearing her story, and she was completely surprised that Amanda was still with them and hadn't demanded to be ferried across the creek. She watched as the two women interacted. *Should have known. Martha adores her, and she's always been a good judge of character.* The heavyset housekeeper had disliked Linda immensely, although the young woman always made sure to be sickeningly polite to Martha whenever Lex was around.

"Lexie?" The housekeeper tapped her arm. "You with us, honey?"

"Uh, yeah. Just thinking." Lex turned her attention to Amanda. "You gonna help Martha here in the kitchen tomorrow?"

"Uh-huh. After we feed the livestock in the morning. Why? Do you have something planned that you need my help with?"

"No, not really. I was just going to ride down and get the Jeep."

Martha, knowing what else she was going to do, piped up. "You're not going to overdo it, are you?"

Lex raised an eyebrow. "Of course not. I'm just going to take a leisurely ride down the road, attach the Jeep's winch to a tree, and then let it do all the work. If it hadn't been raining so damn hard last night, I would have done it then." She hoped she was convincing. "The road should be in good enough shape by tomorrow to bring the Jeep back to the house."

Martha looked less than convinced. "Promise me that you'll not put any undo stress on yourself, sweetheart. I have no desire to try and find a way to get you to the hospital."

Amanda spoke up. "Are you sure you don't need my help?"

"Nah. I was going to check part of the fence first, and I won't be back until late afternoon, at the least. You'd be bored to tears."

"She's right, honey. When Lexie goes out on her horse, time has a tendency to slip away from her." Martha turned her attention back to Lex. "Take your cell phone, just in case you happen to get into trouble, please? You should have taken it with you last night." When Lex rolled her eyes, Martha slapped her arm. "Watch it! Or we'll *both* go with you!"

Lex put up her hands in surrender. "Okay, you win. I remember the last time I got you up on a horse."

"That wasn't a horse. It was a four-legged messenger from the devil! I like transportation that doesn't bite, thank you very much."

Lex couldn't help but laugh. "She didn't bite you. She nuzzled your pocket looking for treats."

"And scared me out of ten years of my life. If you didn't spoil those horses so bad, that would have never happened!" Martha got up to clear the table.

Amanda almost spewed her drink through her nose at Martha's intense dislike for horses. "Don't feel bad, Martha. I don't ride much either because it's a long way to the ground."

"Maybe I'll find you a pony with a seatbelt," Lex teased. The vision of Amanda on a shaggy Shetland pony, buckled into a saddle resembling a child's car seat, made her laugh even harder. She clutched her sore ribs. "Ow."

"Serves you right, making fun of me," Amanda chastised, enjoying the teasing.

"I wasn't making fun of you. I was, uh, simply making a helpful suggestion," Lex said, trying to curb her laughter.

"Oh, you." Amanda threw her napkin into the laughing woman's face.

Lex stood up and carried her dishes to the sink and Amanda followed right behind her. The rancher gently bumped Martha with her hip. "Since we've goofed off all day, let us at least do the dishes." Seeing the housekeeper's resolve weakening, she put on her best pleading look and added, "Please?"

Martha sighed, but backed away from the sink. "Okay, you win. You know I can't resist that look."

Amanda took up her position next to the triumphantly beaming Lex. "Yeah. We'll take care of everything. Why don't you go relax?"

Martha gave in gracefully. "That's not a bad idea. I think I'll go home and take a long, hot bubble bath." She pulled off her apron, hung it over her shoulder, and sashayed out of the room, swinging her hips with an exaggerated motion.

Lex and Amanda looked at each other and burst out laughing. They made quick work of the dishes, Lex washed while Amanda rinsed and dried.

Amanda placed her hands on her back and leaned into the counter with a groan. "I think Martha may have had the right idea. I've found some muscles that I didn't know existed before today."

Lex put the rest of the dishes away. "No problem. You can use my tub. It even has a built-in Jacuzzi." She draped an arm around Amanda's shoulders. "I've got some paperwork that will keep me busy for at least an hour, so take all the time you need." She led Amanda up the stairs.

Once inside the master bedroom, Lex went to the large oak dresser. She pulled several sleep shirts and tee shirts from one of the drawers. "These should be more comfortable than those sweats." She handed the items to Amanda.

"Thanks. But I have no complaints about my other wardrobe."

Lex raised an eyebrow at her and then turned her attention to searching through the massive walk-in closet. "Ah-ha! I knew it was in here somewhere." She pulled out a flowery terrycloth robe, which looked about two sizes too small for her, and handed it to Amanda with a flourish. "My great Aunt Loretta sent this to me for Christmas last year, and I couldn't throw it out. Now I'm glad I didn't. It seems more like you, anyway."

That much was certainly true. Amanda glanced at Lex, and then at the robe. "Mmm, I don't know. I think you'd look rather dashing in it." She giggled at the perturbed cast on her host's face, and decided to give Lex a break. "Thanks. I appreciate the loan."

"No problem. You keep it. That way when I write to Aunt Loretta telling her it's useful, I won't be lying. As it was, I told her on the phone after Christmas that I was enjoying it." She steered Amanda toward the bathroom. "And I was. Every time I pictured myself in it, I had a good laugh." Lex pulled a towel from a nearby cabinet and tossed it to Amanda before heading for the door. "There should be some bubble stuff by the tub." She shrugged her shoulders when Amanda looked at her questioningly. "I enjoy a good soak every now and then myself."

Lex stared at the computer screen and rubbed her tired eyes. She had been searching the books on her accounting program for over an hour trying to find almost ten thousand dollars of missing funds. She flipped over to her Internet access and sent a request to her bank that they send her the bank statements for the last several months. Since Hubert usually handled the paperwork end of the ranch, Lex wasn't about to confront her brother until she had some solid proof. She also decided to personally do a head count of the stock, since it appeared they were losing more than was normal. Exhausted, Lex looked at the clock and blinked. "Amanda's probably upstairs bored to death by now," she mumbled as she shut down the computer and left the office. *Yeah, right. Amanda's bored. Let's face it, Lexington, she's been one floor away for over an hour and you already miss her.*

After navigating the stairs, Lex stopped at Amanda's room, which was dark and empty. She shrugged her shoulders and went into her own room, only to find it vacant as well. Confused, Lex knocked timidly on the bathroom door. "Amanda?" When there was no answer, Lex slowly opened the door. She walked over to the tub, where she spied a damp head poking out of the bubbles. She could see that Amanda was sound asleep, and the only noise in the room was the gurgling of the Jacuzzi. "Amanda?"

When there was no response, Lex raised her voice slightly. "Amanda."

Startled, Amanda's eyes popped open and she sank under the water. She whooshed up out of the water immediately, gasping and sputtering. "Wha—?"

Lex knelt down. "Hey, careful there." She put her hands on Amanda's shoulders and eased her into a more comfortable sitting position. "Didn't mean to startle you like that." Then she started to rub Amanda's back soothingly with one hand while still holding onto her shoulder with the other.

Amanda coughed a couple of more times, then stilled. "I'm sorry. I guess I must have dozed off. How long have I been in here?"

Suddenly aware of where her hands were, a wave of desire spread rapidly through Lex. She pulled back and stood up. "Umm, almost two hours." She put her hands in her back pockets, trying to calm her pounding heart. "I'll just let you get dried off then. You're probably feeling pretty waterlogged." She backed up to the door.

"That would explain the cold water, then." Amanda brushed bubbles off her forehead. She was glad the jets had continued to churn the water, making endless soap bubbles, or else Lex would have had a clear view of her nude body. "Thanks for waking me up. I'll be out in a minute." She watched with some amusement as the usually sure-footed and composed rancher backed directly into the doorframe, blushing furiously.

"Yeah, I'll just, umm. Yeah." Lex beat a hasty retreat into the bedroom, slamming the door behind her.

Amanda giggled as she let the water run out of the tub. She was happy to know she wasn't the only one who felt the electricity between them. She quickly dried off and then looked at her choices of sleepwear. "Hmm. Do I go modest, or do I tease her a little more?" She picked an oversized nightshirt that would hang a little past her knees. "I'd better go modest. She's looking a little too shook up right now. Maybe tomorrow night."

After pulling the sleep shirt over her head, Amanda stepped into the bedroom and saw Lex sitting in the light of the fireplace, slouched down in one of the overstuffed chairs. "All yours." Amanda moved to the other chair and sat down, toweling her hair dry. "Thanks for the loan of the tub. I'm most definitely relaxed now."

"I'm glad. You're welcome to use it anytime you want." Lex shifted uncomfortably in her chair. "I'm sorry I barged in like that, but when you didn't answer me, I got a little concerned."

"No, that's okay. Any longer in there, and I would have turned into a prune." Amanda looked over at Lex. Her face was bathed in shadow, and the firelight turned her usually bright eyes almost black. "You look pretty worn out yourself."

Lex sighed and ran a hand through her hair. "Yeah. Been a long day." She twisted her head to one side, and her neck popped. She stood up slowly. "Think I'll take a quick shower and then jump into bed."

Amanda stood up with her. "Do you need any help?" At Lex's raised eyebrow, she blushed. "Um, I mean, with taking off your bandage?" Lex's other eyebrow shot up into her bangs. "You know what I mean." Amanda didn't think she could get any more embarrassed. Meanwhile, Lex enjoyed seeing Amanda doing all the squirming for a change.

Lex took pity on her. "Nah. I can get it off okay, and I'll probably just leave it off for the night."

"I don't think that's a very good idea. What if you roll around in your sleep? That cut could break open again, and you'd bleed all over the sheets. I really don't think you should go to bed unprotected."

Lex chuckled. "I don't think that I am going to need protection in bed tonight, or will I?"

Amanda's mouth moved, but it refused to form any words. So she blushed instead and looked everywhere, except at Lex, until her brain cooperated a little more. She cast a quick, downward look at her bare wrist. "Ah. Um. Yeah. Time. Wow! Yeah, would you look at the time?" She faked a yawn and then stretched. "Guess I'll let you get your shower. I'll be across the hall if you need me to help you with your bandage."

Amused, Lex watched Amanda flee to the guestroom. *I really should be ashamed of myself, teasing her like that, but the way she blushes is just so damn cute.* Somehow, the camaraderie they shared seemed right, like they had done it for years. And Lex was more than a little intrigued by Amanda's hasty retreat. *I think we may be having the same reaction to each other. At least, I hope so.* Lex walked into the bathroom, whistling and shedding clothes as she went. When she glanced at the tub, her mind automatically supplied her with the image of Amanda's naked body surrounded by the bubbles from her bath only moments before, and she started to breath heavily again. *Get a hold of yourself, woman!* She continued to mentally chastise herself as she set the shower's water temperature to cold.

Amanda had just finished brushing her teeth and was brushing her hair when she heard a knock on the door. "Come in," she yelled, sticking her head out of the bathroom.

A sheepish-looking Lex walked in, wearing a robe and carrying a large elastic bandage. "Hey. Your offer still open?" She seemed like a helpless child. "I can't seem to get this damn thing on right."

Amanda set the hairbrush down and moved into the bedroom. "What's the matter? A torn sheet not good enough for you?"

"No, it's not that. I just remembered that I had this from the last time I broke a rib."

"Really?" Amanda quizzed. "I'll help you, but you've got

to tell me what happened." She looked up expectantly.

Lex shrugged as if dismissing the whole incident. "Nothing, much. It happened last year. Horse threw me into the fence, and I broke a rib. No big deal." Then, like a child, Lex pleaded, "But don't tell Martha. She told me not to try to ride that horse, but I didn't listen. And, I've, umm, kinda kept that accident a little secret from her. Promise not to tell?"

Amanda's heart softened at the look on Lex's face. *God! She is adorable!* "Oh, Lex. You look like a little kid who got caught stealing from the cookie jar." She moved closer and took the bandage from Lex's hands. "Okay, I promise. Now get over here and I'll get you fixed up."

Lex turned her back to Amanda, then removed her robe and laid it on the bed, leaving her in just a pair of flannel pajama bottoms. She tried to empty her mind and body of all thoughts and feelings while she waited for Amanda to wind the bandage around her, both dreading and anticipating her touch.

Amanda couldn't help but notice how beautiful Lex was. She willed her shaking hands to steady as she wrapped the bandage around Lex's body. Broad shoulders led to a narrow waist, with hips that flared just enough to show she was all woman. *Breathe, Amanda, breathe.* For someone who led such a rough life, Lex's skin was softer than Amanda ever imagined. *Not like that! You're about to hyperventilate!* She had to lean into the strong back to wind the bandage around Lex's ribs. Amanda bit her lower lip, trying to rein in hormones that were thumbing their noses at her attempt to keep them under control. Once she finished, she draped the robe back over Lex's shoulders. "All done."

Lex was having control problems of her own. Amanda stood so close that she could feel the heat coming off her. "Thanks." She turned around, missing Amanda's struggle to compose herself. "Guess I'll let you get to bed now." As she passed through the doorway, Lex turned to look at her guest. "See you in the morning." She continued to stand there a moment longer while the two of them recognized the longing in each other's eyes. She gave Amanda a slight nod before walking out and closing the door behind her.

Amanda stood beside the bed and stared at the closed door. "Oh, boy. Lex, my friend, I think we're gonna have to have a little talk, real soon."

On the other side of the door, Lex's emotions washed over her and left her trembling in their wake. *I want her. More than I*

think I've ever wanted anything or anyone. She braced herself
against the wall with one hand and shakily worked her way back
across the hallway.

Chapter
Seven

The next morning, after they finished feeding the horses, Lex and Amanda went into the hay barn. Lex backed the truck up to a tall stack of baled hay, climbed out, and looked around for Amanda. There was no sign of her anywhere. She was about to put the tailgate down on the truck when she felt something drop on her hat and shoulders. "Hey!" Lex looked up and brushed the straw from her body.

"Yep, it's hay," Amanda cheerfully admitted, readying herself for another throw. She had climbed up to the top bale, mainly because she had always wanted to and couldn't resist.

"I thought you didn't like heights." Lex took off her hat and shook the hay free. "Now climb down from there before you get hurt." She put her hands on her hips and glowered.

"No, I don't like *moving* heights. I get motion sickness." Amanda plopped down on the bale, her legs swinging back and forth. "Besides, this isn't that high. Maybe twelve to fifteen feet, at the most." She was about to jump down, when the bale suddenly shifted, causing her to fall.

Lex saw the movement and dropped her hat. She rushed to position herself under the falling woman. "Ooof!" she grunted, catching Amanda in her arms, cradling her as if she were a child. "Are you okay?"

Amanda looked up into frightened eyes and felt the woman holding her tremble. "Yeah." Then she remembered where she was, and how she got there. "Oh, God. Are *you* okay?"

Enraptured, Lex looked into Amanda's eyes. "Uh-huh." She couldn't seem to alter her gaze. Words failed her as she felt Amanda's arms wrap around her neck.

Amanda didn't think, couldn't think. She gave in to her overwhelming feelings for the rancher and pulled Lex's head down. When their lips met, Amanda was amazed at how soft

Lex's lips were. As the kiss deepened, Amanda felt a strong feeling of belonging, and her heart raced.

Lex was having strong feelings of her own. When her lips touched Amanda's, she felt a gentle tickle in the pit of her stomach. And when Amanda deepened the kiss, a jolt of electricity shot throughout her body, which caused her legs to give out. Lex collapsed back into a soft pile of hay, never releasing the woman in her arms.

They spent a few moments just enjoying the kiss until Lex pulled away in order to breathe. "Wow," she gasped.

Amanda laid her head on Lex's chest and sighed. Then she looked up into the eyes so close to hers. "I can't believe I did that."

"Are you sorry that you did?" Lex was terrified to know the answer.

"God, no!" Amanda reached up to caress a tan cheek, trying to calm the erratic beating of Lex's heart. "It's just that I don't usually make it a habit to throw myself, this time quite literally, at someone I've only know a couple of days." She could feel the rancher struggling to pull air into her lungs. "Are you sure you're all right? What about your ribs?"

Lex turned her head slightly and kissed the palm cupping her face. "Never been better." Seeing several emotions cross Amanda's face, Lex kissed her forehead and gave her a gentle hug. "If that's how you're going to react after falling from a stack of hay, remind me to bring you in here more often."

"Works for me. I've always wanted to roll around in the hay." Amanda was immediately embarrassed. "Umm, I mean—"

Lex understood. "Relax. Let's just take things slow and easy, okay? No need to rush."

Amanda's smile lit up her entire face. "Yeah. I guess we'd better finish up the chores, huh?" She saw Lex's face start to relax. "And Martha is expecting me pretty soon."

"True. But first—" Lex leaned down and captured Amanda's lips again, feeling the younger woman's hands tangle into her hair. She ended the kiss slowly, trying without much success to back off. "Whew. I, umm—"

Amanda brushed the hair out of Lex's eyes. "Yeah, that goes double for me." She climbed off Lex's lap and then offered her hand to the seated woman. "Here, since I got you down there, might as well be the one to help you back up."

Lex accepted her offer, allowing Amanda to pull her up.

Not releasing the hand that swallowed hers, Amanda pulled Lex into a very gentle hug. "Thanks." She stood on her tiptoes and kissed Lex's chin.

"For what?" Lex returned the hug, delighted to openly enjoy the feeling of holding the woman in her arms.

Amanda pulled back a little, so she could see her face, which was partially bathed in shadow. "For working on your fence in a thunderstorm. For pulling a complete stranger out of a raging creek, and for catching me when I fall."

I've fallen too, Amanda. Lex kissed the top of her head. "Any time." Her voice broke on the words. She released Amanda, but kept one arm draped over her shoulder. "C'mon. I imagine the cows are about to mutiny."

Sometime later, Amanda was standing in the stable as Lex saddled up the powerfully built Thunder. "Are you sure you don't need any help? I mean, Martha would probably understand if I was a little late today." She reached up and rubbed the large horse's head as he nuzzled her chest.

"Nah. Not that I wouldn't enjoy the company, but I really don't want Martha to try to reach some of those higher cabinets by herself." Lex tightened the cinch. "Martha and stepladders don't always get along." She finished with the saddle and patted the horse on his flank. "Last time she fell and twisted her ankle. I thought she had broken it, and it scared the hell out of me. If you can believe it, she's actually a worse patient than I am." Lex led the gigantic horse out of the stall. "I'd really appreciate it if you could keep an eye on her, if you don't mind." She turned and reached for the saddle horn, but a hand on her arm stopped her.

"I don't mind at all. But you have to do me a favor in return." Amanda grasped Lex's coat with both hands, pulling her closer, which Lex enjoyed immensely.

"Yeah?" Lex could barely keep the silly grin off her face.

"Try to stay out of trouble, and please be careful." She saw Lex open her mouth to argue, and covered it with her hand. "Please? Don't hurt yourself trying to get that old Jeep out of the mud. It's not like we can go very far anyway."

Lex pulled her into a quick hug. "You're starting to sound a lot like Martha." She stepped back and gently chucked Amanda under the chin. "I promise, I'll behave." She climbed into the saddle, causing Thunder to dance sideways. "I'll also be check-

ing some of the fence line by the creek, so I may not be back
until dark."

Amanda patted her leg. "Okay. Just give us a call on your
cell phone if you have any problems." She walked beside the
horse as Lex moved him out of the stable.

"Yes, ma'am." Lex tipped her hat with a smirk. "Do you
want a ride to the house?"

Amanda looked up at Lex and then to the house, which was
only about twenty yards away. An unexpected thrill raced down
her spine, as Lex held an arm out to her. "Sure." She allowed
herself to be pulled up onto the horse behind Lex. Wrapping her
arms around the tapered waist, Amanda leaned into the strong
back with a small sigh. "Now *this* is the way to ride horses."

Delighted, Lex kneed the stallion forward. "Really? Are
you sure you don't want a seatbelt?" She felt the arms around
her waist tighten slightly.

"Nope. This is perfect." She nuzzled her face against Lex's
back.

As they rode the rest of the way to the house, the only
sounds were of Thunder's heavy hooves falling to the ground
and Lex's heartbeat pounding happily in Amanda's ear.

Lex pulled the massive horse to a stop by the back porch
and gave Amanda a hand down. "There you go, ma'am. Door to
door service, as promised."

"Thank you, kind horsewoman." Amanda curtsied. "That
terribly long walk would have worn me out."

Lex winked as she backed Thunder away from the porch.
"Any time." She tipped her hat again before turning the big
horse away.

"Be careful!" Amanda called after her, cringing as Lex sent
Thunder into a full gallop.

Lex charged Thunder through the fields, joyously leaning
over his neck. Feeling only a slight ache in her ribs due to the
activity, she laughed out loud into the wind blowing in her face.
"It's a beautiful day, isn't it boy?" The racing horse snorted in
disagreement. Low dark clouds had begun to cover the sky,
threatening to erupt at any moment, and the cool breeze blowing through the surrounding trees brought a damp chill to the
air. To Lex, the day had never been more beautiful. *I must be
doing something right, 'cause someone up there has certainly
dropped a wonderful gift right into my lap.* "Yah!" She urged

the horse on, absorbing the brisk air around them with glee.

Coming within sight of the Jeep, Lex reined in the large horse, walking him around to cool him off. "Doesn't look like we'll have much trouble here, huh big fella? Let's take a walk down to the creek before get started, okay?" Lex patted his neck as they made their way slowly to the source of a loud roaring sound beyond the trees.

Amanda walked into the kitchen, her cheeks slightly flushed, looking dazed and happy. Martha turned around from the pantry. "Well, well. You must have had a good time feeding the stock. That's an interesting look on your face, honey." She enjoyed the blush that erupted on Amanda's face.

"Oh, yeah. I had a great time." Amanda's words registered in her mind too late, and she lowered her head trying to control her embarrassment.

Martha walked over to her and pulled a few errant stalks of hay from her hair. "Mmm-hmm. Sure looks like it."

Amanda covered her face with her hands. "Oh, God."

The housekeeper's heart melted and she relented. "Sweetheart, calm down. There's nothing to be ashamed of. I'm glad you two have hit it off so well." She took Amanda's arm and pulled her over to the table. "Sit down while I get you some coffee." Martha took a couple of mugs from the cabinet, filled the carafe, and then sat down at the table beside Amanda. "Did Lexie get off to the creek okay?" she asked, pouring them each a cup.

"Umm, yeah, she did. She told me that she would be checking the fence also, and not to expect her back before it got dark." Amanda took a small sip of her coffee.

Martha appeared surprised. "She told you she'd be late?" She gave a slight shake of her head. "She never actually tells anyone when she'll be back. I usually just fix her a big breakfast, and plan dinner for dusk on days when I know she'll be riding fence."

Amanda stared into her mug. "Well, maybe she just said that because she knew that we'd be worried, since she's still injured."

"Bruised ribs and a little scrape? Honey, that's never bothered her before." Martha patted Amanda's hand. "Not that she's unfeeling. It's just that she normally doesn't think about little things like that." Then, with an edge to her voice, she added,

"Not like she can, having to run this place all alone."

Amanda looked up. "Her brother doesn't help her at all?"

Martha scoffed. "Hubert, help? Not in this lifetime. Sometimes I think his sole purpose in life is to aggravate poor Lexie, and, of course, to mooch money off her." She took a sip of coffee. "He's never done an honest day's work in his life. Oh, sure, Lexie lets him keep the ranch's books, and he has that accounting office he runs in town, but he's no good. He's hated Lexie ever since her daddy signed the ranch over to her. And before that, he was just plain mean." She took another sip of coffee. "I normally wouldn't be telling anyone this, but I trust you, and I want you to be aware of just how nasty that man can be." Martha paused to study the young woman across from her.

Amanda had a pretty good idea where Martha was heading with this conversation. She met the wise brown eyes. "Lex told me about Linda." She saw the housekeeper's posture relax somewhat. "Hubert tried to blackmail Lex last night about my staying here. So she decided to tell me about his threat. Did Linda actually dump Hubert for Lex?"

Martha nodded, surprised, but relieved that Lex had been open with Amanda about the woman in her past. "Oh yes. You see, Hubert is quite handsome. Tall, dark, with blue eyes like Lexie's. Only his are lighter and cruel. Women just seem to throw themselves at his feet, until they get to know him. Then the smart ones run like all get out." She finished her coffee and wiped the table with a damp dishcloth. "He's also got Lexie's temper. They both got that from their daddy, but he never learned to control it like she did. I think Linda finally got tired of Hubert taking his anger out on her, and so to get back at him she latched onto Lexie."

Amanda frowned. "She didn't love Lex, did she Martha?"

"Oh, I think she did, in her own way. She just wanted a fancier lifestyle than what Lexie could give her." Martha remembered grimly the month-long bender that Linda's desertion had wrought with the impressionable young woman. Lex would get up before dawn to take care of her chores, then lock herself in the office and drink until late afternoon. Her drinking buddies would arrive then, and they'd all go into town and bar hop until closing, or until they'd land in jail due to their unruliness. Martha would usually find Lex passed out on the front porch, where these so-called "friends" would leave her.

After a month of this sort of behavior, Martha had enough. She found Lex sprawled unconscious on the porch swing and doused her with a large bucket of extremely muddy water. Lex sputtered and cursed, still quite hung over. Martha shocked her by telling her to either clean herself up, or find a new house-keeper, because she wasn't going to tolerate any more self-pity. Heeding the ultimatum, Lex begged for forgiveness and never got drunk again.

"Martha?" Amanda became concerned at the look on the older woman's face. She patted the hand that had been absently wiping the table. "Are you all right?"

The housekeeper shook her head and smiled apologetically. "Sorry 'bout that, dear. I got a little lost in my memories." She placed her other hand on Amanda's. "C'mon. Let's get to work on those cabinets." But Martha hesitated for one more moment while she studied Amanda's face. *This one is no Linda.* She patted Amanda's hand, satisfied that Lex had finally found the real thing.

Lex stood at the edge of the creek, hypnotized by the rapidly flowing water. She shifted her gaze slightly downstream, glad to see the Mustang was still in the same place. Its rear bumper was just barely visible above the water line. Lex looked behind her, mentally calculating the path she would use to pull the car from the water. "How to get it from there to here, that's the sticking point. One of the chains from the Jeep should be long enough, but how in the hell do I get the chain on the car?" She looked at the water, and then down at herself. "Well, I could just tell them I fell into the creek." She smirked, imagining the looks on their faces. Deciding that wouldn't be a very good idea, Lex shoved the problem to the back of her mind, deciding to worry more about it when she got the Jeep out of it's muddy nest. Turning away from the churning waters, she walked back to the patiently waiting Thunder and rode him to her first priority.

An hour later, an angry and mud-covered Lex finally drove the Jeep to the creek. Even while using the winch that was attached to the front of the vehicle, she still had to dig and push to extricate the buried vehicle. She had removed her cowboy hat and duster to save them, but she was almost solid mud from the tip of her head to the soles of her boots, and she was furious enough to spit nails.

Lex backed the Jeep to a large tree several yards from the creek bank, until it was almost touching the heavy oak. She wound a length of chain around the trunk of the tree and the other end around the back axle. Then she pulled a longer stretch of chain from the Jeep and attached it to the steel cable that she unwound from the winch. Lex tied one end of rope to the chain and the other around her waist, muttering, "That's it. I've got to be certifiable, jumping into this damned creek not once, but twice in one week. Martha is going to have me committed." She looked down at her clothes, barely distinguishable under the mud. "At least I can use the excuse that I needed to get the mud off me, so I rinsed off my clothes. I don't have to tell them it was in the creek."

She waded into the creek, thankful that the current had slowed down since Friday. "Damn, but that's cold," she grumbled, as the water slowly made its way to her shoulders. Once again, she let the current do most of the work of moving her downstream. When she got near the partially submerged car, she took over, her strong stroke cutting through the water easily.

She cringed when she bumped into the car. The last thing she wanted to do was put more dents in the vehicle than it all ready had. She lifted herself up on the trunk and pulled the rope across the creek until she had the chain in her hands. Taking a deep breath, Lex slid off the rear of the car and slipped under water. It only took her a minute to wrap the chain around the axle of the Mustang and return to the surface. She pulled herself back across the creek with a sense of déjà vu.

It took Lex over two hours to pull the small car from the creek. At times she feared the old oak would fall and crush both vehicles and her, as well. And though the massive tree creaked and complained, in the end it stood strong. Once the Mustang was safely ashore, she patted the mud-encrusted Jeep on the hood and promised it a nice cleaning. The old vehicle was Lex's pride and joy, since she rebuilt it herself when she was in high school.

After securing the waterlogged car to the Jeep, Lex walked over to the patiently waiting Thunder to remove his saddle and bridle. "Okay, old buddy, I'll race you home." He snorted and started for the trees, content to take the shortcut back to the barn. Lex returned to the Jeep and fished her cell phone out of the pocket of her coat. She dialed the number for the ranch hoping that Martha, and not Amanda, would answer.

On the third ring, her wish came true as the housekeeper picked up the phone. "Walters' residence."

"Martha, it's me."

"Lexie? Honey, is everything okay?" Martha sounded a little nervous. Lex rarely used the device, complaining that she'd rather speak to someone face to face. The fact that she was calling only worried Martha more.

"Everything's wonderful, Martha. I got the Jeep, and I'll be making a stop at the maintenance shed before I get back to the house."

Martha sighed heavily. "Good Lord, sweetheart. Don't scare me like that. I thought for sure something was wrong when you called."

"Sorry. I wasn't trying to scare you. It's just that I sent Thunder on ahead, and I didn't want you to worry when you saw him and not me. The road's still pretty muddy, and I thought it would be too dangerous for him to be led beside the Jeep." Using one hand, Lex tossed the saddle, blanket, and bridle in the back of the Jeep. "I should be in sight of the house in about an hour or so." She hoped that Martha could take a hint and keep Amanda away from the windows.

"That sounds great, Lexie. I thought Amanda and I would go over to my place for a while. I've got some pictures she might be interested in seeing." Martha visualized her face, knowing that Lex knew *exactly* which pictures she had in mind. Martha also knew that the road to the maintenance shed was not viewable from her house. "We'll be back in a couple of hours, so that should give you time to take care of your horse and get yourself cleaned up, too."

Lex laughed a bit nervously. "Uh, well, I was pretty muddy, but it's mostly cleaned off now." She climbed into the Jeep. "I'll see you at the house later, then. Bye, Martha." She disconnected the call before the housekeeper figured out what she had said. "I'm gonna be in so much trouble for that." It was one of her favorite pastimes, teasing Martha to keep her on her toes. "But she gives as good as she gets, that's for damn sure."

Chapter
Eight

"Oh, Martha, these are priceless!" Amanda was seated in the den, with several photo albums strewn on the coffee table in front of her. They had spent the last hour or so talking about their families and enjoying each other's companionship.

Amanda picked up a photo of a teenaged boy who looked like a younger, male version of Lex. He was standing alongside his sister. "Is this Louis?"

Martha nodded as she lovingly ran her finger down the picture and said, "This was taken about a month before he died."

"Look at the way he and Lex are sticking their tongues out at each other. I assume that Louis got along with Lex much better than Hubert did."

"That's the truth, dear. Louis always looked up to his sister. But still, he was fourteen, and he was starting to get a little headstrong. Lexie adored him anyway." Martha paused to reflect for a moment and then added, "I think that's what hurt so much when he died. I swear that girl was as much a mother to her younger brother as I am to her."

"He died the same year Lex's father left the ranch to her?" Amanda's heart started to break for the woman who'd had so much to deal with in her young life. As the puzzle pieces started to fall into place, Amanda came to see a more complete picture of the woman she was falling in love with. She was caught up in her own thoughts until she noticed the dour look that came over the housekeeper's face.

"That's one thing that I'll never forgive Rawson Walters for: the way he just left after young Louis died."

Amanda took the housekeeper's hand and squeezed it. Martha reached for a tissue with the other hand and wiped the tears from her eyes. Then she handed one to Amanda. Amanda sniffled and accepted the tissue. She nodded, and Martha continued her story.

"Rawson had gone off for a week to a rodeo up north. He was on his way back here the day Louis disobeyed his sister and went boating on the lake with some of his friends. Lex had forbidden him to go, but, as I said, Louis was a bit headstrong, and he went anyway. Rawson arrived home right after the sheriff told Lexie about her brother's accident. He never said a word. To Lexie. To anyone. A few days after the funeral, Lex came home after checking the fences to find a note from her father, giving her control of the ranch."

Amanda leaned into Martha's side. Tears ran freely down her face as she felt the heartache that must have been Lex's during that awful time. Martha put her arm around Amanda to console her before continuing on with the tragic memory. "Lexie stood there in the hallway, clutching the letter to her chest and looking like she might shatter at any moment. When she noticed I was close by, watching her, she turned to me and silently gave me the letter to read. Lexie sank down onto the stairs and waited while I read the letter. I'll never forget the part where Rawson told her that he was going back to the rodeo circuit and how there was nothing holding him to the ranch anymore now that Victoria and Louis were gone. He wrote that he couldn't live here day-to-day with Lex's likeness of her mother reminding him of what he had lost."

Amanda felt anger burning inside of her. "How dare he! How could he leave her when she needed him most?"

Martha shook her head. "Rawson wasn't one to worry about what others needed. Not after Victoria died. He didn't need to be a father anymore, that is, in his own eyes once Lex turned 18, so he left the ranch, Lexie, and his memories behind."

Amanda dabbed uselessly at her tears. In a voice thick with emotion she said, "Thank God you were here for her, Martha. What would she have done without you?" She had already felt that her attraction to Lex was something deep and lasting. Learning about this tragedy fueled her feelings for Lex even more.

"My Lexie isn't the one to go about wanting other folks' pity, child. Even though the man who she wanted to please more than anyone in the world treated her as if she didn't matter a bit to him, she lived right up to her new responsibilities. Lex turned into a very capable woman, and she's done her daddy proud. Too bad he'll never know it. In my book, he's the one to be pitied. He'll never know the woman my Lexie turned out to be, despite the way he treated her."

"My heart does hurt for Lex, Martha," Amanda confessed, "And this isn't pity, Martha. It's...it's..." Amanda was sobbing openly now.

"I know, dear child. I know." Martha patted Amanda's shoulder. "I'm glad you came along, Amanda. I can already tell that you're going to be good for Lexie." *And I can tell by the fire in her eyes that she'll never abandon my girl. No, I think this one's a keeper. I sure hope Lexie figures that out.*

Martha looked at the clock on the mantle. It had been almost two hours since she had heard from Lex, and she figured it was safe to go back to the main house. "Amanda? Do you want to help me with dinner tonight? Lexie should be back any time now."

Amanda jumped to her feet, scooping up several of the albums while wiping at her eyes. "I'd love to. What do you need me to do?" She practically beat Martha to the door. Realizing she was still holding the photo albums, she asked, "Oh! Where do you want me to put these?"

Martha relieved Amanda of her burden. "I'll take those, dear." She put the items on a nearby desk. "Come on. I put a roast on earlier today, so let's see what we can find to go with it."

Lex put the Mustang in the shed, deciding to return to work on it after Amanda went to bed. She was surprised at the lack of damage it had sustained. There was only a medium-sized dent in the rear left panel, and, of course, the water damage and the back window now missing its glass. The window was still in one piece, lying on the floor in the tight backseat, so she wasn't concerned about putting it back in place. She had even found Amanda's purse and briefcase and left them and their contents on the workbench to dry out.

Next, Lex brushed Thunder who munched on the hay she had given him. She had actually finished his grooming some time ago, but had allowed the time to slip away from her as she daydreamed about the young woman who had fallen into her creek and then into her arms. Shaking herself from her reverie, Lex decided it was time to get back to the house. She patted the horse on his broad shoulder and left the stable.

Stepping up onto the porch, the tired and dirty rancher

stopped to remove her boots. She hoped to sneak upstairs before Martha was able to see just how filthy she was.

As Lex slowly opened the door and peeked inside, she heard voices in the kitchen. Although she was no longer dripping creek water, her jeans and tee shirt were still damp and heavily stained with mud. She could also feel small bits of mud and debris in her hair, but, thankfully, her hat covered most of her head. Her socks, which had been white this morning, were now a reddish brown. They made a squishing sound on the hardwood floor, causing Lex to wince with each step. She eased her head slowly around the kitchen door, hoping to get past the housekeeper. *Good! They're both busy.* Thinking she was home free, Lex continued down the hallway, walking quickly.

"Lexington Marie! What on earth have you done?" a very familiar voice boomed.

"Uh-oh." Lex spun around in mid-stride, which caused her wet feet to slip out from under her, so that she landed on her rear end with a sodden thump. "Ow!" The muck-covered woman slowly stood up, rubbing her backside with her hands. "Hi, Martha. Did you get your cabinets all straightened out?" she asked, backing up toward the staircase.

"Don't you 'Hi Martha' me, Lexington. You're soaking wet!" The heavyset woman stomped up to Lex, placed her hands on her hips, and cocked her head to one side.

"Umm, well, you see, the Jeep was really buried in the mud, and I, umm..." Lex trailed off, seeing the look in Martha's eyes that said she meant business.

"Yes?" The word was drawn out, and Martha impatiently tapped her foot.

With that one look, Lex felt ten years old again. "Aw hell, Martha. I was covered in mud, and thought I'd better rinse off before I came into the house." Embarrassed, she looked down at her soggy socks.

"I appreciate that, Lexie. But why all the sneaking around?"

Lex looked up, her eyes barely visible under her hat brim. "I wasn't actually sneaking, I just didn't want to disturb you while you were cooking dinner. Yeah, that's it."

Amanda witnessed the entire scene from the kitchen doorway. She covered her mouth with her hand, not wanting to interrupt. Poor Lex looked so cute, standing there with Martha taking her to task like an unruly child.

Martha yanked the black hat off the woman's head. "Good

Lord. What is all of that stuff in your hair?"

Lex closed her eyes and sighed. "I told you I got really muddy. Can I *please* go take a shower now?" She grabbed her hat from Martha and ran up the stairs.

"Dinner should be ready in about thirty minutes," Martha called after her.

"Thanks." Lex squished her way upstairs where she quickly showered and changed her clothes, eager to be in Amanda's presence again.

Martha turned back to Amanda, who was barely containing her giggles. "I swear, that girl can get into trouble just climbing out of bed in the mornings." She sighed as she returned to the kitchen.

Amanda finally lost it. She had to sit down on a nearby stool to remain at least somewhat upright. "She looked so pitiful. Does she do that often? She looked like a drowned cat dragged through too many mud puddles."

"Unfortunately, yes. Mud must be one of her favorite accessories, because she's forever covered in it." Martha stirred a pot of something on the stove. "I swear she could find mud in a drought."

Amanda laughed. "She was rather grimy. But did you really have to fuss at her like that?"

Martha turned away from the stove, meeting her eyes. "No, but if I don't throw at least a token fit, she'll think I don't love her anymore. I think she secretly enjoys the attention."

"Well, I don't think it's hurt her any. She speaks of you with the utmost respect and love." Amanda wanted this sweet woman to understand just how devoted Lex was to her. "She said you were the only mother she'd ever known. She told me the night I met her how much she cared for you."

Martha wiped an errant tear from her eye. "That goes double for me. As a matter of fact, she's one of the main reasons I never married. I had the only family I ever needed right here. Oh, I've had several offers over the years, but I never could bring myself to leave her. And I couldn't see me ever having a child I would love half as much."

Amanda walked over and gave Martha a hug. "Well, for what it's worth, I think you've done a fine job of raising her. Lex is a wonderful person."

"Thank you. I'm very proud of the woman she has become,

although I think she had more to do with it than I did." She patted Amanda's arm. "Now, let's get dinner on the table. She
should be straggling down anytime."

"Martha," Lex admonished, leaning in the doorway, "are
you talking about me again?" Her hair was wet, and she was
wearing jeans and the ever-present tee shirt, which for once
actually had a design on it. However, in her haste, Lex was bare-
footed and had forgotten to put on her bra, which did not go
unnoticed, or unappreciated, by a certain young woman whose
gaze was completely focused on her chest.

Jake's John Deere? Amanda leered. *Bet old Jake would sell
more tractors if his billboards looked like that.* Then, embarrassed that she'd been staring at Lex's body, she turned her
attention to the task at hand and helped Martha move the food
to the table. "So, how did the fence by the creek look? Did you
have to make any repairs?"

Lex reached for a bowl on the cabinet, only to have her
hand slapped by Martha. "Hey, I was just trying to help." She
yanked her hand away quickly and held it to her chest, as if
injured.

Martha shooed her away. "We have it all under control.
Now go sit down." Lex pretended to pout, and Martha turned
her around and slapped her gently on the rear. "Don't give me
that look. You've been out working all day. You need to sit
down."

Lex raised an eyebrow, but did as she was told. "You two
have been working all day, too. What's the difference?"

Amanda looked at the housekeeper, who had a perplexed
look on her face, trying to think of a good comeback. "Because
we actually sat down once in a while and took a break, and we
know you didn't." Martha smiled appreciatively at Amanda's
quick thinking, and at the fact that this young woman seemed
quite capable of handling her Lexie.

"What makes you think I didn't?" Lex locked eyes with
Amanda, who suddenly forgot what the conversation was about
the moment she got caught up in Lexington's intense gaze.

Martha butted in. "Two reasons: One, you *never* take a
break when you work in the field. Two, you look like you can
barely stand up." Lex opened her mouth, but promptly shut it at
Martha's upraised hand. "No. Don't you argue with me, I've
known you far too long." Martha was enjoying having the last
word for a change. "So just sit there quietly while we get dinner
on the table."

Lex knew when she'd been beaten. Besides, one look into Amanda's eyes, and she could barely even remember her own name. All she could do was nod and say, "Yes ma'am."

After dinner, Martha once again refused any help with the dishes, and chased the two young women out of the kitchen, popping her dishtowel at them as she shooed them out.

Lex grabbed Amanda's hand and dragged her from the mock battle, threatening to return similarly armed. She continued down the long hallway, until they came to the doorway to the den. "Do you want to watch a movie?"

Amanda squeezed the hand holding hers. "I think I'd like that very much. But I need to call my grandmother first, if that's okay with you."

"Sure. You know you can use the phone any time." Lex gave a courtly bow, pulling the young woman's hand to her lips. "My castle is yours to do with as you wish." She gave Amanda a slight nudge toward the office. "Go on. Take all the time you need." Lex sat down on the sofa, propped her bare feet on the coffee table, and patted her lap. "I'll save you a spot."

Amanda looked at the office door and then back at the lazily sprawled woman. "You know, it is getting late." She changed direction and moved to the sofa. "And I'd hate to disturb them. My grandfather really needs his rest." Amanda sat down next to Lex and snuggled close. "Besides, I called them from Martha's house today. I'm sure they're okay."

"How's your grandfather doing? I haven't seen him since he got out of the hospital." Lex put her arm around Amanda, who gave her a puzzled look.

"You saw him at the hospital? Why didn't I ever see you?"

"Well, I'd only visit once or twice a week, mainly to make sure Mrs. Cauble was doing okay, and it was always first thing in the morning."

"Oh, well. That explains it. I normally wouldn't get to the hospital until nine or ten, since I would stay so late the night before." Amanda stopped and thought for a moment. "Wait a minute! It was you, wasn't it?"

"What?"

"On Monday and Thursday mornings there were always fresh flowers by Grandpa Jake's bed. You were the one who brought them, right?"

Lex looked somewhat embarrassed. "Uh, yeah. Well, the

florist was on my way in." She felt arms constrict around her. "And Mr. Cauble has always been really nice to me." She pointed to the entertainment center. "He made that, you know." Trying to change the subject a little, she asked her original question again. "How's his leg? Has he gotten his cast off yet?"

"Yep. He's almost back to his old self, but still has a pretty heavy limp. Although he's told us that it's only temporary." Amanda leaned up close to Lex's ear. "But he's doing much," she kissed the tender skin, "much," a slight nibble on the nearby lobe, "better."

Lex moaned, and turned her face to meet Amanda's teasing mouth. They took their time, both enjoying the contact. Lex pulled Amanda onto her lap and was rewarded by hands tangling in her hair, gently kneading her neck.

Lex broke away first, a slightly glazed look in her eyes. "Wow." She cleared her throat. "That was—"

Amanda placed a kiss on Lex's chin. "Oh yeah. It most certainly was. And we're so new at it. Can you imagine when we've gotten some practice in?" She nibbled on Lex's lower lip and said, in her sexiest voice, "Wanna practice?"

She was answered by a quiet growl, as Lex passionately explored the skin on Amanda's throat. She worked her way up to a one ear and gave it a light nip. "Sounds like a plan to me," Lex whispered, enjoying the little shiver she could feel running through Amanda.

They continued almost hesitantly, neither in any hurry to push the other too far. It felt so good to Amanda, and she used her hands to map out the muscles in Lex's back. She was feeling almost overwhelmed by the incredible sensations coursing through her body. She thought that what she had found in the past was special, at least until now. *No, that was friendship, or maybe even infatuation. This is,* a low moan escaped her as Lex found a sensitive spot on her neck, *this is incredible!*

Lex couldn't seem to get enough of the skin under her lips. She bit down gently on the pulse point, eliciting a low moan from the woman sprawled in her lap. Even with her heart pounding in her ears, Lex had never felt such a complete feeling of peace before. When Amanda ran her hands up and down her back, Lex knew deep in her soul that she wanted to feel this way forever.

By unspoken agreement, neither woman took the activities any farther, both wanting to savor the moment. Lex slowly pulled back, trying to prolong their contact while, at the same time, trying to control her desire. "It's getting pretty late. Why don't we continue this *conversation*, tomorrow?"

Amanda ran a trembling finger down Lex's flushed face. "Probably a good idea." She could feel the chest beneath her other hand heaving with effort. "Why don't we go upstairs and get some sleep?" She climbed off Lex's lap, grabbing one of her hands and pulling Lex to her feet. "C'mon. I'll tuck you in." The way Lex looked at her made her realize how suggestive that sounded. Amanda blushed. "Lex!" She slapped her arm. "You know what I mean!"

Lex pulled the red-faced Amanda into a hug. "Sorry. You're just so cute when you blush." She kissed the top of the head tucked under her chin. "But you're right. It has been a pretty long day." She allowed Amanda to step back, but caught her hand. "Can I walk you home?"

"Hmm. I don't know. What would my parents say?"

"They'd say I was incredibly lucky." Lex led Amanda to the door.

Navigating the stairs was an experience, to say the least. Lex took the opportunity to stop at almost every step, citing some unknown house rule about a kiss per step. Amanda didn't want to jinx the house, so of course she obliged. Many minutes later, they found themselves at Amanda's bedroom door. Lex pulled a hand to her lips and kissed it gently. "Goodnight."

Amanda released the hand in hers, and slipped her arms around Lex's neck. She stood up on her tiptoes and zeroed in on a pair of slightly bruised lips. "Goodnight." She kissed Lex with abandon, wanting to send her to bed with something to remember her by. "Sleep well." Amanda used her teeth to lightly tug at Lex's upper lip before releasing her. "See you in the morning." She closed the door behind her, leaving a highly aroused Lex staring after her.

"Oh, boy." Lex turned and headed across the hall. "I need a cold shower." She shook her head. "Nah. I'll just put on my boots and go check out the car. That should calm me down." Lex quietly went back downstairs, her body still tingling from the kiss. "As if I'll ever feel calmed down again, the way Amanda kisses."

Chapter
Nine

Amanda was awakened by another bad dream, and no matter how hard she tried, she could not go back to sleep. She tiptoed to the bedroom across the hall, needing Lex's presence to sooth her frazzled nerves.

Standing in the doorway, Amanda peered at the bed. "Lex?" she whispered, not hearing any movement from the bed. "Are you asleep?"

Not getting an answer, Amanda crept forward, finding the bed empty. She looked in the bathroom, and found it deserted as well. Curious as to where Lex could be, she stepped around to the far side of the bed and sat down, deciding to wait. A few minutes later, completely worn out, Amanda curled up on her side and fell asleep.

Lex crept down the dark stairway feeling somewhat like a teenager sneaking out past curfew. She carried her boots in her hand, not wanting to make any noise that could awaken Amanda. Once outside, she slipped the boots on, shivering as a cold wind ruffled her hair. Looking off to the right of the house, Lex was thankful Martha's little cottage was completely dark. Growing up, Lex wondered if the ever-present housekeeper slept at all. Any time of the day or night the young girl could always count on seeing Martha about, usually in the kitchen.

Lex thoughtfully looked up at the cloudless late-night sky, the full moon illuminating the path in front of her. She hoped that with Amanda's help, they could get Martha to take things a bit easier and not try to do everything herself. Lex stopped in her tracks when she realized what she was thinking. She'd only known Amanda for a few days, and although Amanda's feelings apparently matched her own, she realized her heart had already decided on a life with her. Somehow, she just knew there could be no other outcome to their budding relationship. *There couldn't be. Every time she looks in my eyes, I feel like she's searching my heart. And when she smiles at me, I think she likes and accepts what she sees, and I love the way that makes me feel.*

Upon reaching the shed, Lex opened the door and slipped inside. She turned on the light, then pulled a pair of worn coveralls from their hook and quickly stepped into them.

Three hours later, a dirty and exhausted Lex walked through the silent house. She had spent most of the night taking the Mustang apart, finding out that the water damage was not as severe as she had imagined. Once the vehicle dried out completely, it shouldn't take too much work to get the car running again. Not even bothering with turning on the lights, she undressed in the dark, padded silently into the bathroom and started the shower. Lex stepped inside, moaning with relief when the hot spray hit her exhausted body, almost falling asleep standing up. She quickly rinsed off, climbed out, and wrapped a large towel around her body, patting herself dry on her way back into her room. Lex dropped the towel on the floor beside the bed and slid beneath the sheets, naked. Lex fell asleep, never realizing that she was not alone in the large bed.

Lex awoke to sunlight streaming through the windows, and a heavy weight on her chest. She opened her eyes and was surprised to find company in her bed. Sometime during the night, Amanda had not only found her way into Lex's bed, but had snuggled up against the naked woman under the sheets. Her left arm was slung across Lex's chest, and her left leg was tangled with the rancher's own long limbs. *Oh boy. This could get, interesting, to say the least. Damn, what time is it, anyway?* Lex glanced at the clock on the nightstand. She was surprised to see it was a little after seven in the morning. She carefully slipped out from underneath Amanda, and then walked across the room to the dresser for some clothes.

Amanda felt her mattress move. *Move? What gives?* She slid one sleepy eye open, and spotted Lex's nude form across the room. *Mmm. Nice body.* Amanda jerked awake when the vision before her eyes registered with her mind. *Naked? What is she doing in my bedroom naked?* She blinked, and realized with a start that she was in Lex's bedroom. Peeking under the sheet, she was torn between being relieved and disappointed to see she was still dressed in her nightshirt. Lex opened a drawer and removed a handful of clothes, and Amanda slammed her eyes shut before Lex could turn around. Of course, her imagination promptly took over, describing to her libido what her eyes wouldn't let her see.

Unaware she had an audience, Lex spun on her heel, walked to the bathroom, and closed the door behind her.

Okay. Let's just think about this for a minute. Amanda struggled to remember the events of the night before. The last thing she remembered was sitting on the king-sized bed, wondering where Lex was. "I must have fallen asleep." She looked at the closed bathroom door. "Although, that doesn't explain why *she* was in bed, totally naked." She bit her lower lip. "Maybe she didn't know I was here." *Just my luck I was out like a light!*

The bathroom door opened and Lex stepped out. "I'm awake," Amanda said quietly.

Lex sat on the edge of the bed. "Good morning. I hope I didn't wake you."

"No, not at all." Amanda had trouble meeting Lex's eyes. "I'm sorry. I didn't mean to crash here. I had another bad dream and couldn't sleep, so I came in here, but you were gone." She gave Lex a questioning glance. "Where were you?"

"I had a bout of insomnia, so I went down to the barn."

"Oh. Anyway, I guess I conked out waiting for you. Didn't mean to take over your bed like this."

Lex patted Amanda on the leg. "Hey, no problem. I was so tired when I came in, I just took a quick shower and fell into bed."

Amanda covered the hand on her leg with one of her own. "What time did you get in? I know it was pretty late when I wandered in here."

Lex stood up. "It wasn't that late. Probably right after you came in." She pulled on Amanda's hand. "Come on. Why don't you get up and dress, and I'll meet you downstairs for breakfast."

Amanda went up on her knees on the edge of the bed. She linked her hands behind Lex's neck and pulled her close. "I've got a better idea."

Lex quirked an eyebrow, but didn't complain as Amanda took her time exploring her mouth. She found her hands drifting to Amanda's hips, pulling her closer with one hand while the other moved down to find the hem of Amanda's nightshirt.

"Ahem."

They broke apart quickly, each shooting an embarrassed look at the housekeeper who stood in the doorway with her arms crossed. Lex found her voice first. "Good morning, Martha."

"Obviously," the heavyset woman retorted, causing Amanda's blush to deepen.

"It's, umm, not what it looks like, exactly," Amanda stammered as she tried to explain.

"Right." Martha turned to leave. "You were just checking to make sure that Lexie had no toothpaste residue in her mouth while Lexie was making sure that your nightshirt still fit." She paused for a few seconds while she enjoyed their reaction. "I just wanted to let you know breakfast is ready. I'm sure you've both worked up an appetite." She shook her head, leaving the room and closing the door behind her. Then she leaned against the wall and tried to keep from bursting into laughter at the "deer in the headlights" look that both girls had given her.

Amanda fell back on the bed laughing. "Oh, God. She's not going to let us live this down, is she?"

Lex put her hands on her hips, never feeling more cheerful. "Nope." She once again offered Amanda a hand. "Come on, let's go face the music." Then, wondering if Amanda was feeling any discomfort, she asked, "Does that bother you?"

Amanda stood up, wrapped an arm around Lex's waist and, with a show of bravado that she didn't quite feel, said, "Nope. And I hope it doesn't bother Martha too much either, because I'm not planning on stopping anytime soon."

The only sound at the table was when silverware touched a plate. Amanda was still too embarrassed to speak, and Lex was tired from being up most of the night. Martha bit her tongue to restrain herself because their uneasiness tickled her to no end. "Okay, would you two please relax? I'm sorry I teased you, but I just couldn't resist." She glanced over at Amanda, who gazed back shyly. Then, not being able to refrain from adding one more jibe, she said, "I know not much was going on because Lexie was completely dressed." Amanda choked on her water.

"Huh?" Lex asked, coming back to the conversation with a start. "What did I do?" Amanda, however, turned an even deeper shade of red, and Lex pounded her on the back until her coughing subsided.

"What's the matter?" Martha asked. "Are you not feeling well? You seem to be somewhere else, Lexie."

"No, I'm fine." Lex took a large drink of coffee. She hoped the caffeine kicked in soon, or else the day would be longer than she could handle.

Amanda stopped coughing long enough to take a bite of her food. "Actually, I think someone's just tired. She told me she was having trouble getting to sleep last night."

Martha didn't buy that excuse for an instant and had a pretty good idea why Lex looked so worn out. She glared at the exhausted woman, who gave her an answering shrug. "Uh-huh. So does that mean you're going to take it easy today?"

Lex shook her head. "Nope. I need to start working on the bridge. We're going to run out of supplies pretty soon."

"Lexie, we have enough things to get by on for at least another week, maybe two," Martha exclaimed. "I really don't think you should be messing around with that old bridge. It may not be very stable."

Amanda agreed. "She's right. There's no telling what kind of shape it's actually in. Can't you wait until the creek slows down?" She smiled brightly at them both. "I'm certainly not in any hurry to leave."

"I'm not trying to get rid of you, either," Lex said. "But I would like to have that bridge usable by the end of the week, and I don't know what the extent of the damage is."

"Okay, but I'll go with you."

Lex started to argue, but couldn't get past Amanda's beautiful eyes. "Sure. I'd appreciate the company."

Martha's jaw nearly hit the table. She knew Lex had feelings for Amanda but never expected her to go down without at least a token fight. The gleam in the amused housekeeper's eyes said more than words ever could.

Lex noticed the look on Martha's face. "What?" she asked. The exhaustion was making her irritable. "Something wrong?"

"Nope. Just peachy, dear."

Amanda laughed, nearly inhaling her juice.

Lex glared at her. "You too? Do I have food on my face or something?" Anger colored her tone. *What the hell is their problem?*

Martha joined Amanda in her merriment, and covered her mouth with one hand. "I'm sorry." She stifled a giggle. "But I just can't help it!" She burst out laughing again, even though

Lex's face darkened.

Amanda placed a hand on Lex's arm. "Hey. I'm sorry. I'm not sure why I'm laughing. Maybe Martha's good humor is contagious."

Martha was busy wiping the tears from her eyes. "Oh Lexie, you're just so cute when you get a little flustered. It reminds me of when you were about twelve, and your daddy wouldn't let you go out of town with all the hands to the auction."

This little memory brought Lex back to her senses. "Yeah. I didn't know that young girls didn't stay overnight with a group of grown men. I was so angry." She gave the other women an apologetic look. "Sorry about losing my temper." Lex rubbed her eyes. "Must not be quite awake yet."

Martha stood up and stepped behind Lex, rubbing her shoulders. "Honey, don't worry about it." She carried their plates to the sink. "Are you going to get started on the bridge right away?"

Lex nodded, then stood up and brought her dishes to the sink as well. "Uh-huh. I thought I would load up the truck with lumber right after feeding the stock, so I—" She paused when Amanda cleared her throat. "I mean *we*, probably won't be back until dinner."

The housekeeper turned away from the sink. "After you get finished with the feeding, come back to the house first. I'll have a nice lunch packed for you both."

Lex thought about brushing her off, but considered the woman who was going with her. Even though she didn't always worry about lunch, there was no reason to make Amanda suffer. That, and not putting up an argument, would keep Martha off balance enough for a little fun. "That would be great, Martha. I'd really appreciate it." Lex loved the expression on Martha's face.

Amanda felt sorry for Martha, who didn't have a snappy comeback for a change. "So would I. Do you need any help putting lunch together?"

The housekeeper scoffed. "No dear, you would be more help if you could keep an eye on Grumpy over there." She ignored Lex's outraged look. "Try and keep her out of trouble, if you can."

Lex threw up her hands in disgust. "Okay. I can take a hint. Come on, Amanda. Let's go take care of the stock." She stomped out of the kitchen.

Amanda exchanged amused glances with Martha before following the perturbed woman out of the room.

A few hours later, as Lex drove the old truck back to the barn, she glanced at Amanda who had picked up on her moodiness. Amanda had been uncharacteristically silent for the entire morning. Lex brushed her fingers against Amanda's cheek. "Hey."

Amanda looked away from the window, where she had been studying the passing terrain. "Hmm?"

"I'm sorry I've been such an ass this morning." Lex floundered on unfamiliar ground. She was completely out of her element and wasn't sure how to make things right. Before Amanda could open her mouth to speak, Lex's upraised hand halted her. "No. I'm tired and cranky, and I shouldn't have taken it out on you." She looked at Amanda with an obvious feeling of remorse. "And to top it all off, I have got to go back to the house and beg Martha's forgiveness. She's gonna make me pay big time, let me tell you."

"Yeah, well, I don't think you'll have to work too hard. She's pretty sweet." Amanda reached over and latched onto Lex's spare hand, tangling their fingers. "And you really don't owe me an apology. I can see how tired you are."

"That doesn't excuse my behavior. Martha would be the first one to tell you that she raised me better than that. I would probably be in jail or dead if she hadn't straightened me out years ago." Lex parked the truck behind the hay barn, where a large pile of boards was stacked. "You want to help me load some stuff up?"

"Wouldn't miss it." Amanda put her gloves back on and hopped out of the truck. She waited until Lex stepped out from the other side, and then walked to the back of the vehicle to meet her. Lex pulled Amanda into a hug. They stood there holding each other, reveling in the warmth and closeness blossoming between them.

They finally stepped apart. Amanda cleared her throat, which was choked with emotion from the way Lex had caressed her while they embraced. "Is there any special size or type of these things you want us to load?"

Lex removed her coat and stepped over to the neat, waist-high stack of lumber. Still feeling a little shaky from the intensity of her feelings, she tried to get her mind back on what they were supposed to be doing. "I figure we could take a little bit of everything, so we don't have to make extra trips." She opened a door that led into the back of the barn. "Let me get some tools, and then we'll pile some of this stuff into the truck, okay?"

Amanda opened the tailgate and sat down, swinging her legs back and forth. "Works for me. I'll just keep ol' rusty blue here company."

"What did you call my truck?" Lex asked, mock outrage in her tone. She turned away from the door with her hands on her hips.

"Umm, ol' rusty blue?"

Lex stalked back to the truck, and stepped neatly in between the swinging legs. She put her hands on Amanda's hips, and pulled her closer. "Rusty blue, huh?"

Amanda leaned back on her hands and offered, "Don't forget old—" She was about to continue when her lips were covered by Lex's. Amanda took the initiative and deepened the kiss, wrapping her legs tightly around Lex's hips, and bringing her closer with a strong need.

Minutes later Lex broke off the kiss and cleared her throat. "Great name for the truck." She stepped back to untangle herself from the beautiful woman in front of her. "I'll just go get the, umm, tools now." She stumbled into the barn and leaned against the wall. "Tools. Gotta find the—damn! That woman can kiss!"

Lex parked the truck several yards from the bridge, afraid of getting too close in case the structure wasn't stable or the edge of the creek crumbled. She stepped out of the vehicle, watching as Amanda, with a strange look on her face, did the same. Alarmed, Lex walked around to the passenger's side of the truck, and reached out to Amanda. "Are you—" Before she could finish her question, she found her arms full of a crying woman.

"Oh, God." Amanda latched onto Lex and sobbed.

"Shh." Lex gently rubbed her back. "You're okay." She gently rocked Amanda, not knowing what to do or say.

Amanda buried her face in Lex's chest, sniffling. "S—s— sorry. I guess seeing all this in the daylight brought it all back." She looked up into her friend's concerned eyes. "I could have been killed."

"Yeah, but you weren't. Everything turned out okay." Lex

attempted to soothe her with her voice as she raised a hand to the tear-stained face, wiping under Amanda's brimming eyes. "Do you want to go back to the house?"

Amanda swallowed hard and shook her head. "No. I'm all right. Just had one heck of a wicked flashback, that's all." She hugged Lex. "Thanks." She released a shaky breath and stepped back, wiping her face with her hands. "Let's get started, shall we?"

"Are you sure? I can always come back later if you're uncomfortable." Lex took a step forward and captured one of Amanda's hands. Bringing it to her lips, she kissed it tenderly. "I don't like to see you hurting."

Bringing their linked hands to her face, Amanda rubbed Lex's palm against her cheek. "I think it was just shock. I'm okay now." She kissed the inside of Lex's wrist before releasing it. "Thanks. Let's go see what the bridge looks like. It's not going to repair itself." She shaded her eyes to gaze downstream for any sign of her car. Not seeing it, Amanda assumed it was miles away by now.

Lex shook her head in wonder. "You are an amazing woman, Amanda Cauble."

Shortly thereafter, they stood at the road where it met the bridge, staring down at the rapidly moving water. Lex took a few more steps forward, until she was directly on the edge of the old wooden structure and able to peer down at the shattered boards. She sat down on the edge, swinging her feet below her.

"Lex? Do you really think you should be that close? What if the edge breaks off?" Amanda took a few tentative steps forward then stopped. One of them falling in would be more than enough, and she didn't feel like tempting fate.

Lex looked over her shoulder and without really thinking, said, "Then I guess I'll be going for a swim, huh?" She winked and swung her long body down, disappearing from sight.

"Lex!" Amanda screamed, as she ran for the bridge. Before she could get to the edge, a pair of hands appeared, followed by a dark hat-covered head.

"What?" Lex pulled herself back up on the bridge. She saw the panic in Amanda's eyes and cursed herself. *Idiot! She just got calmed down, and you go and scare the hell out of her. What are you using for brains?* Lex scrambled to her feet and crossed to Amanda, pulling the shaking woman into her arms. "I'm sorry. God, I'm so sorry Amanda. That was stupid of me." She kissed the top of Amanda's head.

Amanda accepted the hug, then stepped back and slapped Lex on the arm. "You could have warned me before you went jumping off the end. I thought you fell!" She grabbed a handful of the rancher's jacket and pulled, hard. "Don't you *ever* do anything like that again, do you hear me?"

"I hear you. I didn't mean to scare you." Lex looked into her eyes, almost losing herself completely. "Forgive me?" Her voice trembled from uncertainty. *Would serve me right if she wouldn't.*

Amanda raised one hand and caressed Lex's cheek. "Oh, Lex. You don't have to ask for my forgiveness. You just scared me, that's all." She placed a kiss on Lex's chin.

Lex couldn't believe how quickly Amanda was ready to forgive her. She hugged her and said, "I'm sorry. It won't happen again, I promise." Then she led Amanda away from the bridge and back to the truck. "If you don't mind helping me dig out some of this lumber, we'll get started, okay?"

The next few hours were spent reinforcing the remaining patch of bridge on their side of the creek. Lex was pleased to find very little structural damage, other than the eight feet missing from the center of the bridge. She decided it would be easier to build a walkway to the other side first, and then worry about driving across later.

She tirelessly sawed and hammered for hours, only stopping when Amanda insisted they have lunch. Her green tee shirt was darkened with perspiration, though the slight breeze stirring around them was cool. Lex stood up from where she had finished with another board and pulled her hat from her head. She looked up at the sky and wiped her sweaty forehead on her shoulder. Realizing there wasn't much daylight left, Lex decided to call it a day. She turned to Amanda, who was picking up the leftover pieces of lumber and tossing them into the truck, as she had been doing most of the day. "You about ready to go back to the house?"

Amanda leaned back against the truck. "Oh, yeah. I think my sore spots have aches, now." She gestured around the area. "I've kept things pretty well picked up, so you just say the word, and I'll be ready to leave."

Lex tossed the hammer into the back of the truck. "Consider the word given." She stepped back to where she had been working and picked up the odd assortment of tools. Carrying them back over to where Amanda stood, she tossed them after the hammer and then opened the passenger side door of the vehicle. "Shall we?" she asked with a bow.

Amanda gave her a somewhat stiff curtsy then climbed into the truck. "Why, thank you ever so much. And here I thought chivalry was dead."

Lex tipped her hat as she closed the door. "Nope. Just dead tired." She crossed to the driver's side and tumbled in. "Let's go home."

As they trudged up the rear steps to the house, Amanda couldn't remember the last time she felt so tired. *And Lex did most of the hard work. I just cleaned up behind her and brought her the lumber.* She spared a quick glance to the woman beside her. *She looks worse than I feel. Maybe I can talk her into a quick shower and then going straight to bed.* A slight blush stained her cheeks after that thought. *Uh, no. Don't think I'll say it quite that way.*

Lex was about to open the door when she noticed her friend's face. *Don't tell me she got sunburned today.* "Amanda? Are you okay?" she asked, while she opened the door and allowed Amanda to precede her. "You didn't get too much sun today, did you?"

Oh, crap. Now what do I say to avoid further embarrassment? "Maybe, I'm not sure. It could just be the exertion." Once in the house, Amanda almost moaned with pleasure at the smells emanating from the kitchen. "And hunger."

Lex pretended to be surprised. "Newsflash." Blocking the expected slap, she poked her head through the kitchen door. "Martha, we're back."

Martha ambled out of the kitchen, wiping her hands on the ever-present dishtowel. "Yes, I can see that, dear." She wrinkled her nose. "You *are* planning on taking a shower before dinner, aren't you?" She reached up and pulled the hat from Lex's head. "How many times have I told you to take your hat off when you come into the house?" She swatted Lex with the hat. "Now go on upstairs and get cleaned up. Ya stink. Dinner should be ready in about thirty minutes." She turned quickly to go back into the kitchen, not giving Lex a chance to argue.

"I can never get the last word in with her," Lex mumbled, while she walked to the stairs. She turned and looked at Amanda. "I bet you're not exactly smelling like daisies yourself." Lex darted up the stairs with a very riled up woman on her heels.

Following dinner, Martha chased them out of the kitchen, and Lex and Amanda sat in front of a roaring fire. The housekeeper had refused their help with the dishes, citing her inability to find anything after they put everything away the day before.

"Amanda? I've got to ride to one of the back pastures tomorrow and check out a few things. Would you like to come along?" Lex asked. Amanda sat on the floor at her feet, with one arm wrapped possessively around Lex's leg. Lex played with Amanda's hair that was tangled in her fingertips. "I remember you saying that you don't like to ride, but—"

Amanda craned her head at an angle, so that she could see Lex's face. "It's not that I don't like to ride, I'm just afraid of falling off. Could we go double?"

"I was just about to suggest the same thing." Lex slid out of the chair, settled beside Amanda and pulled her into her lap. "So is that a yes, or should I try and convince you?"

"Well," Amanda wrapped her arms around Lex's neck. "Your horse is pretty tall." She leaned in for a kiss. "I think you'd better start trying to influence my answer," she whispered, as Lex captured her lips.

After Amanda was thoroughly swayed, she led a tired Lex upstairs and stopped at the guest room door. "Goodnight."

Lex wrapped Amanda in her arms, and kissed her with a quiet intensity. When both of them ran out of air, she broke away. "Yeah." She cleared her throat. "See you in the morning." Lex turned and crossed the hallway to her own room, trying to calm her pounding heart. She stepped inside, closed the door, and then moved to the dresser to get changed so that as soon as Amanda was asleep, she could go work on the Mustang.

Half an hour later, Lex stopped at Amanda's door and listened for a moment. Not hearing anything, she nodded to herself. Then, rubbing her eyes, Lex tiptoed down the stairway, boots in hand.

It took her almost three hours to put the car back together, but she was more than certain she could have it running within the next night or two. Lex couldn't wait to see Amanda's face when she saw the car. She decided she could finish up the engine work the next evening.

The mantle clock in her bedroom chimed twice when Lex finally dragged herself back into the room. *At least I'm getting to bed at a decent hour tonight,* she mused, stripping off her clothes as she staggered into the bathroom. After a quick shower, she walked back into her bedroom, wary of finding a woman in her bed. Seeing she was indeed alone, the exhausted woman pulled a sleepshirt over her head as an extra precaution, in case Amanda had nightmares again, and collapsed under the sheets.

Chapter
Ten

Lex finished saddling up Thunder as Amanda strolled into the barn with a backpack tossed over one shoulder. Amanda leaned up against the stall door, trying to look sexy in her faded jeans and a worn denim shirt that was molded to her body. It worked. The dark green and ivory of Lex's old leather jacket from her high school days brought out the hazel color of Amanda's eyes and made her look even more beautiful. Lex stared at her with an intensity that made her heart pound. She tried her best to appear unaffected and somehow managed to find her voice. "Are you about ready?" The arousal evident in Amanda's voice startled her.

She certainly fills out those clothes better than Louis ever did. "Are you propositioning me?" Lex quirked an eyebrow at the blushing woman, maintaining eye contact with her, and noting the sudden husky quality of her own voice.

"Maybe." Amanda swallowed hard. "Are you accepting?"

Lex led the stallion out of his stall. "Maybe." She tossed the word playfully back to her companion. "Whatcha got there?" Lex asked, pointing to the backpack. "Homework?"

"Nope." Amanda walked in front of Lex, swinging her hips. "Lunch. Maybe I'll share if you're real nice to me." She turned back to Lex and gave her a sexy smile.

"*Maybe* you'll share?" Lex dropped the reins and pulled Amanda close. "Just how *nice* do I have to be?" She leaned down and gently nipped her companion's ear. "And exactly what will you be sharing?" she whispered into the same ear and then ran her tongue around its edge before tenderly tugging on it with her teeth.

Amanda legs went weak beneath her, and she stumbled forward slightly. "Ah." She couldn't seem to form a complete thought since Lex decided to forsake her ear and work directly on her throat. Letting the backpack slide to the floor, Amanda pulled Lex closer, hanging on to her while her arousal took control of every part of her body. She moaned when Lex finally captured her lips. She was on the verge of an all-out collapse when Lex finally relented and gave her a chance to breathe. "God, Lex. Are you trying to kill me?"

"Hmm?" Lex mumbled, burying her face in the sweet smelling hair. "Oh. Sorry. I guess we should be getting on our way, huh?" She stepped back reluctantly.

"Yeah. Just give me a minute to get my legs back. Although I would like to continue this *conversation* later." Amanda ran a shaky hand through her hair and picked up the discarded backpack.

"I'd like that too." Lex gathered up the reins once again and started for the door. "Come on, boy. Let's take Amanda for a little tour."

Once outside, Lex easily mounted the prancing horse, then reached down for Amanda and pulled her up in front of her. "Up, you go. I thought you'd like to be able to see where we're going. Just hang on to the saddle horn, and I'll hang on to you."

"Now that's the best offer I've had in a long time." Amanda leaned back into the warm body behind her. One arm circled her waist as Lex gripped the reins loosely in her right hand.

"Don't worry. I won't let you fall." Lex whispered in Amanda's ear, enjoying the little tremble she felt run through Amanda's body. *Come on, Lexington. Try and control yourself, or it's gonna be one hell of a long day,* she chided herself, giving the smaller waist in front of her a squeeze.

They rode slowly for a couple of hours. Lex took the scenic route to their destination to prolong the pleasant ride as long as possible. They made their way into heavy woods, following a worn path that Lex explained was her favorite. "I usually ride up here to get away from everything," she told Amanda. "I've been known to take a sleeping bag and supplies and just spend the weekend alone."

The terrain became steadily steeper until Amanda saw they were actually in the foothills just north of the ranch. "You have stock that stay up here? What are they, mountain goats?" She felt the body behind her chuckle.

"No. There's a small pass just ahead that opens up into a valley. That's where we keep a small herd of wild horses and cattle. We normally take the road from the north, but we would have to drive through the creek, and that's impossible to do right now."

"I see." Amanda reached back and patted the leg behind hers. "We've been riding for quite a while. Are we going to stop for lunch soon?"

Lex pulled her close again. "Yep. And I know just the right place." She guided Thunder off the beaten path and through the dense trees.

The clearing Lex brought them to was breathtakingly beautiful. There was silence all around, and the sun sliced its way through the treetops to shed light on a small pond. Lex dropped down from the horse and helped Amanda from the saddle. "I hope this is okay. It's one of my favorite spots." She led them to a fallen tree and dropped the backpack beside it, then continued on to the small body of water. A small pit ringed with rocks nearby was the only sign that anyone had ever been there.

"Lex, it's beautiful. This is your hideaway?"

"Yeah. I come up here to clear my mind. It's not too far from the ranch in case I need to get back in a hurry, but it's far enough away that no one knows where it is."

Amanda sat down in front of a log and patted the ground beside her. "Why don't you come over here, and we'll see what Martha packed us for lunch?" She opened the backpack and pulled out a couple of foil-wrapped packages.

"Sure." Lex ambled back over to Amanda and dropped down beside her. She accepted the package that was handed to her and peeled back the foil. "Mmm. Smells like a roast beef sandwich. She knows it's my favorite."

Amanda took a bite of hers, too. "Oh, yum. This is wonderful. I can see why it's your favorite." She reached into the backpack with her free hand and pulled out a bottle of water and handed it to Lex. "Here. She doesn't forget anything, does she?" She sat her sandwich on her leg and grabbed another bottle from the bag and opened it.

Lex, who was happily munching away, shook her head and swallowed. "Nope. She probably thought I'd forget the canteen, but I didn't."

After they finished their lunch, Lex leaned back against the fallen log and held Amanda close to her, wrapping both arms around her. She kissed the top of Amanda's head and enjoyed the squeeze she received in return. They sat quietly and looked out over the pond.

"So, why are we checking the stock? Are you afraid the heavy rains may have done something to them? Could the creek have flooded them out?" Amanda lightly ran her hand up and down Lex's leg.

Lex shook her head. "No, nothing like that. The other night, while I was checking the books, it looked like we were missing an unusually high number of animals."

"Okay, but isn't that somewhat normal on a ranch this size?" Amanda asked, a little confused. Amanda's fingers were now moving in abstract patterns, occasionally drifting higher and closer to Lex's inner thigh.

Becoming more and more aroused, Lex tried desperately to stay on the subject, even though Amanda's fingertips were driving all thoughts from her mind. She cleared her throat and tried to calm her racing heart. "Usually, yes. But not only are we beginning to lose cattle, but sometime recently we've begun to lose money, as well." Lex grasped Amanda's hand before she lost all control. "I don't normally do the books; that's Hubert's job. But I just had this strange feeling something was wrong, and it looks like I was right."

Amanda linked her fingers with Lex's. "So what are we going to do about it?"

We. I like the sound of that. "We're going to do a quick head count in the back pasture. I can compare what we find with what had been reported at the beginning of the summer. That should give us an idea of what's going on." She stood up, pulling Amanda up by their linked hands. "Come on. It's only about another twenty minutes from here."

Lex gave Thunder his head and allowed him to negotiate the narrow pass, which was barely wide enough for two horses.

Amanda shivered, and the arm around her waist tightened. "You okay?"

Amanda leaned back and enjoyed the protective grasp. "Yeah. It's just kinda spooky. I guess because it's so quiet." The only sound was the sodden clump of the horse's hooves, which echoed eerily along the jagged walls. She squeezed the strong leg that was pressed against hers, feeling the muscle jump.

"Don't worry, it's perfectly safe. I ride through here all the time." Lex buried her nose in Amanda's hair. "We're almost through." She kissed the spot she'd just sniffed and then urged her horse onward.

The path suddenly opened up, making way for the more dense foliage. They rode through the thick forest in silence until Lex suddenly pulled Thunder to a stop. "Whoa."

Amanda, who had been daydreaming, came back to herself with a start. "What?" She looked around. "Why are we stopping?"

Lex pointed off to their right. "Smoke." They were on a slight rise and could see over the treetops easily.

"Where?" Amanda strained her eyes. "Are you sure?" She still couldn't see anything.

"Yeah. It looks like it's not too far away, either. We'd better go check it out." Lex kneed the black horse into a faster pace. "Hang on. This may be a little bumpy."

Lex became more ill at ease the closer they came to the smoke. *I don't like the look of this. It appears to be man-made.* She slowed Thunder down to a walk.

Amanda felt Lex go tense. She turned around in the saddle to look up at the rancher's face. "Lex?" She gave the hand on her stomach a squeeze. "Is that it way down there? It doesn't seem like a very big fire."

Lex pursed her lips, then glanced down at Amanda. "I know. I think it's a campfire, only no one should be out here." She swung down from the horse, then reached up to help Amanda dismount. "We're going to walk the rest of the way." Lex loosely tied the horse's reins to a nearby tree. "Stay here, boy. We'll be right back." She rubbed his nose, then reached over and took Amanda's hand. "Let's go check this out."

They walked through the heavy trees for several more minutes before Lex stopped. When Amanda opened her mouth to speak, Lex covered her lips with a finger, silencing her. At her questioning glance, Lex pointed through a gap in the trees. There was a truck with a large trailer in the middle of the clearing with a handful of men milling around. By the condition of the area and of the men themselves they had been there for several days.

Sonofabitch! So this is what has been happening to our stock. Apparently they had driven the truck through the creek and gotten stranded after the heavy rains. Lex checked around. *I count six men. That seems about right.* She caught Amanda's eye and motioned for her to follow.

They hurried back to Thunder, and Lex immediately went to the saddlebags and dug through them. She pulled out the little-used cell phone, turned it on, and then swore. "Damn, I was afraid of this." She crammed the phone back into the bag, buckling the cover angrily.

Amanda placed her hand on Lex's arm. "What's wrong?"

Lex bit back an angry reply, taking a deep breath instead. "Those guys are stealing my stock, and I can't get a signal with the damn cell phone." She looked Amanda in the eye. "I need you to ride back to the ranch and call the sheriff."

"Uh, okay. But what are you going to do?"

Lex gave her a smile that didn't quite reach her eyes. "Teach them that it's not nice to steal."

Amanda took a firm grip on her arm. "What?" She pulled Lex closer, getting right up into her face. "You can't be serious! There are at least half-dozen men, possibly more." She tangled her hands in Lex's coat. "It's too dangerous."

Lex framed Amanda's face with her hands and leaned in to gaze into her eyes in an attempt to calm her. "I have to do something. They look like they're getting ready to move out soon. I'm just going to slow them down until help gets here." She bent down and briefly captured Amanda's lips with her own. "You need to hurry." Lex lifted Amanda into the saddle, and then took a moment to adjust the stirrups. Handing the reins to her, she patted her leg. "Be careful."

Amanda stretched out her hand, waiting for Lex to grasp it. "I will." She pulled Lex's hand up to her lips and kissed it. "You too. Please don't take any unnecessary risks. We still have a *conversation* to finish."

"Don't worry, I won't." Lex released Amanda's hand and stepped away from the horse. "Tell the sheriff they're at the back clearing. He'll know what you mean."

Amanda nodded and turned Thunder around. She led him to the path, turning back in the saddle to look at Lex again before they got to the main stand of trees. She fought the urge to race back to her, before her good sense told her she needed to get going. *Snap out of it, Amanda! You're the only one who can do this for her. If you love her, help her!* Putting on her bravest face, she gave a wave and then turned Thunder toward the trail.

The stallion must have picked up on Amanda's distress, because he moved quickly through the trees once they had made their way through the pass. Oak and cedar trees flew by too quickly for Amanda to distinguish as she hung on to the saddle horn for dear life. Breaking through the dense trees at last, Amanda heaved a sigh of relief to see the barns come into view. They charged past the isolated buildings and headed straight for the ranch house itself.

Amanda practically jumped out of the saddle near the back porch. She fell to her knees as her legs gave out. Thunder snorted, slung his head, and pounded the ground with his front foot. "Thanks, boy. I appreciate you getting me here so fast." She patted his neck before she attempted to climb the steps on shaky legs. She almost screamed when the back door swung open before she could reach it.

"Good Lord, child." Martha pulled Amanda into the house. "What on earth happened? And where is Lexie?" She led Amanda into the kitchen and assisted her into a nearby chair.

"Lex," Amanda wheezed, "is okay." She took a deep breath. "Stealing." Another wheeze, "Cattle." Another breath, "Call...the sheriff." Amanda coughed and took another breath.

Martha sat down next to her and held her hands, trying to warm them up. "Okay. You say someone is stealing our stock?" Amanda nodded, still trying to catch her breath. "And we need to call the sheriff?" Another nod. "Where is Lexie?"

"She's still out there, keeping her eye on them," Amanda got out, her breathing almost under control. "She said to tell the sheriff they were in the back clearing." She paused, "And she was afraid that they were getting ready to leave." Amanda's panic could be seen in her eyes. "She said she was going to teach them not to steal. You don't think she'd do anything rash, do you?"

Martha released her hands and moved over to the phone. After she dialed, she looked back to Amanda. "That's exactly what I'm afraid of." She listened to the phone. "Yes, I need to speak to Sheriff Bristol. This is Martha Rollins." She listened again. "Yes, I'll hold."

Lex watched Amanda ride away through the trees until she disappeared into the dense foliage. "Now let's go have some fun." She jogged back to the clearing while her mind formulated several plans.

As she sat in the tangled underbrush, Lex had a very good view of the entire clearing. A dark shadow passed over her, causing her to jump slightly. She looked up sheepishly. *Just a damn cloud.* A welcome thought occurred to her. *Cloud? Hmm. Looks like rain again. If I can just keep these fools busy for a while, maybe they'll be stuck until Amanda can get the sheriff out here.*

While she kept watch and waited for help to arrive, Lex reflected on how lucky she was to have such a good friend as Somerville's sheriff.

Charlie Bristol had been the sheriff for longer than Lex could remember. He had a knack for always being around when she needed him, especially after her father left. The sheriff showed up for breakfast at least once a week for several years, ostensibly to make sure everything was okay. But only Charlie and Lex knew the main reason – Martha Rollins.

The tall and lanky man was several years older than the heavyset housekeeper, but he followed her around like a little boy with his first crush. He'd bring her flowers, ask her out to the movies on Saturday night, and plead with the sweet woman to marry him at least once a month. She turned him down every time with the reason that she could never leave her "little Lexie" to work the massive ranch alone. Charlie respected that, and in truth it made the gentle woman even sweeter in his eyes.

It took a couple of years, but poor Charlie finally got the hint. Martha cared for him, but she just couldn't bring herself to leave the ranch and settle down. Charlie understood, and he stayed close friends with Martha, taking her to various dances and picnics. He never gave up the hope that someday she'd tire of the ranch life and agree to become his wife. But until that day arrived, he was more than happy to have Martha as a good friend. And the lovestruck lawman never stopped dreaming about settling down with the sweet housekeeper who took care of the Rocking W Ranch.

Movement in the camp brought Lex out of her musings and back to the situation at hand. Deciding that taking closer look was better than daydreaming, she circled around the clearing until she was behind the large truck and trailer. She noticed several of the men were arguing a little distance away. She pulled out her pocketknife and crawled to the parked vehicles, which were empty. Once under the trailer, she positioned herself near the wheels on the farthest side. *Here I go again, Martha...face down in the mud.* Lex poked a small hole on the inside of the tire, which hissed loudly. *Damn!* She quickly wiped a small amount of mud on the neat slice to quiet it and also to slow the speed that the air was leaking out. Lex proceeded to take care of the remaining tires in the same manner, then stealthily made her way back to her hiding place.

The clouds quickly took over the late afternoon sky, thunder rumbling in the distance. Lex was enjoying herself. She could see the trailer slowly sinking to the ground. *Only a matter of time before these assholes notice.* She decided to take care of the truck next. *I wonder how Amanda's doing? I hope she made it to the ranch all right.*

Chapter
Eleven

Martha's face was grim as she hung up the phone. "Charlie's on his way. He said he'd take the back way in." She crossed over to where Amanda sat nervously tearing a paper napkin into tiny bits and touched her on the shoulder. "Amanda?"

Amanda jumped, startled. "What?" She looked down at the mess on the table, then raised her eyes to meet Martha's gaze. "I'm sorry. Wait. Did you say the sheriff is on his way?" She stood up and pushed her chair up against the table. "I've got to get back. Thunder should be rested enough by now." She was almost to the kitchen door when Martha grabbed her arm.

"Now you wait just a darned minute! If you think I'm going to let you go back to—"

"I've got to. She may need me." Amanda felt like crying. "I can't leave her out there all alone, Martha. Don't ask me to."

The housekeeper released Amanda's arm with a heavy sigh. "All right, but you're not going anywhere without a radio." She tossed up her hands in defeat before heading for the office with Amanda right behind her. Martha pulled a handheld radio out of its charging base and gave it to her. "I'll sit here by the base radio, and you can call me if you need anything, okay?" She was about to say more when the rumble of thunder interrupted her.

They both looked up, as if to see something through the ceiling. "Great. Now Lexie will have an excuse to play in the mud again." Martha shook a finger in Amanda's direction. "And you're gonna put on a raincoat before you take off again, right?"

Amanda ducked her head and nodded quietly. "Yes ma'am." Suddenly she was enveloped in a strong hug, which she happily returned.

"Honey, I want you to be extra special careful. Don't take any crazy chances." Martha rubbed Amanda's back. "I have enough to worry about with Lexie always going off half-cocked, giving me heart attacks." She turned around and led Amanda out of the room. "Let's get you bundled up and ready to go."

Lex had just returned to her hiding place after sabotaging the truck when the first raindrops fell. *Great. I knew I should have brought my coat.* The flannel shirt she wore had felt great earlier in the day, but now that the sudden cloud cover hid the sun, the wind was decidedly cooler. She rubbed her hands up and down her arms briskly, trying to keep warm, almost laughing out loud at the scene unfolding in front of her.

The rain started coming down in earnest, causing the would-be thieves to race around picking up their belongings. One of them, a short, stocky man with dark hair, had almost made it back to the truck when he noticed something was wrong. "Hey, Matt," he yelled, looking back at the tall lanky man near the campfire, "is these tires flat?"

Lex nearly gave herself away laughing. *Oh, we've got a regular Einstein among us. Wonder what his first clue was?* She blinked away a raindrop, thankful for the dark cowboy hat keeping most of the rain out of her face.

Another man checked the other side of the trailer. "This side's flat, too." The man they called Matt walked over to the truck and took a rifle from inside. "You guys keep a close watch. I don't like the looks of this."

Lex crept slowly back from her vantage point. *Uh-oh, I think he means business.* She ducked deeper into the brush.

Matt tossed the rifle over to the short, stocky man. "Darrell, take this and do a perimeter check. If anything moves, shoot it!" He turned to face the older man who had checked the far side of the trailer. "Randall, get the other rifle out of the truck and check the edge of the clearing." The gray-headed man nodded and complied.

Lex looked around. *Where did the other three go?* Suddenly, the bushes to the left of her rustled. *Shit!* She ducked down lower, practically lying face down in the rapidly building mud. Man number four stepped out of the shrubbery almost on top of her.

"Hey, Matt, what the hell's goin' on?" he asked, zipping up his mud-covered pants.

Lex slowly lifted her head. *That makes only two left.* She decided not to move until she knew where the other men were.

Looking around, Lex noticed a slight movement in the trailer. *I thought that thing was empty.* As she watched, a younger man, probably still a teenager, climbed out of the trailer and over to the leader.

"Aw, Matt. It's starting to rain again. Are we gonna get out of here pretty soon?" He ran a hand through his shoulder-length brown hair. "I really want to go home."

Matt put his hand on the smaller man's shoulder. "Yeah, we'll just leave the trailer for now. Why don't you go on and get into the truck? We'll be there in a little bit." The young man nodded and walked to the vehicle.

Lex looked at her watch. *The sheriff should be here before too much longer. And knowing Amanda, she's probably on her way back by now, too.* She continued to gradually retreat. *Better get to the pass and wait for her.*

She crept slowly around the outskirts of the clearing, trying to stay out of sight, when, halfway around the area, she nearly crawled into man number six, who was making good use of the thick bushes. He had long blonde hair partially tied into a pony-tail and did not look at all happy to be squatting in the rain.

Lex edged around until she was directly behind him, waiting patiently. *Hurry up, buddy,* she thought to herself, *I really don't want to be watching this.* He grunted a few times and then pulled up his pants. *Ugh. I'd hate to have to do your laundry,* she thought to herself.

The man stood up and turned, coming face to face with a drenched woman in a black cowboy hat, who had a very 'not nice' expression on her face. "Wha...?"

"Say nighty-night!" Lex punched him hard in the face, getting an intense amount of pleasure in watching the man crumple to the ground. She pulled off his shirt, tearing it into two strips. One she used for a gag, and the other to tie his feet together, and then used his belt to tie his hands. She looked down, satisfied with her handiwork. Flexing her right hand, she winced. *Damned hard-headed thief.* Then she continued her journey to the pass. Suddenly, she heard one of the men in the camp shout.

"Hey, Matt! I think I see something." He took careful aim and fired several rounds.

Amanda was almost to the pass when she heard the first gunshots. *Oh my God, Lex!* She pressed her heels to Thunder's sides, urging him to move faster. She knew her friend was unarmed, and she was terrified of what she might find.

Tearing through the pass, Amanda had to pull the powerful horse up quickly, or else collide with the solitary figure on the path.

"Whoa!" Lex tugged at the heaving animal's reins.

Amanda slid off the exhausted horse, stumbling over her feet and almost tackling Lex.

"Amanda? What's wrong? Are you okay?" Lex wrapped her arms around Amanda, who buried her face in the damp material of her chest.

"Am I okay?" Amanda choked back a sob and squeezed Lex tighter. "I heard gunshots." She pulled away from Lex and used her hands to search the drenched form. "Are you okay?"

Lex hugged her in relief. "Oh, yeah, I'm just fine." She took her hat off and shook the excess water from it, even though the rain still fell heavily. "A little damp, but fine."

Amanda wasn't completely convinced. "Are you sure? You're not hiding anything from me, are you?" She continued to search Lex for any signs of injury.

Lex cradled Amanda's hands. "No. They weren't shooting at me; they were shooting near me, and I'm not sure if that rabbit will ever be the same again."

Amanda smiled through her tears. "I heard the shots, and I thought—" She sniffled, trying to regain some composure.

Touched by the concern, Lex pulled Amanda into her arms, and bent down to place a kiss on her forehead, which was partially hidden by a hood. "Were you able to contact the sheriff? I don't think those guys will be going too far right now."

"Yeah, Martha talked to him. He said that he'd come in the back way." Amanda paused. "What do you mean, they won't be going very far? What have you done?"

Lex gave her a devious little grin. "Seems the tires on their trailer went flat." She pulled a piece of wire out of her back pocket, "and this accidentally fell off their truck."

Amanda shook her head. "Never mind. I don't think I want to know." She walked over to Thunder, and untied the duster from behind the saddle and handed it to Lex. "Here, you look half-frozen." Amanda then grabbed the saddlebag and searched through it. "Oh, and Martha sent this." She pulled out the handheld radio and tossed it to Lex.

"Great. Now I don't feel so damn isolated." Lex stuffed the radio into an inner pocket of the large coat. Holding out her hand, she silently requested that Amanda move closer to her.

Happily complying with the unspoken plea, Amanda tucked herself comfortably up against Lex's ribs. "Now what are we going to do?"

Lex looked down at her tenderly. "I don't suppose I could talk you into going back to the house?"

"I don't think so," Amanda said seriously.

"That's what I thought. We," Lex hugged her close, "are going to find a good spot to watch the fun." She sobered. "But we have to be very careful, since these idiots have guns." She held up a warning hand. "And, you have to do exactly as I say, no questions asked, okay?"

Amanda gave her an equally serious nod. "Okay. As long as you understand that I'm not completely helpless, right?"

"Gotcha," Lex agreed, as they headed for the clearing.

It took them almost an hour to walk back to the clearing. The heavy rain and the roundabout route they took hampered their progress. Lex tucked Amanda in the dense shrubbery, then settled down behind her, wrapping her arms around Amanda's waist. They watched in amusement as the man Lex identified as Matt looked under the hood of the truck, apparently having no success in getting it to start.

Lex leaned into Amanda and placed her mouth next to her ear. "I wonder what his problem is?" she whispered, an evil chuckle coloring her tone.

In amusement, Amanda squeezed the hands that were wrapped securely around her stomach.

Another man walked up to the truck and said something to Matt, who looked around the clearing. He pointed in the opposite direction from where Lex and Amanda were sitting, and Darrell walked in that direction, carrying his rifle.

Lex whispered, "Uh-oh. They must have finally figured out that one of them is missing."

Amanda turned slightly in Lex's arms so that she could speak without being overheard. "Missing?"

"Yeah, he's tied up over in those trees to the right."

Amanda's eyes widened. "You?"

Lex gave her a sheepish shrug. "Yeah. I practically tripped over him on my way back to meet you. He was, uh, somewhat indisposed." When Amanda's expression showed that her meaning hadn't registered, she added, "In the bushes."

Amanda's brow creased in a thoughtful manner, then suddenly cleared. "Oh. Eww."

"Yeah. But now that they've figured out he's missing, things could get a little hairy. We may have to get out of here in a hurry, so be ready."

Amanda nodded and reached a hand up to cup Lex's cheek. "As long as we leave together." She pulled Lex's face down for a gentle kiss. "No heroics, right?"

Lex placed a quick kiss on the tip of her nose. "Right." Then she became instantly alert. "Get ready to move. It looks like they're beginning to search for their missing buddy." She released Amanda's waist and grabbed her hand. "Come on. We'll be safer back by the pass." Lex crawled through the bushes, pulling Amanda behind her.

They decided to circle around to the left of the clearing, hoping that the longer path would be free of the searching men. Lex suddenly came to a halt, causing Amanda to slam into her back.

"What?" Amanda whispered, fearing detection.

Lex turned halfway around and placed one hand over Amanda's mouth. "Shh." She motioned with her other hand to the right of where they were standing.

Darrell was searching the underbrush, using the barrel of his rifle to move the heavy shrubbery out of the way. In his other hand he carried a flashlight to help cut the gloom of the heavy rain and the early evening's stormy sky. He was swinging the light in a wide arc, coming dangerously close to the two women.

Lex pulled Amanda to stand directly behind her and hoped that the dark duster she wore would camouflage them. "If we happen to get separated, take Thunder and meet me back at the pond. They'll never find us there," she whispered. A strong squeeze of her hand and an emphatic shake of Amanda's head were her only answer. Lex spun around to face the young woman. "I'm not planning on it happening, but we need to be prepared just in case."

Amanda sighed, then nodded. Lex turned back around to watch the man search, slowly moving the two of them away from him. She froze as the light panned across her body as she felt Amanda's hands clinch tightly on the back of her coat. When the light kept going, Lex relaxed a little. She started slowly backing up again, pushing Amanda back as well. The light suddenly hit her in the face, and the man let out a yell of surprise. "Hey!" He lifted the nose of his rifle, trying to aim it and the flashlight at the dark apparition in front of him.

Lex spun around quickly, still using her body to block his view of her companion. "Run!" she hissed, pushing Amanda forward roughly. Amanda stumbled, but regained her footing and moved quickly through the heavy trees, with Lex right behind her.

Crack!

Bark exploded off a tree near Amanda's head. *Oh, God!* She willed her body to move faster. Through the pouring rain she heard men shouting. She risked a glance behind her and saw Lex a few steps back.

Crack!

Crack!

More shots rang out, and Amanda heard several bodies crashing through the brush right after them.

"To the right," Lex whispered urgently. She pulled Amanda's arm in that direction. They veered off the slight path they were on, into even denser foliage.

Crack!

Crack!

Those shots sounded further away this time, Amanda thought to herself, as Lex jerked her down into some heavy bushes. Panting hard, Amanda looked around, squinting in the dim light. They seemed to be inside a small burrow, so thickly concealed that the falling rain could hardly break through. It was so dark that Amanda could barely make out the large form in front of her, but she knew in her heart who it was.

They sat silently for what seemed like hours, just waiting and listening, trying to hear any noise over the rumbling thunder. Each of them was too tired and too fearful to utter a sound. After half an hour had passed, Lex finally broke the silence.

"Stay put. I'm going to take a quick look around," she whispered.

Amanda grabbed her arm. "Please, don't," she begged, fear evident in her tone.

Lex leaned over until her mouth was beside Amanda's ear. "We can't stay here all night." She reached into her pocket and pulled out the radio, and placed a quick kiss on Amanda's cold lips. "Call Martha and find out where the sheriff is. If I'm not back in thirty minutes, make your way back to the house."

Amanda wrapped her arms around Lex's neck, pulling her close. She gave her a searing kiss, finally breaking off when she ran out of breath. "No! You *will* come back to me!" Her voice trembled. "This is non-negotiable, got it?"

Lex cleared her throat. "Yeah, I got it." She leaned forward and kissed Amanda's damp forehead. "I'll be right back." She turned and crawled out of their hideaway.

Amanda wiped her eyes and turned on the radio. Holding the button down, she whispered, "Martha, can you hear me?" She released the button, and heard a small burst of static.

"Amanda? Child, is that you? I can barely hear you." Martha's voice broke through the static loudly, making Amanda wince, and she hurriedly turned down the volume.

She placed her mouth as close as possible to the microphone. "Yes, it's me. I have to be quiet, though. Have you heard from the sheriff?"

"Yes, I have. He should be at the site any time now, and he's got three deputies with him."

Amanda breathed a sigh of relief. "Martha, you have to warn him that they have guns." She mentally added up what she had seen. "Two rifles that we're aware of. And there's—"

She was abruptly cut off by the sounds of gunfire, although it sounded like it was quite some distance away. *No!* Amanda almost sprang out of her hiding place, with her heart pounding loudly in her ears.

"Amanda? Are you still there?" Martha's concerned voice broke through her racing thoughts.

"Uh, yeah. I'm here." Amanda took a deep breath. "Look, I've got to go, Martha. I'll talk to you later, okay?" She turned off the radio and then sat in the dark, straining to hear anything over the thunder and pounding rain that punctured the stillness.

By the time the thirty-minute time limit was almost up, Amanda was a nervous wreck. *I can't believe I let her talk me into staying here. Where could she be? Is she okay? Oh, God.* She almost screamed when a dark form broke through the dense brush, nearly tumbling in on top of her. "Lex?" She reached out blindly.

"Yeah, it's me," Lex wheezed, trying to catch her breath. "I led them back to the clearing. Those fools will be chasing each other in a big circle for hours."

Amanda let out a deep breath. "Good. Martha said the sheriff should be there with his deputies any time now." She placed her hand on the rancher's shoulder. "Is it safe for us to get out of here?" She was more than a little concerned about her friend. Lex was still breathing hard. "Are you okay? I heard more gunshots while you were gone."

Lex was silent for a few moments while she tried to get her breathing under control. "Yeah, I'm fine. It's just real hard to run in the driving rain wearing boots and a heavy duster. Guess I'm a little out of shape."

Amanda crawled closer, almost sitting in Lex's lap. "Yeah, right. You're still recovering from bruised ribs, remember?" She snuggled into the welcoming arms. "Mmm. This feels really good. I'm a little chilled." She looked up, barely able to make out the outline of Lex's face. "I imagine you're freezing, though, since you've been out in this cold rain longer than I have."

"I've been warmer, that's for sure," Lex whispered, nuzzling the neck below her. "But to tell you the truth, I'm pretty warm right now." She chuckled and fought back a small cough.

Amanda lifted a hand and placed it on the shadowed face above her. "You're feeling a bit warm. We need to get you back to the house and into bed."

Lex gave the hand a small kiss. "I'm fine. Just out of breath from all that damned running." She cocked her head to listen. "But you're right. I think it's safe for us to try and leave now." She climbed to her feet and offered Amanda a hand up.

The walk back was slow, with Lex cautiously keeping them off any real paths. The rain also hampered their progress, even though the heavy tree cover blocked out most of the downpour.

How on earth does she know where we are going? Amanda wondered, keeping her eyes locked on the figure a bare step ahead of her. Lex doggedly made her way through the thick foliage, not hesitating in choosing which direction to take. *She must have some kind of built-in radar.* The object of her thoughts must have felt her scrutiny, because Lex turned her head, giving her a weary smile. Amanda returned it with a smile of her own. *I'm really worried about her. She seems so... washed out.*

They had been traveling for close to an hour when Amanda reached forward and captured Lex's arm. "I hate to sound like an annoying kid on a trip, but how much further?" she asked quietly.

"Do you need to stop and rest?" Lex questioned. "I'm sorry it's taking so long, but I thought it would be a good idea to take the roundabout way, in case those guys are still trying to find us. Let's take a quick breather." She sank to the ground gracelessly, propping her back up against the nearest tree. "I'm afraid that we've still got about thirty minutes of walking to do."

Amanda dropped down beside her, linking her hand with one of Lex's. "Sounds good to me." She leaned her head on Lex's shoulder and sighed. "Is your life always this...interesting?"

"No. Well, at least not until recently." Lex glanced down and could just barely make out Amanda's features between quick flashes of lightning. "I've had more things happen in the last week than in the past couple of years." Lex squeezed the hand in hers. "Guess you brought the excitement with you."

"Oh, yeah. I love driving my car off into a flooded creek, then running around in the cold rain getting shot at. All part of my big plan to bring some thrills into my otherwise boring existence."

"Got more than you bargained for, huh?" Lex released the hand, then wrapped her arm around Amanda's shoulder to pull her close. "Me, too." She gave the damp head a kiss.

They sat there quietly, listening to the sounds around them. Thunder rumbled intermittently, punctuating the bright flashes of lightning. Lex let her body relax, and her eyes slowly drifted shut.

Amanda felt the body next to hers go limp, and she looked up in alarm. Lex's head was tipped forward, with her chin resting on her chest. Reaching up with her free hand, Amanda lightly touched the still face, which appeared unnaturally wan in the flashes of light.

Lex's eyes popped open and tracked to Amanda's face instantly. "What?" Lex blinked, then opened her eyes wide in an effort to become more alert. She wiped a hand over her face. "Sorry. All of this exercise must have worn me out."

"Uh-huh." Amanda pulled Lex's face closer to her with one hand. "Are you getting sick?" she asked, peering intently into the somewhat glazed eyes.

Lex blinked again, shaking her head slightly. "No. Really, I'm okay. Just a little tired." Lex tried to take a deep breath, but felt a sharp pain along her side. *Just what I needed. My ribs want some attention.* She glanced over at her companion and saw the exhaustion on her face. Lex gathered what little stamina she had left and stood up, pulling Amanda with her. "Come on. We're almost back to the pass, and then we can ride the rest of the way home."

Amanda allowed herself to be hoisted to her feet, not missing the slight tremor in the hand pulling her up. "Now that's the best idea I've heard all day." She brushed herself off and resumed her place behind Lex, as the tired woman blazed a trail through the thick trees.

They found Thunder standing under a canopy of leaves, happily munching shoots of tender grass. The stallion looked up and nickered a greeting as the two weary women approached.

Amanda expelled a great sigh of relief. "I never thought I would be so happy to see a humongous horse." She walked over to the animal, and patted his neck.

Lex followed her and checked Thunder's saddle. "Hey, boy. Are you about ready to go home?" She leaned against him heavily.

Amanda wrapped an arm around the weary rancher. "Come on, honey. Let's get you home, too." The endearment had slipped out before Amanda could hold it back. Lex didn't have to say anything in response; the expression on her face said it all.

"Sounds like a plan." Lex climbed up on the horse and pulled Amanda up behind her. "Thought I'd drive, this time."

Amanda wrapped her arms carefully around Lex. "Sure. I've always been told what a great back-seat driver I am, anyway." She felt a chuckle rumble through her friend, and gave the stomach her hands rested on a gentle tickle. "Home, James," she commanded regally. Amanda placed her cheek against Lex's shoulder blade and snuggled up to the strong back.

The exhausted woman leaned back against Amanda. "Yes ma'am." She nudged Thunder with her knees, allowing him to find his way through the dark.

Chapter
Twelve

The ride back to the ranch house was uneventful. Even the rain finally took pity on the two damp and tired women, and slowed down to a light drizzle. The moon was trying to break out of the clouds as Lex pulled Thunder up to the stables.

Swinging her leg over his massive neck, she slowly dismounted, turned, and helped Amanda down. "C'mon, buddy. Let's get you cleaned up and fed." Lex led Thunder into the building to his stall while Amanda went to get a bucket of feed.

When Amanda returned with the oats, she noticed Lex had already pulled the saddle and blanket from the animal and was in the process of brushing him down. She poured the contents of the bucket into his trough, and then stepped into the stall. "Here," she said, taking the brush from Lex's hands, "let me finish this. Why don't you go on up to the house, and I'll meet you there?"

"I'll make you a deal. You can finish with the grooming, and I'll clean up the tack. Fair enough?" When Amanda opened her mouth to argue, Lex continued. "That way we can walk back up to the house together. Deal?" She placed a grubby hand on her friend's shoulder. Deciding on honesty, Lex said, "Besides," she hesitated, looking down at the ground, "I could kind of use a little help with the walk up there. I'm so tired I'm about to fall down."

Concerned, Amanda placed a hand on Lex's arm. "What's wrong?"

Lex shook her head. "Nothing much, I'm just tired, I think." She leaned heavily against the side of the stall.

"If you're admitting to that, it's time to take you up to the house." Amanda wrapped her hand around Lex's arm and pulled her out of the stall. "I'll come back later and finish up with the tack."

Lex meekly let Amanda draw her from the stable, stunned, but happy. *I can't believe I let her get away with this sort of thing. She is certainly something else.*

Amanda pushed open the back door, practically dragging the exhausted woman behind her. "Martha, where are you?" she yelled, pulling Lex into the kitchen. "Here. Sit down before you fall down." She pushed Lex into the nearest chair and gave her shoulder a slight squeeze. "I'm going to go find—"

"What on earth happened to you two?" Martha gasped, standing in the kitchen doorway. "I swear Lexie, I can't leave you alone for a minute." She stomped over to where Lex sat slumped in her chair. Pulling the soaked hat from the rancher's head, the housekeeper scowled. "Good Lord! You're as white as a sheet." She ran one hand across Lex's mud-spattered brow. Turning her attention to Amanda, she asked, "Are you okay, sweetheart?"

Amanda nodded and dropped into a nearby chair. "I'm fine. Just tired and a little damp." She pushed the wet hood off her head.

Martha, who had begun helping Lex take off her coat, stopped. "Is this blood?" She asked, as she gently touched Lex's side.

Lex flinched. "Probably just mud." She tried to bat away the housekeeper's hands, which were pulling at the damp shirt. "Ow! Hey, Martha, cut that out!"

Amanda stood up and went over to squat beside the fatigued woman. "Blood?" She put one of her hands on the dirty denim-covered thigh to balance herself. "Lex?" She forced her friend to look her in the eye. "What happened?"

"I don't know. I think it's just mud."

Martha shook her head derisively. "Honey, if that's mud, I'm a size six!" She pulled the coat off the rest of the way and unbuttoned the filthy shirt. "Let's just take a look, okay?" She turned to Amanda. "Could you go upstairs and get the salve and some clean towels out of the master bathroom?"

Amanda nodded, although there was a worried look on her face. "Sure." She stood up and patted Lex on the shoulder. "Be right back." She kissed the top of Lex's head, then hurried from the room.

The housekeeper turned her attention back to Lex, who was fighting to keep her eyes open. "Lexie?" She tapped her leg. "Now would you care to tell me what happened out there? I didn't want to upset Amanda, but Charlie radioed about twenty minutes ago, said that by the time he got there, all he could find was an abandoned trailer and a stolen truck." She pulled the shirt open and away from Lex's side. "What happened to you?" Martha used a corner of the wet fabric to wipe at the blood on Lex's side. "This looks like a mighty wicked gash on your side here, honey."

Lex tried to shift away from what Martha was doing. "Ouch! Would you please stop that!" She found her hands captured by older ones. "Okay, okay." She cleared her throat. "I think it's a bullet wound. I was grazed by a bullet." She looked into the concerned brown eyes of the woman who was like a mother to her. "Must've happened when they were chasing me." Martha's news finally sunk in. "Wait. Are you trying to tell me that Charlie didn't catch those idiots out there?" She tried to stand up, but was quickly pushed back down. "Damn! How could he let those fools get away? They could barely take a crap by themselves."

"Now you listen to me, young lady! Last I heard he was still looking for them, so you just calm down." Martha tried to pull the shirt off Lex, who fought her again. "Would you please let me take a look at that?"

Lex held the shirt closed stubbornly. "Wait. Can we compromise?" She gave the older woman a pout. "I really want to take a shower. It feels like I'm wearing at least half of the back pasture."

Martha shook her head. "I don't know what I'm going to do with you, Lexie." Then she nodded. "Okay. Compromise it is. But," she held up a warning hand, "it'll be a quick shower, and then you're going to bed. You've spent too many nights staying up late."

Amanda stood in the doorway, requested items in hand. She offered Martha mock sympathy. "I bet it was almost impossible to get her to take medicine as a child, wasn't it?"

Lex scowled, while Martha burst out laughing. "As a child? Sweetheart, I'd rather pull my own teeth than try to get this one to do something that may actually be good for her." She held out a hand to Lex, who had a grumpy look on her face. "All right, let's go upstairs and get you cleaned up."

"I can do it myself, you know," Lex complained, but accepted the help up anyway. "You're not going to bathe me too, are you?" Hearing a giggle from the doorway, she glared at Amanda.

Shaking her head, Amanda cajoled her. "Sorry. You're just

too cute when you act like an overgrown child." Seeing the outraged look on Lex's face, she backed up. "Umm, I'll just go
upstairs and get the shower ready for you." Amanda turned and
took off down the hallway, still laughing.

"You'd better run!" Lex called after her.

It took a while, but Lex finally finished her shower. She
walked into the master bedroom wearing her flannel pajama
bottoms and a large towel draped over her shoulders and down
over her chest. Amanda had returned from her own clean up
effort and was sitting on the bed with Martha when Lex made
her entrance. *Wow, even after the day she's been through, she's
still absolutely beautiful.*

Martha stood up. "Where's your nightshirt? Are you trying
to catch pneumonia or just drive me insane?" She grabbed Lex's
arm and pulled her over to the bed.

"I didn't see any sense in putting it on until you were finished clucking over me." Lex sat down slowly. "It's right here
on the bed and would have bitten you on the butt if it had been
a snake."

"Hrumph. We'll just see about that, won't we, Little Miss
Smarty Pants." Martha pushed her onto her back, so that she
was lying flat on the bed. She turned to address the young
woman who was now standing beside her. "Amanda, don't let
this one here get away with anything. She really is impossible
sometimes."

"Hey," Lex whined, trying to regain some dignity as the
housekeeper spread salve over the long gash across her ribs.
"Ow! Careful there, I'd like to keep myself in one piece, if you
don't mind." She slapped at Martha's hands.

Amanda sat down next to Lex's legs. "What on earth happened there?" She looked at the wound. "If I didn't know any
better—" Her countenance turned stormy. "You were shot?" She
stood up and paced the length of the room. "I don't believe you.
You got shot, and didn't tell me?" Amanda stomped back over
to the opposite side of the bed. "How could you not tell me
something like this?" She sat on the edge, glaring at the injured
woman.

"No! It's not like that. Really." Lex stretched her arm
across the bed, beckoning for Amanda's hand. "I didn't know."
Not seeing any change in Amanda's face, she continued, "Honestly. I didn't. I thought my ribs were just acting up again. And

it's really just a slight scrape."

Martha listened quietly to the women argue. *Poor Lexie. It looks like she's finally found someone who's not afraid to stand up to her. Good!*

Amanda took a calming breath and held Lex's hand. She looked into her eyes and saw nothing but the truth. "Okay, I believe you." She pulled the hand to her lips and gave it a kiss. "But," she squeezed it a little tighter, "next time tell me when you're hurting, okay?"

"Promise." Lex flinched. "Damn it, Martha, I think you're enjoying this a little too much." She gasped as the housekeeper taped a large square of gauze on the wound. "Easy, there. Hey!" Lex squirmed as she got her good side tickled.

"Hush up, you. Now sit up and I'll wrap these ribs again." Martha watched appreciatively as Amanda crawled over to help her patient into a sitting position. "If you would keep these wrapped for more than a day, they wouldn't hurt as much, you know." She pulled the large elastic bandage from behind her back.

"Where did you get that?" Lex asked, her face flushing slightly.

"Honey, I do the laundry around here." Martha wrapped the wide bandage around Lex. "And I know about the last time you broke your ribs." She smirked at the look of surprise and embarrassment on Lex's face. "Teach you to try to keep anything from me."

Lex rolled her eyes, but stayed silent. *Figures. Damn woman has eyes in the back of her head. She can read minds, too.* She glanced over at Amanda, who had covered her mouth with one hand. "What?"

Amanda shook her head, but the sparkle in her eyes gave her away. She sputtered, then finally laughed out loud. "Sorry, Lex, but she's right. You shouldn't try to hide things like that."

"There. All done." Martha tied off the bandage with safety pins. She picked up the nightshirt and slipped it on the injured woman's body. "By the way, Roy called while you were out. He said he and the boys are bringing out a truck tomorrow, and they're going to finish the work on the bridge. They had to wait until all the supplies came in; that's why it has taken them so long." She began buttoning the shirt, much to Lex's annoyance.

"I can dress myself," Lex argued, but let Martha finish. "I'm glad they're coming out tomorrow. The six of them can have it finished in no time." She sat back, exhausted.

Amanda brushed the hair out of Lex's eyes. "I was wondering, where do the hands stay? I've seen Martha's house, the stables, and the hay barn, but—" she stopped when Lex squeezed her hand.

"The hands stay at the bunkhouse, which is just up the road from here. It's closer to the main cattle pens." She took a pained breath and closed her eyes. "It can hold up to fifteen, but there's only six of them right now. We hire extra help when we start tagging in the spring."

"Actually, there's only five real hands. Lester is mainly the cook, right, Lexie?" Martha looked up when there was no answer, and saw that Lex had fallen asleep. Shaking her head, the housekeeper said to Amanda. "Let's go get you something to eat. I still have some roast and potatoes left." She stood up and covered the sleeping woman with a blanket.

Amanda let go of Lex's hand reluctantly and climbed off the bed. "Okay, then I'll come back and sit with her for a while." She followed the Martha from the room, glancing back at the doorway at the sleeping woman. *She looks so fragile when she's asleep.* "I'll be right back," she whispered.

After finishing at the stables, Amanda ate a quick dinner. She raced back up the stairs after Martha chased her out of the kitchen. "Just see that she stays in bed tonight. Don't let her take any more trips out to the stables," the housekeeper had commanded.

Stopping at the doorway to the master bedroom, Amanda leaned against the doorframe and sighed. Lex was still sleeping peacefully, although she had kicked off the blanket and was now curled up on her good side, facing away from the door. Amanda tiptoed into the room, and went quietly to the bed. She picked up the blanket from the floor, and was about to cover the sleeping woman with it when Lex rolled over and sat straight up in bed, sweat dripping from her body.

"Damn," she muttered, visibly trembling. "Amanda?" She looked at her friend in dazed surprise.

Amanda placed the blanket around her shoulders and then felt her forehead. "You're burning up, Lex. I'd better go—"

Lex grabbed her hand. "Don't leave me," she pleaded in a hoarse whisper. "I'll be okay." She trembled again. "Could you just stay with me for a while, please?"

"Of course I can. Just let me get you some aspirin for that

fever, okay?" Amanda quickly stepped into the bathroom and brought a glass of water and two white tablets. She sat down on the edge of the bed and handed the pills to Lex. "Here. Take these, then I'll get you tucked in. I seem to be doing that a lot, huh?" she said, teasingly.

Taking the aspirin, Lex finished the water and sat the glass on the side table. "Yeah." She leaned back into her pillow. "Does that bother you?"

"No. In fact, it makes me feel really good that you let me." Amanda pulled the covers over the trembling woman. She ran her hand gently through the damp hair.

Lex partially closed her eyes and relaxed. "Thanks." The feel of Amanda's fingers combing through her hair was very soothing. "Mmm." She closed her eyes the rest of the way and drifted off to sleep.

Amanda sat by her side for a long while, running her fingers through Lex's hair. She knew she needed to go to bed, too, but really had no interest in leaving the sleeping woman's side. She laid her hand along Lex's jaw line, noticing with relief that the fever seemed to be easing. Standing up, Amanda was about to walk out the door when she heard Lex moan slightly in her sleep. *I really don't want to leave her.* She compromised with herself by crossing to the other side of the bed and crawling under the covers. *Much better.* Lex moaned again, and Amanda turned on her side and took a hand in hers. "Shh, it's okay. I'm here," she whispered, which calmed Lex down immediately. Pulling the hand up to her face, Amanda tucked it carefully under her own cheek as she lay there, just watching her friend sleep.

Chapter
Thirteen

Martha walked into the master bedroom with a tray in her hand, humming softly to herself. She looked at the bed and stopped dead in her tracks. The sight that greeted her warmed her heart.

Lex was sound asleep, although it was almost eight o'clock in the morning. She lay flat on her back, her left arm uncovered and wrapped securely across Amanda's back.

Amanda was curled up beside her with her head tucked under Lex's chin. Her arm was outside the covers and across Lex's chest.

The housekeeper walked to the bed and set the tray down on the side table. Seeing that both women were deeply asleep, she placed her hand on Lex's forehead. *Thank the good Lord that she's not running any fever this morning. I was a little concerned about that bullet wound, but I guess I cleaned it up okay.* Not wanting the sleeping women to be disturbed, she turned off the ringer to the telephone. Satisfied that her job was complete, Martha quietly exited the room and closed the door behind her.

She was lying on her back in a field of wildflowers, the sun soaking into her body. The silence would normally be alarming, but it filled her with a contented peace she rarely felt. She enjoyed the gentle fragrance of the flowers around her as a warm breeze passed through her hair, bringing with it another heavy dose of the flowery scent. Knowing she should get up, her body rebelled, embracing the warmth of the quiet spring day with decadent pleasure.

Lex took a deep breath and inhaled another lungful of the fragrant bouquet. She opened her eyes, somewhat surprised that she was indoors, and even more surprised to find that she was in bed. *But I could swear that I smelled flowers.* Her brow creased in confusion, and then she noticed the source of the delightful fragrance. A tousled head was tucked directly under her chin. Lex decided she needed to compliment Martha on her choice of shampoo for the guestroom. She also decided that the dream was nice, but reality was much better. Although she didn't want to disturb Amanda, her body reminded her that it was well past her normal wake up time. Lex carefully rolled Amanda off her, which got her a small sigh in return. She was finally able to maneuver herself into a sitting position, and was charmed when Amanda rolled back over and snuggled into her pillow. Lex eased herself off the bed, biting her lower lip to stifle a groan. *Getting too old to play all day in the rain, Lexington,* she admonished herself, stepping slowly into the bathroom.

A nearby smell woke Amanda, and she became aware that she was lying in the big bed alone, hugging Lex's pillow. She turned her eyes to the bedside table, which had a large tray sitting on it. "So that's where that wonderful smell is coming from," she mumbled, taking another deep breath, closing her eyes in bliss.

"Gee, thanks," Lex drawled, stepping out of the bathroom.

Amanda blushed then pulled the pillow over her head. "I can't believe you heard that."

Lex walked over to the bed and sat down. "Good morning to you, too."

One eye peeked out from under the pillow. "Morning," Amanda grumbled, then sat up. "How are you feeling?" She reached out to the other woman. "You look a lot better this morning."

Lex accepted the hand and pulled it to her lips for a little kiss. "Must be the company I'm keeping."

Amanda's blush deepened. "Umm," she pointed to the tray trying desperately to change the subject, "isn't that breakfast?"

"Yeah. Martha must have just brought it up a few minutes ago. The food is still steaming."

"She was in here when we were asleep?" Amanda stammered.

Lex winked at her. "Yep. And now she probably knows that I didn't need any extra blankets last night." *Ooh...you're bad, Lexington, very bad. But look at her blush!*

To her surprise, Amanda just stretched and said, "That's funny. Neither did I." She crawled over to Lex, wrapping her arms around her neck. "Good morning," Amanda whispered, leaning in and planting a sensuous kiss on Lex's mouth.

Lex moaned and deepened the kiss almost instantly. She put her hands on the small of Amanda's back to pull her closer, so that their bodies melded together.

Amanda buried her hands in Lex's thick hair. She gasped when Lex finally broke away, her heart pounding so hard she just knew the other woman could hear it.

"Goo..." Lex had to clear her throat before she could continue. "Good morning." She pulled back slightly. "Certainly makes waking up worthwhile."

Amanda leaned forward until her forehead was on Lex's chest. "Oh yeah. I think I've just become a morning person."

Lex pulled Amanda close again. She nibbled on the nearest ear, then whispered suggestively, "I'm more of a night person, myself." The body in her arms trembled in response. "You cold?"

"N...n...no. As a matter of fact, I'm pretty darned warm right now." Amanda tilted her head back as Lex's lips worked down the slim neck. "Ahh...oh." She couldn't seem to put together a coherent thought with Lex taking tender bites of her throat. "Oh, God." Amanda found that she couldn't sit up any longer, so she fell back onto the bed.

Lex followed her, never giving up on her quest to know every inch of the young woman's throat. "So sweet," she mumbled, then turned on her side to get more comfortable. Her injured ribs complained at the motion, and she let out a gasp.

Amanda turned to get a look at her companion's face. "Lex? What's the matter?" She could see the pain in Lex's eyes as she stroked the pallid face with gentle hands.

Lex felt herself guided onto her back against the bed. "Sorry. Guess I turned wrong or something. Just give me a minute to catch my breath." Closing her eyes, she concentrated on trying to will the pain away.

Brushing her hands slowly across the strained face, Amanda leaned down and kissed Lex on the forehead. "Shh. Just lie still for a little while. Let me go get Martha." She started to get off the bed, but was stopped by Lex's hand on her arm.

"No. Stay, please." The barely spoken plea slipped through Lex's lips before she could stop it.

"Okay, I'll stay." Amanda positioned herself with Lex's head in her lap, gently stroking the pale face and running her hands through Lex's hair. The caring touch caused Lex's eyes to close and allowed her to relax somewhat.

A quiet knock at the door made Amanda look up. "Come in."

Martha opened the door slowly, uncertain if she had interrupted a private moment between the two women. She saw the look on Amanda's face and Lex apparently asleep in her lap. A few steps later, she was next to the bed and could see worry in Amanda's eyes. "What's going on? How's Lexie this morning?"

"She was doing pretty good earlier." Amanda flushed at the double meaning. "I mean, she was feeling better than she was last night." Embarrassed, she looked down at the still face in her lap.

Martha sat on the edge of the bed and placed a hand under Amanda's chin, forcing the young woman to look at her. "And?"

"We were, uh...just," Amanda bit her lower lip to contain her tears. "She turned wrong and I think it hurt her ribs, or maybe pulled at the bullet wound." Her hands, though shaky, kept up their gentle tracing.

"Oh, honey." Martha wiped a stray tear from Amanda's cheek. "Everything's going to be just fine." She looked down at Lex, who now looked completely relaxed in sleep. "Darn fool kid. Why don't you come downstairs with me, and we'll let Lexie get some rest?"

"No, I can't. I promised her I would stay with her, and I don't want her to wake up alone."

Martha was about to argue with her when she heard the phone ring downstairs. She leaned over to the bedside table and plucked the cordless phone off the base. "Walters' residence, Martha speaking."

"Martha, this is Charlie. Is Lex around?"

"I'm sorry, but she's resting right now. Is there something I can do?"

"Sweetheart, I hate to be the bearer of bad news, but we've lost track of those damn thieves. The last trail we had, looked like they were headed up to the main house."

Suddenly very afraid, Martha's face lost some of its color. "What exactly does that mean?"

Charlie was sounding tired, but resolute. "It means that you need to get everything locked up tight. I had to send most of my men back to town because of some trouble there. But don't you worry. Joseph and I will keep looking until we find them. I'm sorry to be calling with this right now, but I really wanted to let you know what was going on."

"No, I appreciate you calling. I'll tell Lexie."

"Are you sure you'll be okay? I really wish I could be there with you, but I think I'll have better luck out here searching, instead of sitting around the house waiting." He paused. "Besides, I know Lex is more than able to handle whatever comes her way."

Martha took a moment to think about what Charlie had just said, hoping that it was true, given Lex's condition. "We'll be just fine. The boys should be back by late this evening, hopefully."

"Okay, then. You take care, and call me if you need anything. I'll still have the radio on the same channel."

Martha looked down at Lex's face, still sleeping peacefully in Amanda's lap. "Yes, we will, Charlie. Thank you." Her hand shook as she hung up the phone.

"What was that all about, Martha?" Amanda noticed the slight tremble to the older woman's actions. "Was that the sheriff?"

"Yes, that was Charlie. He wanted us to know they haven't been able to find those thieves yet. They lost their trail earlier this morning."

Amanda's brows knit in confusion. She couldn't understand why Martha was so shook up, just because the men hadn't been apprehended. "Well, that's rotten luck and all, but why do you look so upset? I mean, he's going to keep looking, isn't he? And they weren't able to get away with anything, right?"

"Before they lost the trail, the thieves were headed this way." Martha's normally calm voice shook slightly. "And, unfortunately, something's going on in town, so Charlie had to send some of his men back. Now, he and one deputy are the only ones still searching."

"But, these men have guns. Why doesn't the sheriff just come to the house?"

"He can't be sure they're still headed this way. Charlie won't give up until he finds them, I promise you that."

Amanda felt a little better at Martha's confidence in the local law enforcement. She was quiet for a moment, and then a thought suddenly occurred to her. "What if they found out that Lex was the one who sabotaged their truck? Do you think they would be stupid enough to come up here looking for her?"

"I don't know. That's why Charlie wanted me to tell Lexie. He said she's more capable of defending this house than most of his deputies are. He tried for several years to get Lexie to join his department, said she was stronger, smarter, and a heck of a lot better shot than those college boys who work for him." She reached down and brushed the tangled bangs from the sleeping woman's face. "Let's give her some time to rest, and I'll tell her about Charlie's phone call when she wakes up." She was about to stand when the sound of thunder caught her attention. "That's just dandy. Just what we need, more rain." Martha stood up and spotted the untouched tray. "Next time you two get involved in something, eat your breakfast first."

Amanda closed her eyes in embarrassment. "Oh, good Lord."

When Martha reached the doorway, she turned back. "Might as well get started on it. Breakfast, I mean. You can feed Lexie when she wakes up." She sauntered out of the room and started down the stairs.

Amanda scowled down at the sleeping face in her lap. "You are in so much trouble when you wake up." She kissed Lex on the lips, then eased out from under her, covering the still form with a blanket. "She's not going to let us live this one down, and you made me face her alone. Not to mention I think we're about to have more trouble around here."

Another deep chord of thunder rattled the windows, punctuating her observation.

Chapter
Fourteen

Martha spent the remainder of the morning doing her housework and smiling from time to time over her parting shot when leaving the master bedroom. She was almost back to the kitchen when there was a knock on the back door. "Now who could that be?" She grabbed the nearest weapon, which happened to be a mop out of the utility room, and went to the back door. After a peek through the curtains covering the small glass windows in the door, she sighed in relief. "Charlie! Get yourself in here before you catch your death." Martha swung open the door and pulled the tall man inside.

"Thanks, Martha. I just wanted to stop by and give you a report." He removed his drenched hat and shook it outside before closing the door. Happy to be in out of the rain, Charlie followed her into the kitchen.

She placed the mop in a corner, daring him to say something. "Let me fix you something to eat."

Charlie Bristol had been coming out to the ranch long enough to know that tone in her voice. As much as he wanted to tease Martha about her choice of weapons, he quickly changed his mind. "That would be great, Martha. Thanks." He took off his coat, sat his hat in a nearby chair, and then dropped down into a seat. "Damn, it's been a long night. Is Lex doing okay? You told me earlier that she was resting."

Martha began to cook him something to eat, turning her head every so often to talk. "I guess you could say that. She got shot, but it just grazed her side. She's upstairs now sleeping." She tried to sound nonchalant, but he could hear the tremor in her voice.

Charlie got up from his seat and walked over to the stove, gently wrapping his arms around the trembling woman. "Shh, it's okay sweetheart. Let it out."

Martha spun around, and tucked her head into Charlie's chest, sobbing quietly. "Damn it, Charlie, I could have lost her." She felt his arms wrap tightly around her, as she let days of stress break free.

The quiet lawman just stood there, loaning his strength to a woman who rarely needed any. *She's the strongest woman I know, yet she lets me see this side of her. God, I want to take care of her for the rest of our lives.* He bent his head down, and placed a tender kiss on her graying head. "I know, honey, but she'll be fine. Our Lex can handle just about anything." He always thought of the young rancher as his adopted daughter, and he knew that she was the child Martha never had.

Martha enjoyed the embrace for a few moments more, then stepped back and wiped her eyes with the edge of her apron. "Thanks, Charlie. I guess I must have needed that." She gave him a light kiss on the cheek and turned back to her cooking. "So, any luck in finding those thieves? We had to practically sit on Lexie to keep her home last night."

Charlie moved back to the table and sat down. "Not really. Seems they broke up into two different groups and then went in opposite directions. Joseph went after one group, and I'm looking for the other." He waited until Martha turned around to face him. "Like I told you earlier on the phone, one group may be coming this way. That's why I'm here."

"I was a little afraid of something like that. Amanda told me what Lexie had done to them. They'd have to be totally stupid not to figure out who did it." She carried a plate of food over to the table and set it down in front of him. "Do you think they'd really come after her?" She picked up the carafe of coffee and brought it to the table, along with two mugs.

"I'm not sure. Part of me thinks they'll just try to get transportation out of here, but I don't think they know that the bridge is out." He speared the food, speaking in between bites. "What bothers me most is the fact that they're so good at hiding. They could be right outside, and I may never find them." He was one of the best trackers in the area, and that these thieves had the skill to elude him made him justifiably nervous.

Martha sat down, looking into her coffee mug. "I'm afraid," she whispered.

"Honey, I'm not gonna rest until I catch these bastards, and you can take that to the bank." Charlie grasped her hand. "No matter how long it takes, I will not let them hurt you."

The housekeeper looked at him with sad eyes. She finally

spoke what had been in her heart for the last few days, not knowing how much more she could take. "I'm not afraid for me, but for Lexie. I don't want anything to happen to her, but she's so stubborn. This week has nearly killed me."

"This week? What else has happened, Martha?" he asked, forgetting his food and scooting his chair closer to hers.

"Where do I begin? It seems like if it's not one thing, it's another." Martha leaned into Charlie's sudden embrace. "Friday night, she was down by the creek checking the fence, when she saw a car get washed from the bridge. Damn fool child could have drowned, jumping in like she did. But she did bring us a blessing in disguise, you could say. Not expected, but certainly welcome."

"Good grief. I thought you raised her with more brains than that. I knew that the bridge was washed out, but—" Charlie squeezed the hand in his. "What kind of blessing are you talking about? Who did she pull from the creek?"

"You know Jacob and Anna Leigh Cauble, right? Well, their granddaughter Amanda was in the car that was knocked into the creek. She's such a sweet girl, too."

Charlie knew that look. *Uh-oh. She's got that Martha Matchmaker face on again.* "Really? I've never met her, but old Jacob talks about her all the time, and she sounds like a wonderful girl. Is she still here?"

"Oh yes. She's upstairs right now, taking care of Lexie."

The sheriff's eyebrows rose at that statement. "Taking care of Lex? You've got to be kidding me. We are talking about the same person, right? Tall, dark, and obstinate? The Lex I know wouldn't allow anyone to take care of her."

Martha squeezed his hand again. "You'd be surprised what Lexie has allowed that young girl to do. She even lets her win arguments. I never thought I'd see the day when that would happen." Her wistful expression faded as she got serious again. "I just hope Lexie will stay in bed for a day or so, to get her strength back. She's been so tired lately, and this last little adventure has about worn her out."

"I don't know if that will be possible, Martha. If my suspicions are right, half of that group of thieves could be on their way to the house as we speak. And they could be looking for trouble."

A voice from the kitchen door interrupted their conversation. "They're headed here? Are you going to leave us some protection?"

Both people at the table looked up. A concerned young woman stood in the doorway, looking somewhat disheveled in the oversized maroon sweats she was wearing. She walked into the room and sat down at the table next to Martha.

"Amanda, what are you doing downstairs?" Martha asked, as she got up to get another coffee cup from the cabinet.

"I can't stay long, I just came downstairs to get Lex something to eat." Amanda hoped that Martha would appreciate her sneaky tactics. "I made her promise to stay in bed today." She blushed slightly, remembering what the rancher had told her. *"Only if you keep me company. I tend to get bored, otherwise."* It had been said with a diabolical air, which had sent shivers of excitement up and down Amanda's spine.

Charlie smiled tiredly at Amanda. "Miss Cauble, I really wish I could stay here and personally guarantee your safety, but the truth is I can't even justify keeping a man on this case."

"Please, call me Amanda." She looked at him closely. "And who says you can't stay on the case?"

The sheriff shook his head sadly. "City politics, Miss...Amanda." He saw her frown at the more formal way that he'd addressed her, and figured that if Martha had her way, she was practically his "daughter-in-law", anyway. "The county commissioners don't much care for Lex. She really hacked them off a few years ago, and the bast...err...excuse me, old coots haven't gotten over it yet."

Amanda was shocked. "And, because of their hurt feelings, they won't allow you to help? That's absolutely ridiculous!" She slapped her hand down hard on the table.

Martha stopped working on the tray for Lex and walked over to stand behind the upset woman. "You're right, it is. Charlie, don't lose your job over this. I'm sure Lexie can handle things just fine."

Charlie leaned back in his chair with a smug expression. "It just so happens my vacation starts today. And Joseph just happened to get sick last night. He said he owed Lex a favor, and he'll keep looking for those thieves as long as he needs to." He stood up, and took his hat off the extra chair. "Martha, if you wouldn't mind, we'll keep in touch with you on the radio. Channel six."

The housekeeper handed the sheriff two thermal containers full of coffee and gave him a kiss on the cheek. "I'll carry the portable with me. Now you be careful out there. We've got a date next Saturday night, and I hate to be stood up."

Charlie blushed. "You know I'd never stand you up, sweetheart." He gestured with a Thermos. "Thanks for the coffee. I'll keep in touch." The lawman left the kitchen with a happy smile on his face.

Martha glanced over at Amanda, who was smirking. "Now don't you look at me like that. We've been friends for years."

"I didn't say a word." She shook her head solemnly and pretended to zip her lips.

The housekeeper walked over and swatted her on the arm, then turned around and moved back to the counter without speaking.

"Hey, it's not my fault your boyfriend is so cute." Amanda chuckled when Martha actually blushed. Having gotten even for being embarrassed upstairs earlier, she enjoyed the small victory.

Martha rolled her eyes. "I guess I deserved that." She opened the refrigerator and poured a glass of orange juice, adding it to the finished breakfast tray. "How is Lexie feeling?"

"Much better, I think. She's only running a slight fever this afternoon, and her coloring is almost back to normal." Amanda stood up and checked out the tray. "That sure looks like a lot. Does she normally eat that much?"

"Not usually, but you tell her she had better finish every bite, or I'll come upstairs and feed it to her personally." Martha handed the tray to Amanda. "Good luck, you're gonna need it."

Lex stood in the bathroom, her nightshirt unbuttoned and opened. Turned to one side, her right side was an easy view in the bathroom mirror. She had removed the elastic bandage from her body and was now gingerly trying to peel the tape covering the wound. "Ah, damn. When will someone invent tape that can be taken off without ripping all your hide off in the process?" she grumbled as she continued to slowly pull the tape from her skin, wincing with every tug.

"Ahem."

Startled, Lex spun her head around to face the open doorway. "Oh. Hi."

Amanda stood in the doorway with her hands on her hips, one foot tapping impatiently. "What do you think you're doing?"

"Um, well, I had to go to the bathroom."

With a scowl on her face, Amanda stepped into the room.

"And you had to unwrap your ribs to do that?" She stood directly in front of Lex, looking up into her eyes.

Those same eyes rolled. "No. But my side was aching a little bit, so I thought I'd change the bandage."

Amanda pulled the shirt aside and glanced at the gauze taped over the wound. ""Okay. But the bandage is still on. Do you need some help reaching it?" She ran a light hand over the area in question, then looked back up.

"To tell you the truth, I was having some trouble removing the tape."

Amanda bent down so that she was at eye level to Lex's waist and pulled the shirt back. "Hold this." With one hand on Lex's hip for balance, she gently pulled the tape back. When the skin beneath her hand flinched, she admonished, "Stay still."

Lex jumped again. "Ow! I'm not gonna have any skin left at this rate," she hissed.

Amanda looked up at her and with amusement said, "Bruised ribs don't bother you. Gunshot wounds don't slow you down, but try to put medicine or bandages on, and you yelp like someone is trying to kill you." She patted the flat stomach. "You are such a big baby." After a short pause, she placed a kiss on the bare abdomen. "I really like that." Amanda stood up, the tape temporarily forgotten. "I really like you." She wrapped her arms around Lex's neck and slowly pulled her head down for a kiss, trying to show what her heart desperately wanted to say.

Lex accepted the kiss and the feelings that went along with it. She pulled back slightly, noticing the sparkle of emotions on Amanda's face—emotions that were reflecting how she was feeling as well. "I really like you, too." She leaned down and captured soft lips again, prolonging the contact until they both broke away, breathless.

Amanda leaned into Lex's body and took a deep breath. "Whew. Okay, let's get you taken care of, and then I'll serve you lunch in bed." She reached for the tape again. "And if you're a really good girl, I'll tuck you in." She started to pull on the tape, but felt Lex tense up. "Easy. It'll be over soon, I promise." Amanda removed the tape, and slowly tried to pull the gauze away from the wound, only to find it stuck. "Oh, Lex, it looks like it bled quite a lot." She looked up and saw the pain in her friend's eyes. "I don't think I can get this off without hurting you more."

Taking a deep breath, Lex closed her eyes. "Yeah, I know." She braced herself against the counter. "I need to clean up anyway. Let me just get into the shower, and maybe I can peel it off easier."

Amanda stood up and placed a hand on Lex's arm. "I've got a better idea. How 'bout you let me run you a nice warm bath? Maybe soak for a while and rest?"

Lex opened her eyes slowly and rubbed them. "That sounds like a great idea. I'm still pretty beat."

"I can tell. Why don't you go sit down for a minute, and I'll start the water." Amanda led Lex into the bedroom and helped her sit on the edge of the bed. She kissed the top of the dark head before disappearing into the bathroom. "Be right back."

Over an hour had passed since Lex had gotten into the tub. Worried, Amanda tapped lightly on the outer door. When she didn't receive an answer, she slowly opened the door and peeked inside. *Aw, poor sweet Lex.*

Lex had slipped down into the tub, her head barely visible above the water. The bubbles that filled the bath were long gone, and the water must have been cold, but she continued to sleep peacefully.

"Just like Sleeping Beauty," Amanda marveled quietly, as she walked over to stand beside the tub. "Well, it worked for Prince Charming," she mumbled. She leaned over and placed a soft kiss on the lips of the reclining woman.

Surprised, Lex almost slipped beneath the water. She blinked several times and peeked up at Amanda. "Hey."

"Hey, yourself," Amanda countered. She wiped the damp hair away from her friend's eyes. "I was afraid you had drowned in here."

Lex couldn't help but smile. "Not quite. How long have I been in here?"

"Over an hour."

"Damn. I can't believe I dozed off like that." Disgusted with herself, Lex started to stand up.

Amanda couldn't help but stare at Lex's wet body as the water sluiced off her slender form. Her mouth went dry, and she lost the ability to speak. She stood there, mouth partially open, staring until Lex cleared her throat.

"Would you mind handing me the towel that you're standing on?"

"Hmm?"

Lex grinned and held out her hand. "Towel. That soft thing

lying under your feet." Although she enjoyed the glazed look on Amanda's face, she snapped her fingers to break her trance. "Earth to Amanda. As I'm sure you can tell, I'm getting cold."

Amanda's eyes widened, and she hurriedly bent down and picked up the towel. "I'm sorry. I just, umm, well—" Her eyes, which had been studying Lex's chest, focused on the floor.

Quickly wrapping the towel around her body, Lex guessed that her teasing might have gone too far. "Hey." When Amanda continued to stare at the floor, she caressed her cheek and then the back of her head until she looked up. "It's okay."

Mortified at herself, Amanda swallowed hard, then finally met Lex's eyes. "I'm sorry."

"Don't be sorry. I'm flattered." Lex winked. "Besides, you showed a lot more control than I would have." She stepped out of the tub and leaned over to leave a kiss on Amanda's cheek. "Thanks."

The smile didn't leave Amanda's face as she watched Lex walk out of the bathroom, clad only in a short yellow towel that Amanda thought was still about an inch too long. She gathered up the medical supplies and followed her friend from the room.

Lex pulled on a pair of gray sweatpants and was about to slip a tee shirt over her head as Amanda came out of the bathroom. She turned around, shirt still over her head, when Amanda spoke.

"What do you think you're doing?"

"Getting some clothes on, why? You don't expect me to run around in a towel all day, do you?" The shirt was almost on when Amanda grabbed it and stopped the movement.

"Smart ass. You forgot to put another bandage on." She raised and removed the garment, then swatted Lex with it. "Go lie down on the bed."

Lex stepped away, but stopped before she got to the bed. "I really don't think that's necessary, Amanda." She twisted her head so that she could look at the bullet wound. "It's hardly bleeding at all, now."

Amanda sighed and pushed the rancher back onto the bed. "Yeah, right. And I'm sure Martha wouldn't mind you going without putting anything on it."

"What makes you say that? I'm perfectly capable—"

"Of not taking care of yourself," Martha finished for Lex, as she stood in the doorway. "What kind of bull pucky are you spreading now, Lexie?"

Lex rolled her eyes and glared at the housekeeper. "I was

just telling Amanda that I don't need a babysitter, and I'm more than capable of taking care of myself." It was hard trying to look tough while sitting on the bed in just sweatpants and the shirt hiked up high, so Lex crossed her arms over her chest to appear a bit more intimidating.

Martha couldn't help but laugh. "Of course you are. But, just to help you along, I've brought some antibiotics that you conveniently forgot to take with your last injury. This should help stave off any infection." She popped a pill into Lex's mouth before she could argue. "Hush." Turning to Amanda, she started to hold out her hand for the bandages, but stopped. "You look like you can take it from here. I'll just run back downstairs and finish up some laundry."

"Thanks, Martha. I'll let you know if she gets out of line," Amanda teased, expecting and receiving a disgusted look from Lex. She waved her fingers at the retreating figure, then turned her attention back to her friend. "I promise to be gentle."

"Uh-huh." Lex looked doubtful, but laid back and raised her arms over her head. "Do what you will with me. I'll suffer in silence."

Amanda's hand froze in mid-air. She looked at the bare skin in front of her and suddenly forgot what she was supposed to do. *Don't tempt me, Lex. If I do to you what I want, you certainly won't be silent.*

"Hello? Hey, Amanda? Are you okay?" Lex waved her hand in front of the other woman's face.

Shaking her head, Amanda blinked. "Oh, yeah. Sorry about that." She opened the jar of homemade salve and dipped her fingers inside. "I'll try not to take too long."

A short while later, Lex dozed peacefully, and Amanda walked downstairs, only to find herself alone in the house. Martha had obviously gone to her own home for a while, so, not knowing what else to do with herself, Amanda went over to the kitchen phone and picked up the handset. She dialed the number of her grandparents and waited patiently until the phone was answered.

"Hello?"

"Gramma? How are you? How's Grandpa?" The gracious tone in Anna Leigh's voice made Amanda want to curl up on her grandmother's lap like she did when she was a little girl.

"We're fine, Mandy. How are you? I was a little concerned when we didn't hear from you last night, but Jacob said that you were probably worn out from your horseback ride."

"It was a long day, that's for sure." She sniffled to try and get her emotions back under control.

Not fooled for a moment, Anna Leigh heard the soft sniffle and became instantly alert. "What happened? You didn't have a fight with Lexington, did you? I know she can be a bit abrupt sometimes, but she really is a dear girl."

"No, no. Nothing like that. We just ran into some trouble when we were out riding yesterday. There were these thieves, and—" Here, Amanda lost it and began to cry softly.

"Mandy honey, calm down." Concerned, Anna Leigh's tone hardened, and her voice rose, something that Amanda rarely heard. "That does it. We're driving out there right now, and I don't care if I have to swim across that damnable creek!"

"No," Amanda exclaimed, then softened her tone. "No, Gramma, I'm okay. It's just been a bad week, that's all. And with Lex getting hurt like that, I guess I'm just a little on edge."

"Hurt? What happened? Was she thrown from her horse?"

"Um, no," Amanda hedged, knowing her grandmother would really get upset if she knew what had happened. But she had always been honest and open with her grandparents. "She was shot, but it only grazed her. But with the way her ribs are acting up, it's—"

"Shot?" Anna Leigh yelled. "Are you okay, sweetheart? My goodness is Lexington okay? Do we need to send a doctor out there?" She stopped her questions when the phone was taken away from her.

"Peanut? What's going on? Your grandmother is white as a sheet. Are you okay? Did I hear her correctly, was someone shot?" Jacob Cauble's deep voice took over the phone, causing a wave of relief to wash over Amanda.

"I'm fine. Lex got a little hurt, but she's okay now."

Jacob sighed. "A little hurt? If she was shot, that's more than a little hurt, Peanut. Do you want to talk about it?"

Amanda ran her hand through her hair. "Yeah, actually I would. Got a few minutes? Maybe get Gramma on the other phone?" She had to talk to someone about this. Her emotions were too strong and she didn't know what to do.

"Mandy, we have all the time in the world for you." Anna Leigh had picked up the extension and spoke from the other phone. "Talk to us."

Amanda wiped the tears from her eyes and told her grandparents everything. She started with the wonderful tour of the ranch on horseback, then graduated to when they came upon the thieves. Her voice shook again when she told of the frightening ride back to the clearing after she alerted Martha and the sheriff, and then the hiding in the thick bushes to wait for Lex to return. Finally, she told them of her feelings when she found Lex had been shot, and of the fear she had of losing someone who had already become quite special.

Jacob and Anna Leigh were very supportive as they talked Amanda through her bouts of tears and laughter. They listened as she told of meeting Sheriff Bristol, and of her finally being able to catch the unflappable Martha off guard. When Amanda told them how deep her feelings were becoming for Lex, they gave her their blessings as well.

After her emotional phone call, Amanda went upstairs to check on her patient. Since Lex continued to rest peacefully, she walked out onto the balcony to enjoy the break in the rainfall. Heavy clouds still filled the late-afternoon sky, but the lightning had stopped, and there was only an occasional rumble of thunder shattering the still silence as she leaned against the railing.

Amanda was so wrapped up in her thoughts that she didn't hear when another person joined her on the balcony. Strong arms wrapped around her waist and hands rested lightly on her stomach.

"Penny for your thoughts," a soft voice whispered in her ear, while lips nipped at the soft lobe.

"Mmm." Amanda leaned back into the warm body behind her, covering the hands on her abdomen with her own. "Just daydreaming."

"About anything in particular?" Lex asked as she nibbled a path down Amanda's neck.

Amanda leaned her head to one side to give Lex better access. "Uh." Her knees weakened. "Hmmm?" She turned around, and wrapped her arms around the other woman's neck.

Lex felt hands clench in her hair as she took the opportunity to blaze a fiery trail down Amanda's throat. The body she held trembled. "Cold?"

"N...n...no. It's just...ahhh." Amanda released a deep breath. "C—can we take this inside? I seem to be having trouble standing."

Lex halted her exploration of the soft skin under her lips, leaning back just enough to look into slightly glazed eyes. "Really? Think you're coming down with something?"

"Could be." Amanda unlocked her hands from the silky hair and covered the hands that were settled on her waist, bring-

ing them both indoors. After the close call of the day before, she
didn't want to waste one precious moment of their time
together. "Maybe you should tuck me into bed."

Lex followed, her legs suddenly weak. "I think it may be
contagious. It sounds serious." She kept the playful banter alive
while Amanda guided her to the edge of the bed.

Amanda slowly raised Lex's shirt, pushing the rancher gently onto her back. "Oh, yeah. I'm going to need lots of special
attention." She pulled her own shirt off. "Think you can handle
it?" She watched as Lex's eyes darkened. "Let me demonstrate."
Amanda leaned down, covering the mouth under hers with a
searing kiss.

When they finally broke apart, Lex pulled in a shuddering
breath. "Let me see what I can do." She let her hands explore
the supple body above her with tender caresses. Taking special
care, she slid her callused hands across the dips and curves,
mapping out her intentions with gentle desire.

She teased and tormented Amanda with her touches as her
own desire flamed well beyond anything she had ever experi-
enced before. Amanda was so responsive to her that it caused
her own body to demand as much of Amanda's as possible.
Each moan from Amanda was reciprocated by one of her own;
each woman giving herself completely to the other.

Amanda felt a burning fire course through her veins as Lex
memorized her body by touch, stopping at different points to
leave a heated kiss, or a gentle nip. Their bodies moved together
as if each motion, each touch, had been practiced for years.
Amanda reveled in the freedom to show Lex what had been in
her heart from the moment they'd met. *It was never like this
before,* was her last conscious thought before she rode out a
wave of ecstasy as brightly colored lights exploded beneath her
closed eyes.

Much later, Amanda awoke with a warm body wrapped
around hers, a dark head pillowed on her stomach, and two long
arms stretched protectively across her body. She lovingly ran a
hand though the disheveled hair, while her other hand gently
clasped a tanned arm. *I don't know what got into me, but I don't
think Lex is going to complain.* She smiled in remembrance. *It
was so intense. But I don't think I've ever felt so...loved before.*
She sighed. *That's what this is, I think.* She looked down fondly
at the sleeping woman in her arms. *No. I know that's what this*

is. She felt a strong surge of emotion hit her deeply. *I wonder how Lex feels about it?*

The object of her affection stirred and tightened her hold slightly. Lex nuzzled the smooth skin under her cheek and opened one eye to focus on the shining eyes above her. She reached up with one hand to wipe away a single tear trickling down Amanda's cheek. "What's wrong?" she asked, attempting to sit up.

Amanda held her down gently with an arm. "Nothing. I'm just being stupid." She took a deep breath to try and get her roiling emotions under control.

Lex kissed the flat abdomen her head rested on. "Are you regretting—" her voice broke.

"Oh God, no." Amanda guided Lex's face upward until they were inches apart. Placing a trembling kiss on her lover's lips, she whispered, "No regrets. I'm just a little overwhelmed." She added another kiss and touched her forehead to Lex's. "Okay, a lot overwhelmed. I've never felt anything like this before."

Lex completely understood. Her own feelings were all over the place. "I never thought I'd feel anything like this. Ever." She swallowed hard and cupped Amanda's cheek, wiping away another stray tear with her thumb. "I—" she paused, trying to find words to express the incredible feelings coursing through her body. Unable to find any, Lex gave Amanda a soft kiss. The young woman promptly deepened it, conscious of the unspoken words and adding her own.

Their bodies were able to articulate what their voices couldn't. Amanda pulled back just far enough to gaze into Lex's eyes. Swearing to herself that she could see directly into the other woman's soul, Amanda matched her intensity, while her eyes sparkled with unshed tears. "I love you." The words were spoken so softly, she barely heard them leave her mouth.

But Lex heard them. Her eyes widened and she stopped breathing. Then her eyes closed, silent tears tracking over her features. She opened her mouth to speak, but was unable to utter a sound. Finally taking a large gulp of air, Lex opened her eyes again.

Amanda placed concerned hands on the other woman's face, searching her eyes intently. "Lex? Honey, what's the matter?" She used her thumbs to brush the tears from Lex's face. "Please, talk to me." She could feel her lover tremble, still not able to speak.

Lex pulled Amanda tightly to her, burying her face in her hair. "No one has ever said that to me before," she rasped, her throat thick with emotion. "And," she pulled back until she could look Amanda directly in the eyes, "just so there's no confusion—" She placed a light kiss on Amanda's lips. "I love you, too." Lex pulled her into her arms then rolled over to lean back against the headboard.

Amanda snuggled happily into Lex's embrace, content to just lie there and absorb the warm feeling bubbling up between the two of them. Even now, the increasingly loud rumbling of thunder couldn't ruin the euphoria she was feeling. She felt a kiss on the top of her head, and the arms holding her tightened.

"I hate to disturb you," the familiar voice whispered in her ear, "but if we don't get downstairs pretty soon, Martha's gonna come looking for us."

In no hurry to move, Amanda took a small bite out of the shoulder conveniently located nearby. "And this would be a bad thing?" She nibbled her way over to Lex's throat. "Would it bother you, her seeing us like this?"

"Of course not. I just didn't want you to get embarrassed, that's all."

"Well, I don't think she's going to pick on me much, at least for a little while anyway. We sort of called a truce this morning."

Lex pulled up Amanda's face so that she could see into her eyes. "Truce? Did you two have an argument?" She didn't want any bad feelings between the two women in her life, and the last thing she wanted was for Martha to dislike her new lover.

"No. Nothing like that." Amanda patted Lex on the stomach in order to calm her. "I caught her in the kitchen with her boyfriend."

"Charlie was here?"

"Yeah, early this morning." Amanda went on to explain everything he had told them, and how he refused to stop looking until the thieves were caught.

Lex released a heavy sigh. "Damn, I was afraid of something like that." She kissed the top of Amanda's head. "Come on. Let's get cleaned up and go downstairs. I'm starving."

Amanda climbed off Lex. "And I thought that noise was thunder. I didn't know it was your stomach growling." She smirked and held out her hand, which was taken immediately. "Want to conserve some water?"

"Sure." Lex allowed herself to be pulled off the bed and led into the bathroom. "Although I don't know how much we'll conserve. This could take a while."

Martha stood at the kitchen window, staring silently out at the darkened sky. Amanda was about to call out a greeting when Lex covered her mouth with her hand. Giving her companion a devilish look, she sneaked up behind the housekeeper and wrapped her arms around the ample waist.

"Evenin' Martha," she boomed, squeezing her quarry tight.

"Aah!" Martha screamed and then spun around. Quickly recovering from her fright, she slapped Lex on the arm. "Blast it, I swear I'm going to keel over dead one of these days!"

Amanda was only a few steps behind Lex, bent over laughing. She finally stopped long enough to catch her breath. "Good one, Lex." She missed the fond look bestowed on her by the housekeeper, who finished blustering and was now all business.

Martha aimed Lex at the table. "Sit down and I'll get you something to eat." When she saw that they both had damp hair, a wicked thought crossed her mind. "You, too, Amanda. I'm sure you both worked up quite an appetite." She enjoyed the dark blushes that spread over both women's faces.

Despite her red face, Lex looked up impishly. "As a matter of fact," she raised an eyebrow at Martha, "better give me double helpings." She winked at Amanda, who just covered her face with her hands. "Right, Amanda?"

Amanda uncovered her face and stuck her tongue out at her lover. "I'll get you for that."

"I certainly hope so. I'll be looking forward to it."

Martha walked up to the table and lightly slapped Lex on the back of the head. "Behave yourself, Lexie." She then gently ran her hand through the damp hair. "You look like you're feeling better."

Lex leaned back into the caress, guiltily enjoying the attention. "I am, Martha. Guess all that sleep did the trick. I feel almost as good as new." She looked tenderly at Amanda. "And I had a really good nurse."

Martha touched Lex's forehead, relieved to find it cool. "How's your side? Do you want me to change the bandage?"

"It's great. Amanda took care of it earlier."

Amanda met Martha's gaze and nodded. "Yep. It had bled some during the night, but other than that it looked pretty good. I just re-bandaged it a few minutes ago. There doesn't seem to be any infection."

Lex reached across the table for Amanda's hand. "Must be all the good care I've been getting."

"How's your ribs?" Martha asked, setting the platters of food on the table, then sitting down to join them.

"Good as new," Lex bragged, then looked up when a loud crash of thunder rumbled outside.

"Teach you to try and fib to me."

"Yeah, right." Although she was enjoying the banter, Lex knew it was time to get serious. "Not to try and change the subject, but have you heard anything else from Charlie?"

Martha's smile faded. "He radioed in a couple of hours ago. No luck so far, but a couple of deputies rode in by horseback and said they were going to take over while he and Joseph went up to the bunkhouse for a rest."

"Good. I didn't want him to stay out there indefinitely. He's begging for pneumonia as it is." Lex thought for a moment, then asked, "Any word on how the work on the bridge is coming along? Have you heard from the boys?" She started eating, her appetite coming alive when she swallowed the first bite.

"They called right after lunch and said the bridge should be finished by sometime tomorrow." She turned her attention to Amanda. "I'm sure Lexie will give you a ride back into town."

Amanda looked up from her plate with a surprised look on her face. She saw the mischief in Martha's eyes and decided to play along. "Well, I really do need to check on my grandparents." When Lex's face fell, she didn't have the heart to go on. "But, I'd like to just go and pick up some clothes and things and come back here to help out. At least until someone is completely healed." She squeezed Lex's hand and received a look of relief in return.

Lex picked up her glass of ice tea, trying to appear nonchalant. Amanda's teasing comment scared her more than she cared to admit. With her previous track record, Lex feared that her new love would leave at the first available opportunity. She lifted the glass to her lips. "You don't have to work. You know you're welcome to stay here as a guest for as long as you want."

"I know, it's just that—" Amanda paused, seeing the glass shake slightly in her friend's hand. *Why is her hand trembling like that?* She looked into Lex's eyes and saw a thinly veiled fear. *She thought I'd leave? After today?* Amanda felt a sharp jab of pain in her chest with this realization. *We're going to have a nice long chat later, my friend.*

"Amanda?" Lex called her out of her reverie. "You with us?"

Amanda blinked, then shook her head. "Uh, yeah. Sorry about that." She stood up, taking her empty plate to the sink. She looked at Lex, whose face was impassive. "I need to go call my grandmother, if that's okay with you."

"Sure, go ahead. I was going to go out and check on the horses." Lex stood up as well, leaving her hand on the empty chair back.

Amanda crossed the kitchen to place her hand on Lex's. "Martha and I fed them pretty late last night, so they should be okay." She pulled the hand to her lips and kissed it. "Don't be gone too long, all right?"

Lex finally allowed a smile to cross her face. "Right. Give your grandparents my best." She gave Amanda's hand a squeeze, then made her way to the door. "Martha, lock the door behind me just in case, okay?"

The housekeeper was running water into the sink. She gave them both an innocent look. "Amanda, honey, could you do that for me? I've already gotten my hands stuck in this dishwater."

Amanda walked over and placed a light kiss on the round cheek. "Okay, but I think you should work on your subtlety." She followed Lex out of the kitchen.

They walked silently down the hallway, hand in hand, until they reached the back door. "Do you need any help? I could wait to call my grandmother." Amanda watched as Lex put on her heavy duster and placed her black hat on her head. "Do you ever leave the house without that hat?" She reached up and pushed it back off Lex's head and tousled her hair.

"Well, actually no, I don't. Guess it's like my security blanket. My dad gave it to me right before he left." Lex paused in thought. "Makes me feel like he's here with me, watching."

Amanda buttoned the coat closed. "How long has it been since you've spoken to him?" She looked up and saw a fleeting sadness in Lex's eyes.

The rancher took a deep breath, then released it slowly. "'Bout a year, I guess. He called asking for some money, said the circuit was pretty tough." She let her gaze turn inward for a long moment. "Haven't heard from him since, so I guess things are going better for him." She shook her head, not wanting to share her negative thoughts with Amanda. "Anyway, guess I'd better go check on the horses." She pulled the other woman into her arms. "See you in a little bit." Leaning down, Lex slowly captured Amanda's lips, feeling her arms wrap tightly around her neck.

"Hurry back," Amanda whispered when they finally broke apart. Thunder interrupted her, followed by a nearby flash of lightning. She ran a loving hand across Lex's jaw. "Be careful."

Lex leaned into the caress, closing her eyes. She took a shuddering breath then looked down into the pools of light that were Amanda's eyes. "I love you."

"I love you, too." Amanda placed a kiss on Lex's lips. She deepened the kiss, pouring her heart and soul into the connection. When she stepped back, she could see the same emotion in her lover's face.

Lex opened the door and stepped out. "I've got a key, so go ahead and lock the door." She started down the steps. "I'll be back in about an hour or so. I just want to look around and make sure everything is okay."

Amanda stood at the open doorway. "Don't be too long, or I'll come out after you." She winked at her lover. "I know of several better activities than messing around with a bunch of horses."

Lex bit her bottom lip. "Hmm. Hold that thought. I may have a surprise for you later." She tipped her hat and started for the barn.

Lex made a short check of the horses, then moved quickly into the maintenance barn. The Mustang looked just like she had left it. She slipped off her coat and hat, then stepped into the greasy coveralls that she had left hanging by the door.

An hour later, Lex was certain that the car suffered no serious damage due to the flood. She put a couple of gallons of gas in the tank then sat down in the drivers' seat to turn the key. The engine grumbled, then finally sputtered to life. "Yes!" she yelled aloud, pumping a hand into the air in triumph. Leaving the engine running, Lex walked over to the telephone that was hanging on the wall.

Two rings later, Martha answered. "Walters' residence, Martha speaking."

Feeling mischievous, Lex lowered her voice. "Hey, baby, you sound hot. What are you wearing?" She had to cover the mouthpiece with her hand to muffle her laughter.

Martha recognized the voice immediately. "Oooh. You sound absolutely marvelous. What are *you* wearing?"

Lex lost it. Laughing hard, she replied, "Greasy overalls, baby."

Martha laughed as well. "Hmm, a little too kinky for me, I think. But let me ask my friend in the other room. I think she's into nut cases like you."

"Wait! Don't get Amanda just yet. I need you to do me a favor. Ask her to look out through the window in the sitting room. I want to show her something."

"Got it running, did you?" Martha knew how much Amanda treasured the classic car. "She's going to fall to pieces, you know that, right?"

"That's okay. I'll pick them up." Lex stripped the coveralls off, using one hand. "I should be up there in about five minutes, okay?"

"Okay, Lexie. I'll make sure she's ready." Martha hung up the phone and went in search of the young woman.

While Lex was busy getting the Mustang in running condition, Amanda had gone into the office to call her grandparents.

She greeted the deep voice that answered the phone. "Hello, Grandpa Jake."

"Hey there, Peanut. How's everything going?"

"Great. How are you feeling? Is your leg still bothering you?" Amanda asked. She remembered how badly Jacob would limp, barely able to walk on his newly healed leg.

"Not bad at all now, sweetheart. I'll be back on the jogging track in no time." He was about to say something else when another voice broke in on the conversation.

"I'll second that, Mandy. Your grandfather has been chasing me all over the house." Anna Leigh's voice was filled with happiness at her husband's quick recuperation. "How's Lexington feeling?"

"Much better, Gramma. She's gone out to check the horses right now." She took a deep breath. Although her grandparent's already gave her their blessing, she knew what a big step she was about to take. "Once everything gets back to normal, I'd like to invite her home for dinner, if that's okay with both of you."

"Does this mean what I hope it means?" Anna Leigh asked.

"Yes, I think it does, Gramma. I've never felt like this with anyone else before." Amanda paused for a moment, trying to convey her seriousness. "I love her."

Jacob was the first to speak. "Wonderful! I've always liked her, especially after the way she took care of my Anna Leigh during that whole escapade with the Taylor house."

"Oh really? Guess I'll have to get her to tell me all about that, huh?" Amanda enjoyed her grandfather's exuberance. "Anyway, I just wanted to call and let you know that the bridge work should be finished sometime tomorrow. I'll probably be home in the next day or so." Cutting off any other questions, she continued, "I told Lex I wanted to stay out here for another week or so, until she's healed up from this past week's activities. I want to pick up a few things and see both of you."

They spent the next half-hour talking about inconsequential things, with Amanda promising to bring *her* rancher to dinner in the next couple of days. *They sound almost as thrilled about all of this as I am. I wonder if that's possible? I wonder what my own parents will think? Uh, no. I don't think I want to know right now.* Her grandparents had always been very supportive of how she lived her life, even when her parents couldn't seem to comprehend that she preferred the company of women to men. She always felt more loved and happy during her childhood summers, spending them with the two most important people in her life. Jacob and Anna Leigh had treated her as their own child, with all the love and support she had been missing at home.

Amanda hung up the phone with a bittersweet pang in her chest. Her grandfather's recent accident had reminded her of their mortality, and she always became a little sad after these types of thoughts. *Stop it.* She repeated her grandmother's mantra, which kept her sane during those long nights at the hospital. *Don't dwell on the bad things, just think about all the good things.*

Amanda was still drifting in her thoughts when the phone rang. Martha must have picked it up immediately because it only rang one time. A few minutes later, the housekeeper bustled into the room.

"There you are. I'm sure glad I found you. Lexie has a surprise for you and wants you to look out the front window." Martha took Amanda's arm and led her into the sitting room.

The room was delicate, Amanda noticed. Queen Anne furniture surrounded a baby grand piano that stood proudly in one corner. The large bay window had delicate lace curtains, and

soft watercolor paintings graced the room. "Martha, it's beautiful," she whispered, looking around the room in awe.

A sad look crossed Martha's face. "This was Mrs. Walters'
favorite room. I remember when she used to sit at the piano and
play for little Lexie." She wiped a tear from her cheek. "Lexie
used to sit in here for hours, practicing. She was really good at
it, too, until her daddy told her it was useless to play the piano
when she should spend her time learning how to run a ranch."
Taking a deep breath to bring herself back to the present, Martha continued, "She still comes in here every once in a while
and plays. I think it relaxes her."

"Lex plays the piano?" Amanda was surprised. The rancher
didn't seem like the type to spend time with something that had
to be done indoors.

"Oh, yes." Martha's face took on an angry tint. "But that
no-good father of hers teased her until she quit." She was about
to comment further when a honk outside the house interrupted
her.

Amanda rushed to the window, then gasped. "Oh, my." She
hurried out of the room and through the front door before Martha could say another word.

Martha peeked through the window to see a light blue Mustang sitting in the front circular drive. "Well, I'll be," she muttered, before shaking her head and going back to the kitchen.

Amanda stood on the front porch, tears streaming down
her face. Lex stepped out of the vehicle and stood on the
driver's side, door still open. Amanda walked slowly down the
steps, unable to say a word.

All the sleepless nights were suddenly worth the effort
when Lex watched the emotions that crossed her lover's face.
She barely had time to brace herself before Amanda wrapped
her body around Lex and squeezed with all her might.

"I can't believe this. I thought it was lost forever," Amanda
murmured, her faced tucked securely in Lex's shoulder. "Was
this what you were doing all those nights?"

Lex buried her face in Amanda's hair. "Yeah. Surprised?"
She sighed in contentment when Amanda squeezed tighter. The
slight pain it caused her ribs was quickly forgotten. "It's got a
small dent on the left rear panel, and the upholstery needs to be
cleaned, but other than that I think it's okay." She pulled away,
momentarily, to reach into the back seat. "I found this on the

front floorboard." She handed over a purse and an old leather briefcase, dotted with dirt, but reasonably intact. "I didn't look at anything, but I laid everything out on a workbench to dry."

Amanda looked at the items, then back at Lex. She grabbed her lover around the neck, kissing her soundly. "Thank you." She couldn't begin to explain the emotions thrumming through her and began to cry. "You have no idea what this means to me."

Lex held her close, kissing the top of her head. "I have a pretty good idea. I know that you and your grandfather found this car and rebuilt it together, yet you never complained when you thought it was gone."

Amanda stepped back, looking Lex directly in the eyes. "The car is very important to me, that's true. But as long as I was alive, I knew things always have a way of working themselves out. My grandparents taught me that." She framed the face above her with her hands. "And as long as I have you, nothing else matters." Amanda leaned up and placed a kiss on Lex's chin.

Lex closed the car door, and led Amanda back to the house. "I'm just glad you dropped into my life." She opened the front door, then handed Amanda the keys to the car. "Here. You can drive us into town tomorrow."

Chapter
Fifteen

The two women sat in front of a roaring fire in the den. Lex was ensconced in a chair, and had Amanda sprawled in her lap. They had been snuggling for well over an hour, and neither one seemed to be in any hurry to move.

"Are you sure I'm not hurting you?" Amanda asked. As comfortable as she was, the last thing she wanted to do was to bring any discomfort to the woman she loved.

"You've got to be kidding." Lex nibbled on a convenient ear. "I've never felt better." She was about to get a little more serious about it when Martha walked into the room.

"Excuse me, Lexie, but I've gotten dinner ready, if you can tear yourself away from what you're doing." She worked hard to keep the smirk off her face. "If not, I guess I can just throw it out."

Amanda practically jumped out of Lex's lap. "Wait! You wouldn't throw out perfectly good food, would you?" She seemed horrified by the thought.

Lex rolled her eyes and stood up as well. "Pul-lease. This is the same woman who would save my plate and make me finish it later when I was growing up. She never throws food away."

Martha slapped at her as she walked through the door. "That's only because you would barely stand still long enough to eat. Then come back an hour later whining about being hungry."

She made sure both women were seated at the table before joining them while Lex faked an innocent look. It didn't take very long for the three of them to pass around the platters of food, filling their plates quickly.

"I've been meaning to ask you Martha, when do you find time to cook all these wonderful meals?" Amanda asked, enjoying her food with gusto.

"It's not really that big of a deal, Amanda, and it doesn't take that long at all." Never one to be afraid of storms, even Martha jumped when thunder rumbled a little too close by.

Lex looked up at the ceiling and shook her head. "I swear, I'd almost welcome a drought after this past week." Another crack of thunder shook the house.

Amanda scooted her chair closer to Lex's. "Sounds like it's getting closer."

"It's only weather. There's nothing to be worried about." Lex wrapped her arm around Amanda's shoulders and pulled her close. Then she quieted, and listened carefully. "Did you hear something?"

Martha looked at her quizzically. "I hear another storm approaching, why?" She listened as well, but couldn't hear anything out of the ordinary.

"Shh," Lex warned. She stood up from the table and walked over to the kitchen window. "Something isn't right out there."

Suddenly, there was another crash of thunder and the lights went off in the house.

"Damn!" Lex groped around in the darkness. She reached into a nearby drawer and pulled out a flashlight. "Amanda? Martha? You two okay?" She aimed the beam of light onto the table, highlighting two pale faces. Walking over to the frightened women, Lex squatted down between them. "I don't like the feel of this." She saw her lover tremble slightly. Grasping Amanda's hand, Lex squeezed it to offer some sort of comfort. "Hey, it's okay. Probably just the storm."

Amanda knew Lex was only saying that to make her feel better. She didn't like the feel of things either, and was afraid they were in serious trouble. "Yeah, sure." She looked over at Martha, who had a concerned look on her face as well. Amanda was about to reassure the housekeeper when the sound of breaking glass assaulted their ears.

Lex jumped up, looking at Martha. "You two get into the storm cellar, I'll go check it out." She was about to go to the back door, when two sets of hands caught her from behind.

"Are you crazy? Come down into the cellar with us," Martha begged, suddenly afraid of the unknown. "I've got the portable radio here in my apron, we'll call Charlie."

"She's right. If it's those thieves, they have guns, and you don't. Please don't do this," Amanda pleaded quietly, knowing in her heart that Lex couldn't and wouldn't do as she asked.

Lex kissed her lover on the lips. "Go with Martha. I've got to check this out." She turned to look at Martha. "Go to the cellar, please." She stared at the older woman for a very long moment. "Call Charlie and tell him to come in through the back door." She walked over and grabbed a nearby skillet. "You always said I was dangerous in the kitchen."

Martha nodded bleakly and grabbed Amanda by the arm. "Come on, Amanda. The cellar is very well hidden and we'll be safer there." She looked up at the woman she had raised from a small child. "Join us soon, okay?"

Lex set the skillet down and scooted the table off to one side so that Martha could move the rug underneath and open a trap door. "You two go on in, I'll cover your tracks." She leaned over and gave Martha a hug. "I'll see you in a little bit."

Martha nodded, then stepped down into the dark passage. "You'd better." She continued down until she reached the bottom. There she picked up a lantern and lit it with a book of matches kept nearby for just such an occasion. "Thank the good Lord I clean this place up on a weekly basis."

With tears of worry running down her face, Amanda looked at Lex. "I'd rather stay with you." She leaned into the hand that caressed her face. "I don't think I can stay anywhere without you."

Lex pulled her close for a deep kiss. "I need you to take care of Martha for me." She jumped as the back door was kicked opened, and the sound of splintered wood and glass echoed in the quiet house. "Hurry. I'll see you soon. I love you," she whispered, then sent Amanda down the stairs and closed the trap door behind her.

The rancher rearranged the rug and placed the table back over it, careful not to block the door in case Martha and Amanda needed to escape. She dusted off her hands and started for the doorway, armed with only a flashlight and a cast iron frying pan. Lex could hear voices in the hall, so she raised her makeshift weapon and stood with her back flat against the wall.

"Shut up, damn it," a deep voice barked low, just inside the house. "They know we're here now."

A younger voice broke though the silence. "Why do we have to do this, Matt? Wouldn't it be easier to just steal a car or something?"

"Because I don't like being made a fool of, and that damn woman did just that," Matt snapped, as he walked carefully down the hall. "You still with us, Darrell?"

"Yeah, I'm here. Why, I don't know." He cocked the rifle, making sure a round was in the chamber.

Lex leaned closer to the wall, hearing the three men move closer and closer to the kitchen doorway. She closed her eyes to gather her courage, and sent a silent prayer to keep Martha and Amanda safe, should she fail.

Amanda watched with a sense of dread as the trapdoor closed, then turned to look around the small room. The lantern's flickering light painted the walls, which were covered with open shelves filled with canned goods and other items.

Martha sat with a heavy sigh on a wooden bench that ran down the middle of the room and patted a spot next to her. "Come over here, Amanda." She pulled the small radio from her apron pocket as Amanda sat down beside her. "Charlie? Do you read me?" Her whispered voice sounded horribly loud in the gloom.

A small burst of static answered before a faint voice replied, "Martha? Read you loud and clear. What's up?"

The housekeeper glanced at her companion. Amanda's face mirrored her relief. "You need to get to the house, pronto. We've got some unexpected visitors."

"Roger that." After a short pause, the sheriff continued, "Where are you? Are you okay?"

Martha thought a moment before replying. She didn't want to give away too much, just in case the thieves were monitoring the radio. "Amanda and I are *weathering* it out just fine. Lexie said for you to come in the back way. The electricity is off, so be careful."

There was a short pause, then Charlie spoke. "Roger that. I'm on my way now." He understood the need for caution. "Sit tight, sweetheart."

Light thumping from above caught both women's attention. Martha bit her lip as she looked up at the ceiling. "Sounds like they're in the hallway now." She glanced over at Amanda, whose shadowed face held a look of alarm.

"I hate just sitting here," the young woman exclaimed, standing and pacing the length of the small room. "There's got to be something we can do."

Martha stood and took a firm grasp on Amanda's shoulders. "I don't like it much either, but we are helping in a way." Seeing Amanda take a breath to argue, she continued, "With us down here safe, Lexie can concentrate on those men and not have to worry about us." She pulled the young woman back over to the bench to sit down. "The best thing we can do is stay calm, in case she needs our help."

Amanda took a deep breath and wiped a tear from her cheek. "I know that what you're saying makes sense, but I can't help but feel that I should be doing more." Another loud thump from above made her look up at the ceiling. She was about to say more when a sharp bang was heard. "Oh, God, no. Lex!"

While she waited next to the doorway, Lex listened as the three men continued to argue.

"Okay, listen. If we split up, it won't take as long to search."

"Matt," a younger voice interrupted, "I don't want do this. It ain't right."

"Shut up, Ronnie." Matt sounded as if he was walking a fine line, and the smallest thing would set him off. "Fine. You stick with me, and we'll check upstairs. Darrell, you look around down here. Shoot anything that moves, got it?"

A resigned sigh was his answer. "Yeah, yeah. I got it." He watched as the other two headed up the stairs. Flashes of lightning through the windows and the broken back door were the only illumination in the silent house.

Lex hugged the wall tighter. She heard two of the men move past the door and down to the darkened stairway, as the third stood in the hallway, grumbling to himself.

"Check the downstairs," he mumbled, "shoot anything." He peered into the kitchen.

The rancher raised the frying pan over her head, preparing to swing downwards as soon as the thief stepped into the room.

Darrell stood in the doorway, holding his breath and listening carefully. A close lightning strike lit up the entire room, and he could see that it was empty. Shaking his head, the thief continued down the hallway to the front of the house.

Lex exhaled, a little angry that the man didn't walk into the kitchen. *Guess I'll just have to follow him.* She spun into the doorway, slowly looking around the doorframe with one eye. She could barely make out the dark form, which was going into the den. *Time to play hide-and-seek,* she said to herself as she sneaked down the long hallway.

Darrell stepped into the den, waving the rifle back and

forth, peeking around the heavy furniture. As he approached
the office, Lex slowly crept up behind him, and raised the frying
pan over her head. Sensing another presence in the room, the
nervous man started to turn around when another flash of lightning lit up the room, highlighting a tall form barely two feet
away from him. He raised his rifle to fire at the apparition,
which suddenly appeared to be swinging something at his head.
  Crack!
  The gunshot echoed throughout the silent house, leaving a
deathly still quiet behind it.

  Amanda jumped to her feet, prepared to race up the stairs
when a strong hand on her arm stopped her. "Let go of me," she
cried, struggling to break free.
  Martha held the squirming young woman. "No, honey.
We've got to stay here." She wrapped Amanda in a tight hug.
"We don't know what's going on up there."
  Realizing she wouldn't be able to break out of the strong
grasp, Amanda finally relented. "But she may need me. She
could be hurt." A shudder ran through her body. "Or—" She
couldn't even finish the horrible thought.
  "Honey, you can't think like that." Martha continued her
strong hold. "Our Lexie is one of the strongest people I've ever
known. Now come over here with me and sit." She pulled
Amanda back over to the bench and pulled her down beside her.
  Amanda calmed, thinking about what the woman who had
raised Lex had said. *She is very capable – I'm not giving Lex
enough credit.* Looking at Martha, Amanda could read the fear
in her eyes as well. *I never thought about what this is doing to
her. Lex is practically her daughter. I've been pretty selfish here.*
She linked their hands and squeezed. "You're right, as usual. I
can't help but be on edge. It's been a pretty wild week."
  Martha was about to reply when the radio crackled.
  "Martha? You there?"
  She hurriedly pulled the device once again from her apron.
"We're here, Charlie."
  "I'm right outside. Did I hear a gunshot just now?" Ner-
vousness was quite evident in the sheriff's tone. "Are y'all
okay?"
  Martha took a trembling breath then looked over at
Amanda, who was chewing on her lower lip. "Amanda and I are
fine. We're still hidden. I'm not sure about Lexie, though." She

felt an arm wrap around her shoulder in support.

"She's fine, I'm sure of it," Charlie assured her. "I've got reinforcements on the way. We caught one group of those damn thieves hiding near the stolen vehicles. Damn fools."

Relieved at the news, Amanda pulled Martha close. "That means there's only three left." She gave a forced little laugh. "No contest."

The silence hung heavily in the air over the crumpled body sprawled in the center of the office floor. The tall figure stood over the still form for a moment, then squatted down beside him to check for a pulse. *Still breathing. Guess that's a good sign.* Lex tossed the frying pan off to one side, then removed the laces from the unconscious man's workboots. She made quick work,using the laces to tie his hands and feet, in case he came to. She picked up the rifle and was about to leave the room when she heard heavy footsteps on the stairs. *Goody. One down, and two to go.* Lex crossed stealthily across the den, until she was just inside the doorway. A quick peek around the corner showed two forms: one at the foot of the stairs, and the other standing in the kitchen door.

"Matt, I'm scared," the younger man whined as Matt stepped into the kitchen. A moment later he returned, then walked over to the back door, which was still partially open, and stepped through it.

"Shut up! I swear to God, if you don't quit whining, I'll shoot you myself." Matt opened the door to the utility room and quickly checked inside.

The smaller man sat down on the bottom step, with his arms around his knees, rocking back and forth. A large clap of thunder startled him, and he began to cry. "Matt, I want to go home."

Lex watched as Matt walked back over to the stairs.

Slap!

"Ssh! Quit being such a damn baby. You're fifteen years old, so grow up for Christ's sake." Matt shook the younger man's shoulder. "Now come on. Stay behind me and keep your mouth shut." He walked down the hallway, heading straight for the den where Lex stood waiting.

Come on, you bastard. Just a little closer, Lex silently urged him on. *Dragging a poor kid into this mess. I'm gonna enjoy this.* She turned the rifle around in her hands, so that she held it like a club.

Another rumble of thunder shook the house, then the back door swung open as lightning lit up the sky once again.

"Hold it," a man's voice yelled, as a beam of light flashed down the hallway. "Sheriff's department!"

Matt whirled, careful to keep the young man between him and the deputy, who had raised his gun.

"No!" Lex screamed, not wanting to see the boy shot. She jumped out of the den brandishing her rifle like a club. "Hold your fire," she yelled at the deputy, while she swung the gun downward.

Crack!

Crack!

The lights came on just as the shots rang out.

Chapter
Sixteen

"Okay, I've got men at all of the doors, and I've found the outdoor breaker box where they threw the electrical switch. As soon as my men are in position, I'll turn the lights back on, and we'll go in."

Amanda quickly took the radio from Martha's shaking hands. "Do you really think that's wise? We don't know where Lex is, or what the situation is up there."

"Normally I'd agree with you, but I don't want my men to be shooting at shadows. Someone could get hurt." He paused, trying to get his point across without unduly upsetting either woman. "And, if Lex is hurt, it'll be easier to find her if the lights are on."

Before Amanda could reply to that dark thought, two more gunshots rang out upstairs just as the electricity came on, illuminating the cellar with the dull, weak light of a dusty old bulb.

"Charlie? What's going on?" She screamed into the radio. "Charlie?" Amanda handed the radio to Martha, and started up the stairs. "That's it! I'm not spending a single second longer down here!"

Before she could reach the top, the trapdoor opened. The bright light from the kitchen temporarily blinded the two women. Amanda had to shade her eyes from the glare, since the light in the storm cellar was so dim. "Lex?" she whispered, begging in her heart for it to be true. Not waiting for an answer, she charged up the stairway, Martha quickly at her heels.

Lex was practically bowled over by the excited women, finding herself almost flat on the floor. "Hey, take it easy."

Charlie stood in the doorway, beaming at the sight before him. "Damn, Lex. I've been meaning to ask you how you're able to attract the most beautiful women."

Martha got off her knees and took a near-leap at the lawman. "Oh, Charlie, you've always been such a sweet-talker." She forgot where they were and gave him a passionate kiss.

Lex looked up at Amanda, who was leaning over her prone body. "I guess this means you missed me?"

Amanda leaned down and gave her a long kiss. "Yeah, I guess you could say that." She sat up, looking Lex's body over carefully. "Are you okay? We heard several gunshots." She ran her shaking hands across the beautiful body beneath her.

Lex sat up and wrapped her arms around her lover. "Not a scratch. How are you holding up?"

Amanda enjoyed the strong arms holding her close. "Just great, now." She placed a kiss on Lex's neck. "But I guess I should let you get off the kitchen floor." She stood up, hauling the rancher with her. Amanda pulled Lex close, then wrapped her arms around her and squeezed. "I really don't want to go through anything like that ever again."

Lex kissed the top of Amanda's head. "Come on. Let's see if they need any help with the clean up." She walked them both out of the kitchen.

Charlie and Martha were already in the hallway; the housekeeper maintained the grasp she had on the sheriff's weathered hand as he watched his men finish up their business.

Amanda's eyes popped open wide. There were deputies everywhere. One was at the back door, another was speaking to a young teenager who was seated on the stairway, and several more were leading away two men in handcuffs. One of the men bled from a head injury, and he scowled at Lex as he was led out through the front door. The other man complained about a headache and gunshot wound to his leg. He glared at Lex and questioned her parentage under his breath as he was led outside.

One deputy, with his hat in his hands, walked up to Lex. "Uh." He looked down at his feet, embarrassed. "Lex, I want to apologize again for shooting at you." The big man looked like he was about to cry.

Amanda stiffened, and would have probably attacked the poor man had Lex not tightened her hold on her shoulders. "Jeremy, I don't blame you. All you could see was a person with a gun." She winked at him. "I'm just glad you can't shoot worth a damn."

He shook his head and beamed. "Yeah. Me, too." They all looked to the front of the house as a loud rumble assaulted their ears. "That would probably be your men. It took two of our guys with riot gear to keep them away after they finished the bridge." He was about to say more when the six muddy men stomped into the house.

The man in the lead was older, with a scraggly dark beard liberally sprinkled with gray. The evident leader of the group, he limped up to Lex with worry in his eyes. "Miz Lexington." He looked her over carefully, seeming not to even notice the beautiful woman tucked up against her side. "You look like you're still in one piece. We'd heard on the radio there'd been some shooting." After he finished his careful perusal, his eyes lit on Amanda standing next to his boss, and he blushed slightly. Yanking his hat off his head, the older man mumbled, "'Scuse me. I, umm—"

Lex took pity on the grizzled man. "Lester, I'd like you to meet Amanda Cauble. Amanda, this is Lester. He takes care of the boys down at the bunkhouse."

Amanda held out a hand, giving him a firm handshake. "Nice to meet you, Lester. Martha has spoken highly of you." She smiled brightly, ignoring the mud liberally covering his bent form.

This caused his blush to darken. "Ah, now I know you're pullin' my leg." He gave the housekeeper a shy nod. "I'm just glad y'all are all right. Me and the boys are gonna go on up to the bunkhouse and get cleaned up." He nodded at Lex, put his hat on, and shuffled to the door. Turning, he tipped his hat at Amanda. "Real pleasure to meet you, miss. Hope we'll be seeing more of you around." He started back to the door again, ushering the other men outside. "Come on, you damn fools, let's get out of these folks' way."

Amanda waited until he closed the door, then burst out laughing. "He's cute." She looked up at Lex, who looked exhausted. *Hmm, how should I handle this? Subtle? Yeah. Why not?* Amanda turned her attention to the sheriff. "Do you think anyone would mind if we went upstairs?" She gave the rancher a pleading look. "I really need to go sit down. My legs won't stop shaking." Although the statement was true, she knew this was the only way to get Lexington to take a break. "Could you give me a hand up the stairs?"

Lex worriedly scanned her lover's face. "Are you okay? Should I call a doctor?" She felt a hand pat her stomach.

"No. I'm just tired, and more than a little shook up, I guess. I'm not used to so much excitement." Amanda looked at Charlie and Martha, hoping that they wouldn't ruin her attempt to get Lex to relax. "Well?"

"Uh, yeah. You go ahead and get some rest, we'll get this all straightened out down here." Charlie felt Martha's hand tighten around his, and his heart swelled.

Amanda pulled Lex up the stairs. "Thanks. We'll see you both in the morning." She gave a little wave, then tightened her grip as she felt Lex lean against her slightly. "Come on, honey. Let's get you into bed."

Lex pulled her closer. "Now that's the best offer I've had all day." She leaned down and gave Amanda's ear a light nip. "Or at least all evening."

Once into the master bedroom, Lex went directly to the bed and sat. "Damn. I feel like I could sleep for days." She ran a hand through her tangled dark hair.

Amanda knelt at her feet and pulled off Lex's boots. "Sounds like a great idea to me." She stood up, unbuttoned her lover's shirt, then pulled it off and touched the bandage wrapped around her ribs. "Let me go get something to—" She didn't finish, as she found herself sprawled across Lex's body. She returned Lex's attention kiss for kiss and caress for caress.

"I thought you were tired," Lex whispered in her ear, then started to nibble across her throat.

Amanda sat up, and moved back slightly. "Well, I, umm—" She lost her train of thought as Lex's eyes captured hers.

Lex ran a hand down her lover's cheek. "Sorry. I really shouldn't tease you like that, but you're so cute when you get flustered."

Amanda leaned into the touch, then turned and placed a kiss on the callused palm. "Yeah? Well, normally I don't like it when people tease me, but with you it's different, somehow." She reached down to unbutton Lex's jeans. Seeing Lex raise an eyebrow, she blushed. "Now don't be getting any ideas. I just want you to be comfortable before we go to sleep."

Lex gave her another look, but didn't argue as Amanda slid the jeans off and then raised the sheet and comforter over her prone form. She fought to keep her eyes open as she watched as Amanda removed her own clothes, then crawled into bed. "Damn, but you're beautiful," she mumbled, eyes closing against her will.

Amanda continued to blush, then rolled over on her side and propped her head up with one hand. The compliment embarassed her since she never really considered herself attractive before. "Obviously you are so tired that your eyesight has been affected." She brushed dark bangs off the resting woman's forehead. "Lex?" When there was no answer. Amanda sighed. "Sleep well, my love." She edged over and snuggled up against the rancher, kissed the tan cheek, and joined her in sleep.

Lex slowly opened her eyes, unsure why she was awake. It was still dark outside, and a glance at the bedside alarm clock showed it was just a little after five o'clock in the morning. She started to get up, but she had been effectively pinned to the bed by Amanda's body. Her left arm was numb, and she realized that the lack of feeling was what caused her to awaken. Using her free hand, Lex slowly pulled the covers back, exposing their upper bodies to the cool air in the room. Amanda moaned slightly, then snuggled even closer, allowing Lex to free her arm. She was quite proud of herself until the extremity began to tingle painfully.

Amanda woke up, feeling a definite cool draft. Opening her eyes, she saw that somehow the comforter and sheet had been pushed down around her waist, leaving her upper body bare to the room. Glancing up at her companion, she saw that Lex was awake as well, biting her lower lip with a pained expression on her face. Shivering slightly, Amanda pulled the covers up over them both, and ran her hand along her lover's clenched jaw. "Lex? What's the matter? Is it your side?"

With a pained shake of her head, Lex tried to relax. She flexed her left hand and flinched. "No. My arm fell asleep, and now I'm trying to wake it up."

Amanda sat up to lean comfortably against the headboard and reached under the covers for Lex's arm. She tenderly massaged the muscles, enjoying the feel of Lex's smooth skin. Finishing up, she leaned over and gave Lex a kiss. "How's that?"

Lex pulled Amanda over until she was lying on top. "Mmm. Seems to be working just fine." She wrapped both arms securely around Amanda and squeezed. "But it may need extensive physical therapy," she continued, rolling over until her mate was under her. Lex placed light bites on Amanda's neck. "Better safe than sorry," she whispered in a nearby ear, leaving a kiss behind.

"Ooh, yeah." Amanda gasped, and threaded her fingers in the thick hair above her. "I'll be glad to, oh, boy." She trembled as Lex traced a fiery path down her body with small bites and kisses. Amanda's last coherent thought was that Lex's hand seemed just fine to her.

Lex and Amanda strolled into the kitchen hours later, both looking quite happy and rested. Charlie sat at the table talking with Martha, who was at the stove cooking breakfast.

"Well, well. Look who finally decided to get up," Martha teased.

Lex recovered first as she sat down next to Amanda. "Well, we woke up earlier and just decided to take it easy for awhile."

Charlie snickered into his coffee cup, as Amanda blushed. "Roy stopped by earlier, said he and the boys were going to take care of the horses for you for the next week or so." He looked over at the housekeeper, who had a smug look on her face. "They felt bad you had to do all the chores lately, and they want to make it up to you."

Lex looked at Martha. "Sounds like a certain someone has been busy this morning."

Martha turned away from the stove and placed her hands on her hips. "Now you just listen to me, Lexie." She stalked over to the table, putting one hand under the rancher's chin and tilting her face upwards. "You *are* going to take it easy for a few days, or at least until these dark circles disappear from under your eyes." Seeing a stormy look appear on Lex's face, she leaned over and placed a kiss on her forehead. "Please? For me?"

Lex's face lightened immediately. "Aw, Martha. Don't look at me that way." She looked over at her companion, who was trying to control herself. "What's so funny?"

Amanda had one hand covering her mouth. "Nothing." But her eyes were sparkling.

Lex tilted until she was inches away from Amanda's face. She waited until her lover's eyes locked with her own, then in a quiet voice said, "I have ways of making you talk, my dear."

Amanda's eyes widened and then glinted with something other than humor. "I'm looking forward to seeing you try." She leaned over and placed a quick kiss on the surprised rancher's nose.

"She's got you there, Lexie," Martha chortled as she went back to the stove and piled two plates with food. "I'm sure you girls are ready for breakfast, right?"

Charlie looked at them, then at his watch. "Wow. It's almost ten o'clock. Getting closer to lunch, isn't it?"

Lex glared at him. "You really don't want to go there." She stared down at the plate Martha placed in front of her. "Good Lord, Martha. Do you actually expect me to eat all of this?"

The older woman sat back down at the table after placing a similarly laden plate in front of Amanda. "As a matter of fact, I do." She gave her charge a long stare. "You haven't been eating enough to keep a bird alive, and I'm putting a stop to it."

Amanda giggled. "I was wondering how she could run a ranch on what she ate. Now I know." She ignored the nasty look Lex gave her.

"Fine. But don't blame me for the mess in the kitchen when I explode from eating all of this," Lex grumbled as she started on her breakfast.

"Poor baby. You'll probably be bedridden for days." Amanda patted her leg in mock sympathy.

Lex grumbled again, but she couldn't disguise the affection in her eyes. "And this would be a bad thing?"

Ducking her head, Amanda prudently didn't answer, but continued to eat her breakfast while humming delightedly.

Charlie cleared his throat and eyed at Lex. The innuendo embarrassed even him, and he decided it was time to change the subject. "Since you don't have any chores to do, what are your plans for what's left of today?"

Setting her coffee mug back on the table, Lex glanced over at her companion. "Well, I thought if Amanda felt up to it, we'd make a trip to town. I need to pick up my other truck, and I thought we could put her car in the shop to get the interior cleaned up."

"That would be great! My grandparents will be so excited!" Amanda took Lex's hand in hers. "Think I could talk you into staying there for a few days?" Looking into her lover's eyes, she felt the room recede until it seemed that only the two of them were there. "Even though you know Gramma and Grandpa Jake, I'd really like to introduce you to them, if you know what I mean."

Lex was so absorbed in the eyes across from hers that she didn't hear Martha and Charlie make their exit. She swallowed hard, trying to put her thoughts into words. "Are you sure about that?" She saw the shock, and then sadness cross Amanda's expressive face.

"What?" Amanda looked into the sad eyes inches away from her own. "Why wouldn't I want to show you off?" She used shaky hands to cradle Lex's face. Leaning forward, she placed a kiss on Lex's trembling lips. "I love you," she whispered, "and I want the entire world to know it."

Lex felt the sadness squeeze her heart painfully. "I love you, too. But I don't want to see you get hurt." Taking a deep breath, she continued, "People in town have very long memories, and I've got a pretty checkered past." Her voice broke as she felt the soft touch of Amanda's fingertips brushing the tears that fell from her eyes.

Amanda stood and moved to sit in Lex's lap. She wrapped one arm around Lex's shoulders, and used her free hand to capture one of her hands. Bringing it to her lips, she placed a kiss on the knuckles, then pulled their linked hands to rest between their bodies. "I've already told my grandparents about us," she whispered, making eye contact with Lex, "and they couldn't be happier." She kissed her lover's forehead. "And I really don't give a damn what anyone else thinks. So get used to it."

Lex started to speak. "Are—" She cleared her throat and tried again. "Are you sure about this? You're going to hear a lot of nasty stuff, and most of it's probably true." Seeing the fierce determination in Amanda's eyes, she relented. "I just want you to know what you're getting into." She was about to add more, but was interrupted when Amanda's lips found hers.

Amanda poured everything she had into that kiss, transferring all her hopes, dreams, and love to the woman who had so thoroughly captured her heart. When she pulled back, she could see the love shining in Lex's eyes, and she felt her own eyes begin to fill with tears of happiness. "So you'd better get used to the fact that you're stuck with me, because I'm not going anywhere."

Taking a shuddering breath, Lex closed her eyes and pulled Amanda against her with all the strength left in her shaking arms. She buried her face in her hair, trying to come up with something, anything, to express the feeling in her heart. "Oh God, Amanda," she whispered hoarsely, "I love you with all that I am." She felt the return squeeze and felt something that had been missing her entire life fall into place in her soul.

They sat in the kitchen silently, tangled together, for what seemed like hours, neither speaking, yet not quite ready to let the other go. Finally, Amanda pulled back slightly and ran her hand down Lex's cheek. "Well, now that we've gotten that settled, are you ready to drive into town so I can show you off?"

"Not much to show, but yeah, I guess so. Let me go get a bag together, since we'll be there for a few days." She waited until Amanda climbed off her lap. "I've also got a few errands to run while we're there, if you don't mind." She stood and wrapped an arm around Amanda's shoulder.

"Sure. I've got some things to take care of, too." *Like requesting some more vacation time, and of course thanking that slimeball Rick for sending me out here,* she mused. *I can't wait to see his face when he finds out his little scheme backfired.* A small giggle escaped her.

"What's so funny?" Lex asked, as the headed for the stairs.

"I was just thinking about Rick."

"And?"

"I'm just picturing the look on his face when I stand up in front of the entire office and thank him for sending me on a wild goose chase."

Lex stopped in the middle of the stairway and looked at her as if she had completely lost her mind. "Thank him?"

"Yep." Amanda nodded, prodding Lex forward once again. "I'm gonna say, 'Rick, if it hadn't been for you, I may never have met the love of my life. So thank you,' and then watch him pass out from the shock."

"That would certainly do it." Lex allowed Amanda to enter the master bedroom ahead of her. "But when he gets up, he's mine. That bastard and his little games nearly got you killed, and I have a few choice words of my own for him." She was almost to the closet when the light touch on her back stopped her. Turning around, Lex saw a quiet look of determination on her lover's face.

"No. Please don't." Seeing Lex's confusion, Amanda continued, "I would gladly go through all of that again for what I have gained this past week." She enjoyed the look of comprehension, then pure joy suddenly covering Lex's face.

Lex was ecstatic. She scooped Amanda up into her arms. "Funny, I feel the same way." She spun them around, enjoying Amanda's startled laughter as it floated in the air.

"Lex, you nut! Put me down before you hurt yourself." Amanda linked her hands around Lex's neck to keep from flying out of her arms. When she saw that she was in the unique position of finally being able to physically see eye to eye with her lover, Amanda took advantage of the opportunity presented and captured Lex's lips with a vengeance.

Lex happily returned her offering, accepting the deepening of the contact wholeheartedly. She loosened her grip on her lover slightly as she felt her own legs begin to weaken. "God,

Amanda," she whispered huskily, "it's amazing what you make me feel with just one kiss."

Amanda smiled against her mouth. "It's only fair, considering what you can do to me with just one look. You in much of a hurry to get into town?" She slid down Lex's form slowly, then led her lover to the bed. "I thought we could leave sometime after lunch."

"Yeah? You have something in mind to do until then?"

"Yeah," Amanda tugged on Lex's hand and drew her toward the bed. "Wanna practice?"

Lex shrugged, her eyes slightly glazed with desire. "You're the boss."

Chapter
Seventeen

It was with a growing sense of unease that Amanda drove the Mustang up to the bridge. The closer they got, the more she shook. *Oh, God...I don't know if I can do this.* She was starting to feel physically ill, until a strong hand covered hers.

"Stop the car for a minute, Amanda." Lex spoke quietly, but with authority, and Amanda was unable to deny the request. "Please?"

Lex stepped out of the vehicle as it rolled to a stop, only a few yards from the edge of the newly reconstructed trestle. She walked over to the driver's side and opened the door, offering Amanda her hand. "Come here," she beckoned, concerned when her companion's cold clammy hand grasped hers. "We're gonna take this slow and easy, okay?"

"No, it's okay," Amanda managed to choke out.

"Just let me know when it gets to be too much." She slowly led Amanda to the newly rebuilt structure, pulling her closer against her as they walked forward.

Amanda took a deep breath, and walked with Lex up to the edge. Before she could feel any panic, however, the arm around her shoulder tightened slightly, and she felt the fear melt away. When she got one foot on the wooden surface, she trembled. *Stop it. Lex is here, and she won't let anything happen, so just get over it.* Amanda was angry that an inanimate object could instill such fear into her.

"Shh. Easy, sweetheart." Lex spoke quietly into her ear, as she would to a spooked horse. "Everything's going to be okay, I promise." They walked halfway across before she felt Amanda begin to relax.

Feeling her heartbeat calming, Amanda risked a glance at her protector. Having Lex beside her was like having her own personal security blanket, and she felt her anxiety melt away.

She stopped in the middle of the span and turned to envelop herself in Lex's embrace. "Thank you." She placed a kiss on the chest her face was buried in. "I'm going to be okay now." Looking up at the shadowed face above her, Amanda brightened. "Let's go get the car and get out of here."

The rest of the drive into town was uneventful as the two women shared humorous anecdotes from their childhood.

"...And then he said, 'How in the hell did that calf end up wearing my boots?'" Lex finished, while Amanda wiped her eyes from too much laughter.

Amanda shook her head. "Stop it, please! I'll never get that picture out of my head. Poor Charlie." She turned the car onto a beautifully landscaped street, where trees draped over the road. Amanda glanced over at her lover, who was beginning to look a little spooked. "We're almost there. Are you okay?"

Lex had been looking out of the window, remembering the last time she had driven down this street. *Been almost eight months,* she thought. *Not much has changed.* "Yeah, I'm fine. Just feeling a little bit intimidated, I guess. I haven't been to this part of town in a while."

"Really? So you've been over here before?" Amanda remembered her grandmother saying that Lex was on the Historical Committee, but hadn't known she had been to their house.

"Yeah, a couple of months before you moved back here, there was a meeting of the Committee at Mrs. Cauble's home, and I happened to attend." Lex took a moment to gather the courage to tell her story. "Anyway, the ladies were chatting about some old barn north of town, when the alarms on their cars went off. We all went outside to look, and there were a couple of kids trying to break into the vehicles." She looked down at her lap, unable to meet the gaze across from her. "I wasn't really thinking, just ran outside while Mrs. Cauble called the police. I caught them, but they tried to get away, and I—" she stopped, unable to continue.

Amanda pulled the car over when Lex started relating her story, realizing she was having more trouble than she cared to admit telling her tale. "You don't have to—"

Shame weighed heavily on her heart, and it took several seconds before Lex could finally looked at her. "Yes, I do. You really need to know what kind of person I can be." She took another deep breath and rubbed her eyes. "They were just a couple of punks, trying to get a little extra money from stuff they could steal. I lost it. Here they were, two dirty teenagers, stealing from ladies I considered friends." Unable to look at Amanda any longer, Lex closed her eyes. "I beat the hell out of them. It took five deputies to pull me off them, and they both spent weeks in the hospital." She slumped down further into her seat. "I've been ashamed to show my face in town ever since. I'd just get done what I needed to and get out of town quickly, hoping not too many people notice when I'm here."

"Oh, Lex." Amanda felt sympathetic tears welling up in her eyes. "You have nothing to be ashamed of. You protected people you care about." She reached a hand over and clasped the distressed woman's arm.

Lex opened her eyes and looked at Amanda. "I'm not sure I can agree with you. If you could have just seen the looks on those ladies' faces." A single tear fell down her face. "I see them almost every night in my dreams. They were horrified, and for good reason." She ran a hand through her hair nervously. "I guess I'm just afraid of seeing that look on your grandmother's face when you show up with me on her doorstep. I don't think I could handle that."

Amanda unbuckled her seat belt so she could get closer to Lex. "No! My grandmother thinks the world of you. We've spoken on the phone quite a few times since I've been staying with you, and she has said nothing but wonderful things about you." She gave Lex a kiss on the lips. "And if she felt any different, you know she would have told me."

Lex sat for a minute, just absorbing what Amanda said. Anna Leigh Cauble was no wilting flower, and if she had a problem with Lex, she certainly wouldn't have allowed her granddaughter to stay at the ranch, damaged bridge or not. "Yeah, you're right." She cupped Amanda's face in her hands and kissed her. "You wanna take me home, now? I think I need to tell Mr. and Mrs. Cauble my intentions toward you."

Amanda gave her a puzzled look. "Intentions? Why do I have this sudden vision of you standing under my window serenading me?" She laughed nervously, then became somewhat alarmed at Lex's smug expression.

"Damn. You figured me out." Lex couldn't help but chuckle after seeing the shock on her companion's face. "Don't worry, I'll cancel the Mariachi Band."

Slipping back into the driver's seat, Amanda laughed again.

"You wouldn't." She looked at Lex's semi-innocent face. "You would! Don't you dare!" Amanda buckled back up and steered the small car back onto the street, laughing all the while.

Amanda drove into the tree-lined drive and parked behind a shiny Suburban. "Looks like they're home." She got out of the car and walked around to the passenger's side, waiting for her lover to climb out. "Come on, let's go give them a big surprise." She took Lex's hand, practically running up the walkway to the door.

Before she could open the door, it swung wide open, and her grandmother stood smiling in the doorway. "Mandy, you're home!" She rushed outside, wrapping her arms around Amanda in breathless abandon.

"Urk. Gramma, calm down," Amanda gasped, as her grandmother squeezed the breath out of her.

Jacob Cauble stood just inside the doorway, watching with an amused air. "Well, Peanut, we can never accuse you of not making an entrance." He enjoyed the scene until Amanda released her grandmother and came at him full force. "Ugh. Okay, I'm happy to see you, too."

Anna Leigh looked at Lex, who stood a few steps away with a bemused look on her face. "Lexington? Are you just going to stand there, or are you going to say hello?" She stepped closer to the silent woman.

The smile on Lex's face was small, but genuine. "Hello, Mrs. Cauble. It's been a while, hasn't it?"

"You scamp. Get over here!" Anna Leigh pulled Lex into a strong embrace. She whispered into her ear, "I could never thank you enough for what you have given us. And I'm glad you're here."

Amanda and Jacob stood arm in arm, watching the scene on the front porch with joy and satisfaction. "I'm glad you got her to come back with you, Peanut. Your grandmother has been very worried about her since your last talk."

"Is the guest room still available? I actually got her to agree to stay in town for a few days, and I want to get her to visit Dr. Anderson while she's here."

Jacob let go of his granddaughter and reached for the woman standing next to his wife to pull her into a hug. "Welcome back, Lexington. I hope you will stay with us a few days, so we can get caught up." He led her into the house, with

Amanda and Anna Leigh close behind.

Lex followed him into the living room and sat down on the loveseat he gestured to. "Well, if you don't mind me hanging around, I'd like that. I have some business to attend to here in town that will take a couple of days."

Amanda plopped down next to her, almost sitting in Lex's lap. She took her lover's hand and squeezed. "Like I would let you out of my sight for any amount of time."

Jacob sat in the large recliner, with Anna Leigh perched on the arm. "Looks like our little Amanda has gotten her hooks into you, Lexington." His eyes shone in response to the blushes coloring both young women's faces. "Not that I'm complaining, mind you. As long as Mandy is happy, we're happy. Right, Anna?" He took his wife's hand and pulled it to his lips for a kiss.

Anna Leigh looked at her granddaughter, then at the woman seated next to her. "I couldn't agree more, Jacob."

"That's good, because I've fallen completely, totally, and irreversibly in love with Lex, and I couldn't be happier." Amanda snuggled closer to her embarrassed companion.

Jacob and Anna Leigh exchanged amused glances. "So, Lexington," he drawled, trying to keep a straight face, "what are your intentions toward our granddaughter?" Between the shocked look on Amanda's face and Lex's apparent struggle with her thoughts, he could barely keep a straight face. "Well?"

Lex looked at Amanda, then at Jacob and Anna Leigh. So that they knew she was serious, she stood up to address the two older people. "Mr. Cauble, Mrs. Cauble, my intentions are purely honorable. I love Amanda with my entire being, and if I were able, I would ask you for her hand." She looked back at her lover, who had tears floating in her eyes. "But since I can't, I want to stand here right now and give you my word that I will treat Amanda with the greatest respect, and honor her for as long as she will have me." She felt Amanda's hand slip into hers. "We've known each other less than a week, yet it feels like a lifetime. She brings out the best in me, and I will do everything in my power to make her happy." Lex's free hand flexed into a fist as she tried to control her nerves. The small speech was more difficult than she could have ever imagined, yet she knew deep in her soul that she'd do it again in a heartbeat.

Anna Leigh stood up, followed by Jacob. "Lexington," she said sternly, watching the emotions flicker across Lex's face, "welcome to our family." She walked over and brought the ner-

vous woman into an embrace. "And call me Anna Leigh. Mrs.
Cauble sounds so impersonal, don't you think?" She felt the
body she was holding shake with silent sobs, and she rubbed
Lex's back in a comforting motion. "Shh. It's okay, dearest."

Lex drew a deep breath and slowly edged away. "Thanks,
Anna Leigh. You have no idea what it means to me to hear
that." Embarrassed, she ran a hand over her eyes.

Amanda stepped up beside her and gave her a one-armed
hug. "That was beautiful, Lex. I didn't know you were so elo-
quent."

"Well, Lexington, it appears that you're stuck with us."
Jacob walked over and embraced the young woman. "And if you
call me Mr. Cauble again, I'll have to get tough. You can call
me Jacob, Grandpa, or old fart. I'll answer to just about anything." He chuckled at her look of surprise. "Although 'old fart'
is usually reserved for my Anna Leigh to call me." He flinched
as his wife slapped his arm lightly. "See what these Cauble
women are capable of? Are you sure you want to be subjected to
this?"

Lex laughed in agreement, and looked down at Amanda.
"Yeah, I know. She's already popped me a couple of times. I
guess it's in the genes." She winced as the expected slap came
her way. "See what I mean?" Her comment broke the seriousness of the conversation, to her relief. *Damn, that was harder
than breaking a wild horse. Glad I'll never have to go through
this again.* Then her thoughts sobered. *Oh, shit. I've still got to
meet her parents!*

It was late evening, and Lex and Amanda were snuggled up
on the sofa in front of a roaring fire. "You know, I always knew
your grandparents were special. I never fully appreciated how
special they are until today." She felt a kiss on her collarbone,
where Amanda's face was tucked.

"Yeah. It may sound strange, but they're closer to me than
my own parents. I love my mom and dad, but we were never as
close. I've always felt like I could tell Gramma and Grandpa
Jake anything."

Lex kissed the top of her head. "I know what you mean. I
feel the same way about Martha. She's always been there for
me."

They sat for a while longer, staring as the flames burned
down, enjoying each other's company. Amanda dozed off, and

Lex thought about her visit to the bank the next day, as well as her trip to the county jail to sign the complaint against the five thieves. She had refused to press charges against the teenager, especially when Charlie told her he was an orphan under the care of his older brother, Matt. When she asked him what they were going to do with the boy, the sheriff said they would probably have to put him in juvenile hall. Lex was going to see the boy tomorrow, and ask him if he'd like to work on the ranch. She didn't know if it was the right thing to do, but her conscience wouldn't let a boy go to jail when he'd been forced to follow his brother.

Anna Leigh glided quietly into the room, in case the two women were sleeping. She noticed her granddaughter was sound asleep on Lex's lap, and the rancher was staring pensively into the dying fireplace. She edged over to the arm of the sofa and perched on top of it. "Lexington? Is everything all right?"

Lex looked up at Amanda's grandmother and understood where her lover got her beauty. She kept her voice low so she wouldn't wake the sleeping bundle in her arms. "Yeah, fine. I was just going over in my head the things I have to do tomorrow."

"From what I hear, that means a trip to the doctor as well, doesn't it?" Anna Leigh didn't know how else to bring such a subject up. "Amanda said over the phone that you have bruised ribs and had been shot?"

Sighing, Lex ran her free hand through her hair. "Yeah. She'll badger me until I go, I guess." She looked up at Amanda's grandmother. "It's really not that bad. I'm sure she made it sound worse than it actually was."

Anna Leigh gave Lex's head a gentle pat. "Of course. But you forget how well I know you." Then her face took on a pensive look. "Why haven't you been by recently? I've missed the conversations we used to have on the patio Saturday evenings." The two women would sit outside, drinking iced tea and discussing everything from politics to the price of cattle after the Historical Committee meetings, but that had stopped after the incident eight months ago.

"I...I—" Lex stammered, looking one of her worse fears in the face. "I just figured you didn't need me around your little gatherings. I'm not exactly tea party material."

"Lexington, I was never so proud of you as I was that day you stopped those horrible thieves. What if one of the ladies had decided to leave early? Do you think they would have just run away?" Her tone of voice forced Lex to look her in the eye. "I don't think so. I believe that they would have seriously hurt someone, and yet you jumped to our defense immediately. Don't be ashamed of the fact that you protected us from an unknown danger. Yes, they were just boys. But you know as well as I do how vicious young men can be. Don't underestimate what you did. The ladies still talk about how very proud of you they are."

Lex was caught speechless. She hadn't looked at the incident from that point of view. "Mrs., umm, Anna Leigh. Thank you. I've been worried all this time about what happened then. I'll still worry about it, but you've helped me put it more in perspective."

Anna Leigh leaned over and kissed the top of Lex's head. "Lexington, there's nothing in this world I wouldn't do for you. Now why don't you get yourselves upstairs and into bed? Unfortunately, the guestroom is still under repair, so you'll have to share with Amanda. I do hope that's all right." She patted the arm closest to her before getting to her feet. "Get some rest, and we'll see you in the morning." As Anna Leigh left the room, she was unable to suppress the chuckle that escaped her lips due to Lex's startled expression.

Lex looked after Anna Leigh with a renewed fondness. Her sneaky ways weren't lost on Lex. She glanced down at the sleeping woman in her arms. *Wonder if I can get her awake long enough to make it upstairs?* "Amanda?" she asked quietly, gently shaking the relaxed body.

"Mmm?" Amanda tucked her head tighter against Lex's chest, but didn't awaken.

The rancher shook her head in defeat. *Can't say I didn't try.* She stood up, cradling the sleeping form gently. *Okay, now where the hell is her bedroom?* Lex started walking up the stairs, remembering from a previous tour of the house that all the bedrooms were on the back area of the second floor. Just as she reached the top, Amanda woke up slightly.

"Lex?" Amanda looked up into her eyes, then noticed where they were. "You didn't carry me up the stairs, did you?" She used one hand to push the hair from her lover's eyes.

"Yep. And your grandmother told me the guestroom was being repaired, so we'll have to share." Lex shifted her grip on the bundle in her arms. "So where should I take you?"

Amanda raised her arms and locked her hands behind her lover's neck. "Anywhere you want to."

Other books in this series available from
Yellow Rose Books

Faith's Crossing

Lexington Walters and Amanda Cauble withstood raging
floods, cattle rustlers and other obstacles to be together...but
can they handle Amanda's parents? When Amanda decides to
move to Texas for good, she goes back to her parent's home in
California to get the rest of her things, taking the rancher with
her. She discovers someone in her family will go to any length
to keep Lex from Amanda, no matter what the cost.

Available in Fall 2003
ISBN 1-932300-12-0

Hope's Path

In this next look into the lives of Lexington Walters and Amanda Cauble, someone is determined to ruin Lex. Attempts to destroy her ranch lead to attempts on her life. Lex and Amanda desperately try to find out who hates Lex so much that they are willing to ruin the lives of everyone in their path. Can they survive long enough to find out who's responsible? And will their love survive when they find out who it is?

ISBN 1-930928-18-1

Love's Journey

Lex and Amanda embark on a new journey as Lexington redis-
covers the love her mother's family has for her, and Amanda
begins to build her relationship with her father. Meanwhile,
attacks on the two young women grow more violent and deadly
as someone tries to tear apart the love they share.

ISBN 1-930928-67-X

Strength of the Heart

In the fifth story of the series, Lex and Amanda are caught up in the planning of their upcoming nuptials while trying to get the ranch house rebuilt. But an arrest, a brushfire, and the death of someone close to her forces Lex to try and work through feelings of guilt and anger. Is Amanda's love strong enough to help her, or will Lex's own personal demons tear them apart?

ISBN 1-930928-75-0

Also fromCarrie Carr
and
Yellow Rose Books

Something To Be Thankful For

Randi Meyers is at a crossroads in her life. She's got no girl-friend, bad knees, and her fill of loneliness. The one thing she does have in her favor is a veterinarian job in Fort Worth, Texas, but even that isn't going as well as she hoped. Her supervisor is cold-hearted and dumps long hours of work on her. Even if she did want a girlfriend, she has little time to look.

When a distant uncle dies, Randi returns to her hometown of Woodbridge, Texas, to attend the funeral. During the graveside ser-vices, she wanders away from the crowd and is beseeched by a young boy to follow him into the woods to help his injured sister. After coming upon an unconscious woman, the boy disappears. Randi brings the woman to the hospital and finds out that her name is Kay Newcombe.

Randi is intrigued by Kay. Who is this unusual woman? Where did her little brother disappear to? And why does Randi feel compelled to help her? Despite living in different cities, a ten-tative friendship forms, but Randi is hesitant. Can she trust her newfound friend? How much of her life and feelings can Randi reveal? And what secrets is Kay keeping from her? Together, Randi and Kay must unravel these questions, trust one another, and find the answers in order to protect themselves from outside threats— and discover what they mean to one another.

ISBN 1-932300-04-X

"An excellent story about two women who've gone through the School of Hard Knocks. You can't help but root for Kay and Randi as they try to make sense of their lives. This is Carrie Carr's best novel yet!"

~Lori L. Lake, author of *Gun Shy* and *Different Dress*

Carrie is a true Texan, having lived in the state her entire life. She makes her home in the Dallas/Ft. Worth metroplex with her partner AJ and their teenage daughter, Karen. She's done everything from wrangling longhorn cattle and buffalo, to programming burglar and fire alarm systems. Her spare time is spent writing, traveling, and trying to corral the latest addition to their family, a Chihuahua named Nugget. Check out her website at www.carriecarr.com for information such as merchandise, personal appearances, and personalized bookplates for her books.

Breinigsville, PA USA
16 November 2009
227655BV00003B/153/A